Arm Candy

Arm Candy

T.C. Littles

www.urbanbooks.net

Urban Books, LLC
300 Farmingdale Road, N.Y.-Route 109
Farmingdale, NY 11735

ISBN 13: 978-1-945855-63-4
ISBN 10: 1-945855-63-0

First Trade Paperback Printing December 2018
Printed in the United States of America

10 9 8 7 6 5 4 3 2 1

Distributed by Kensington Publishing Corp.
Submit Orders to:
Customer Service
400 Hahn Road
Westminster, MD 21157-4627
Phone: 1-800-733-3000
Fax: 1-800-659-2436

Arm Candy

by

T.C. Littles

Chapter One

Samira

"Word on the street is that this party is gonna be slapping tonight!" Jamila puckered her lips in the vanity mirror. She coated them in pink lipstick. "The whole city is coming out for K.P.'s light work album release party. It's been getting major play all over social media."

"They better act like they know all of the time! My baby out here doing the damn thang, so I can't wait to see him shining bright tonight." I stepped in front of the mirror and admired my curves. I'd gone all out for my bae's big night and gotten a fire-engine red dress custom made. There was no way in hell I was about to be caught half-stepping. "I can't wait to bust these bitches' heads tonight. I'm killing 'em!"

"Yeah, I've gotta give you that. No hate or shade this way, Samira. You're rocking the hell out of that dress! I don't think any chick in the place is gonna be walking close to stepping on your level." She pumped my ego up more. "K.P. better know what he's got!"

Continuing to get ready for the night, Jamila made sure my makeup was flawless and that nothing about my appearance looked like I was overdoing it. She was a beast at her craft and could beat a face beautiful. Jamila wasn't half-stepping with her swag, either. She was dressed in a white crop top, high-waist pants, and six-inch stilettos that made her booty stand out more. If she weren't my ace, I might've been jealous.

Neither of us had brought it up per se, but the elephant was definitely in the room. King's mistress was supposed to be in the building tonight, and we all knew when the other bitch was involved, shit could get messy. Not knowing why K.P. couldn't keep his dick in his pants but more importantly out of her, I had to keep my front game up tonight, making sure my man stayed focused on me. I wasn't trying to be embarrassed having him check for side meat in my face.

Finally ready, I slipped on the newest pair of Daffodile spiked platform red sole pumps I treated myself to the last time King pulled a week hiatus from home. Then I grabbed my purse and keys to hit the door.

"Damn, girl! King is looking hella good tonight I see." Jamila scrolled through her social media pages from my passenger seat. "You're damn right to be focused on trying to get him down the aisle. You better get wifed before the next bitch does."

"Don't I know it!" Whipping my fully loaded platinum-white MKS through traffic, I wasn't trying to show up even a minute late for the red carpet event. There was no doubt in my mind that Rayna would jump at taking pictures like she was the leading lady if I wasn't there to defend my position. Trust, I'd been fighting for a ring for far too long to go down without one helluva fight. Me and King had been together for seven long years, and I'm not talking about on-again, off-again, "just kicking it" type shit. This rock I was getting ready to floss in Rayna's face was more than enough proof that I wasn't a blast from the past, but more like a guaranteed lifetime.

"Here, bitch, you're hella tense. You need to take one blow of this cookie goodness and get right." She passed me the blunt she'd been puffing on. I hesitated because smoking wasn't normally my thing. Don't get me wrong, I'd join the rotation from time to time if I was around my crew, but to roll up and blow for the fuck of it on a solo dolo tip definitely wasn't going to happen. But tonight I wasn't turning her down.

"Fuck it, why not? This is a celebration for us too, for finally getting our business off the ground."

"No doubt! Everybody in our clique is doing hella good right about now. 2014 is about to bring big things for me and you though, fa'sho!" Leaning back, sipping from the EverFresh lemonade bottle, she was really getting beyond faded because it was more than half spiked with Cïroc. Even though she was tilted, Jamila was right. Everyone we rolled with had major things about to pan out for the New Year. I couldn't wait for me and Mila to drop our proposal on the table. Shit for us two was most definitely geared to be epic. Who said you shouldn't mix business with family?

I checked my phone. King hadn't called to check for my whereabouts. He'd left a few hours earlier with his Versace fit and blood-bottom shoes, promising that when we met back up tonight, he'd be on his best behavior. Only seconds from my exit, I privately asked God to walk with me 'cause only He knew how hard I'd clown if K.P. tried anything slick to embarrass me.

Pulling into the valet of Flood's Bar and Grille, we saw it was already crowded with a line that wrapped around St. Antoine onto Lafayette Street. Even high-rolling gamblers from Greektown Casino wanted to know what was taking place across the median. Jamila made sure her reflection was on point while I busied myself checking for K.P.'s boy Johnie's custom-painted whip. King made a big deal of having to ride with him. Seeing it a few spaces deep into the middle of the valet's reserved parking lot made me know without a doubt that their asses had roamed the streets before coming here. *This nigga is always trying to play me for dumb. He ain't gonna be happy until I start doing the same trife-life shit behind his back.* I threw my car into park, and the valet attendants rushed to open our doors. I was too busy texting King. "Fuck me walking in like some regular common broad. He better bring his ass out here to escort me in."

"Do you, girl. I'll just fall back to follow your lead." Jamila waved the attendant away, letting him know we'd be a few minutes.

Finally, King stepped out the door, walking straight toward my car and looking happier than ever to see me. I straightened up the mean mug expression on my face, not wanting to stir up trouble unnecessarily.

"What up, boo, you good?" He held the door open for Jamila, and she grabbed his hand and stepped out, smiling.

"What's up, Mila? You good, my baby?" He gave her a friendly hug that seemed to last a second too long, but since Jamila was my ride-or-die best friend it went over my head.

"Yeah, K.P., I'm all good. Ready to get spent! I'm proud of you, bro!"

"Shit, you already know it's bottles popped and flowing. It's King the Producer's night, my baby!"

He walked around the front of the car, and my headlights put him on front. He looked into the car, smiling at me. I was buttered up already. Damn, I loved this man. Opening my car door, King held his hand out for me to grab. "Come on, my lady, let's do this."

"I wouldn't have it any other way." I slid my manicured hands into his and stepped out into his arms. Hugging me tightly, he slid his hands down my curves to smack my delicious ass. He gripped it tightly, letting everyone watching know I was taken. I didn't mind the public affection, because with all the cheating King did, these hoes needed to be reminded who really held his heart.

"Can you cum all in that tonight?" Being nasty, I knew he loved a true freak, but my real intentions were to make sure he planned on coming home.

He licked my ear then whispered into it, and I was ready to climb back into the car for a quickie. "I'm talking about making a baby with you, girl. The King has arrived." Giving me a kiss, I made a mental note to make sure he raw dogged me hard tonight. I'd do anything to birth his seed. Pulling me back, he nodded with utter approval. "Oh, yeah, ya man will most certainly be ramming, slamming, and cumming all in that tonight."

King led me to the entrance of where the red carpet was letting us get our shine on as a couple. In the mix with the hired photographers, there were paparazzi from small-time internet magazines, bloggers, and those just looking to get pictures. They were lined up, snapping away. I couldn't wait until the photos started to make a buzz on people's feeds. I made sure each look I gave was fierce, cute, and worth studying in the roll back. King was more nonchalant with the crowd but never let my hand go. Jamila modeled a few feet from us, loving the limelight. I was glad my girl was here.

Walking into the scene, I was blown away. Jamila had been right. This place was slapping for sure. My man and his entourage had Flood's filled to capacity, with only a few tables reserved for random parties. I'd expected King to be the Diddy of his city, but this party was major fa'sho! Dough boys and pretty girls had turned out in heavy numbers.

"Damn, baby, you're doing it big out here. I'm so proud of you, like your number one fan." I leaned in and kissed him on the lips. He surprised me by slipping his tongue inside of my mouth.

"I wouldn't be shit without my woman holding me down. I love you, Samira, to the motherfucking moon and back." I was in la-la land. King had me spinning on cloud nine with the public attention and devotion. Nothing else in the world mattered because I had my soul mate by my side.

"I wouldn't have it any other way." Blushing, smiling from ear to ear, and more than ready to party hard, it wasn't shit you could tell me. It was gonna be Samira and King the Producer forever.

King led me to the back where the majority of his reserved booths were. Jamila had already made herself comfortable at the back booth, pouring herself a glass of gold-bottle Moët. She was more than ready to get tipsy, but I couldn't lie, with King on his best behavior, I was ready to celebrate too. The hostess was a headlining dancer at King of Diamonds, Miami, so you already knew the venue was hype. Turquoise Barbie was the baddest redbone Guyanese Sicilian stripper to climb, twirl, and stunt on the pole. Me and King had the pleasure of cashing her out on our last vacation. I guessed his sneaky ass kept in touch.

"It looks like Jamila's got your glass on deck. Go ahead and turn up with ya girl. I've gotta go network with the crowd, but I'm gonna be watching your fine ass." Giving me a quick peck on the cheek, he dipped out, joining a few of his partners before I could contest. Stuck for a moment watching him, I saw King throw handshakes up, taking pictures with a few guys he'd been producing. Johnie, the newest artist to King's team, stood out to me with his yellow self. Not to hate, 'cause he had the face to make you wanna fuck, but I wasn't into "light skin be like" dudes. With a neatly trimmed beard, goatee, and sideburns, maybe his pretty boy swag would be perfect for Jamila. When he looked my way, I tried playing it off like I wasn't plotting on him.

"So I see you're enjoying yourself. Hand me my glass so I can get tilted too!" I joined Jamila in the back, and we both started bouncing to the mixes the DJ was spinning of King's new album.

"I would be too if I were you. K.P. been giving you hella star power. It brought a tear to my eye seeing y'all so in sync."

"I know, right? I wish his ass could be like that all the time." Scanning to find him in the club, I saw he was still networking with other artists from the underground music world. I knew this was also his way of getting potential clients, more venues to entertain at, and more fans, so I decided to stop hawking him and start actually enjoying my baby's success. He'd put in a lot of hard work, and I'd invested more than enough of my money and time to deserve this celebration too.

"Girl, don't trip until he trips. He's doing good so far, so give him credit."

"I ain't trying to stunt on K.P. I'll give him his credit, but I already know this bubble I'm living in gonna be popped soon." No matter how hard I tried, I couldn't help but be a realist. King got down on a level no one knew of, no matter how much I shared.

"Bitch, bye with your negative ass. Don't fuck up my vibe! You better turn that glass up, guzzle it down, then get with the program. Besides, you've gotta get out here and stay relevant to these hoes. Your man is definitely the man tonight, Samira!"

"Ain't he though?" Turning my glass up, taking her advice, I used the liquor to build up my ego. I could stop the room's movement with just my entry alone, so by the end of the night everyone would know who I was and my relevance to King.

Me and Jamila made sure to work Flood's Bar & Grille inside and out. From working up a sweat hustling on the dance floor, to doing shots at the bar with a few other ladies who dated King's artists, everyone in attendance seemed to be having a great time. I'd finished almost a half bottle of Moët champagne with plans on taking the rest out shortly. Everyone in our section had personal bottles, living like bosses for the night. Turned all the way up, I hadn't drunk this much in a long time. Feeling woozy, I sat down in the first available chair I saw, grabbing my head and trying to get myself together. My shit was spinning like a merry-go-round!

"You straight?" Jamila yelled into my face, still dancing.

"Yeah, I'm good. I ain't trying to kill your vibe or nothing, but can you grab me a water real quick?" I wanted to do it myself, but I was feeling too lightheaded.

"I got you. Be right back." As Jamila hurried to the bar, I tried to play it off like I wasn't drunk, but I was pretty much done for the night. *Where the fuck is King's ass? He know I can't handle my liquor.* Barely holding my head up, I grabbed the bottle from her hand and sipped it slowly because my stomach was starting to do cartwheels.

"Damn, boo, you might've gone too hard in the paint," Mila laughed, rubbing my back. "Are you feeling totally tapped out?"

"Naw, I'm just gonna get this water into my system. Let's go to the bathroom so I can pee out some of the liq." I stood up. Making sure I could actually walk, Jamila locked hands with me, leading the way to the restroom. All things happen for a reason, so me spotting King's lowdown doggish ass nibbling on a bitch's neck was not by sheer coincidence but meant to motherfucking happen. "Oh hell naw, I'm on one hundred. You see that crap over there, Mila? K.P. ain't never gonna be shit!" Sobering up quickly, I was ready to take him and ol' girl's head off.

"Yeah, I was hoping you didn't. Damn, bro." Shaking her head, hanging it in defeat, Jamila knew I was right about King bursting my bubble sooner or later. I hadn't seen that nigga since he'd gone to the other side of the club, and apparently, this was why. "I've got your back, sis, even if I've gotta usher your drunk ass over there."

"Oh, you good. I've got this." Not thinking twice, I took two steps, grabbed a bottle out of a passerby's hand, and quickly launched it across the room at King and who I assumed to be Rayna. Taking off my red bottoms, running quickly through the crowd, I followed the bottle, attacking King like a pit bull in a skirt. I hit him in the back a few times with the heel of my shoe. Scaring him was the least of my worries.

"Ahh, what the fuck!" King yelled and swung around to see what was going on and most importantly who had hit him. I was ready to pop this buster's eyes out no doubt. The commotion of me tossing the bottle had popped off behind me, but I was totally focused on the fight ahead of me.

"You want me to handle this bitch, babes?" Rayna called herself stepping around King ready to confront me.

"You ain't handling shit this way, believe that." Jamila ran up, grabbing ol' girl by the arm and making sure she didn't hit me.

I was stuck in shock, couldn't move, and could only see red. Jamila knew it, and that's why she ran to cover me from any blows Rayna could serve my way. King pinned my arms to my side and marched me toward the back, trying to keep me calm, but I was already on ten.

"Is that bitch carrying your baby, K.P.? 'Cause if so, it's about to be off with her motherfucking head!"

"Calm down, Samira, this ain't the time." He didn't deny that he'd gotten the side piece pregnant. People finally realized it was King who had a catastrophe going on, and they focused all their attention on us. Drinks were still getting poured because everyone knew this would be a video clip most worthy for WorldStarHipHop. "Mila, back up off ol' girl, 'cause she was just leaving."

Throwing commands, K.P. still felt like he had enough weight right now to do so.

"Fuck calming down, nigga. You better start explaining this nonsense. Guess you didn't have time to get her an abortion either, huh?" I tried lunging over him. With a swollen belly, she was truly invested in having his first kid, but the only way I wanted that kid to come up out of there was through miscarriage. "You don't knock up dusty-knee dick suckers fool!" Slapping spit from his mouth, I was hotter than fish grease wanting him to feel every bit of anger my heart was feeling.

"You ain't gonna keep putting your hands on me, Samira." He grabbed then twisted my arm. "A nigga wrong, no doubt, but I'm gonna have to lay your ass out if you rise up again!" By this time, his whole crew had come from the back area to see if King was okay. Coming up on the scene, they fell back a little, not wanting to get in the middle or called out seeing it was him getting caught up. I guessed I was the last one to find out.

"Baby or not, daddy, I'll handle her if you want me to," Rayna giggled, sipping her water from a wineglass, giddy that she had one up on me. I knew about her for sure. The baby, I did not.

"You want me to bang this bitch or what, sis? You already know I ain't caring about this situation right here!" And that, my friends, was why I rode with Jamila through thick and thin.

"Bang her out!" I shouted, smacking King again with all my might. This time I felt him slap me back. All hell broke loose in the club.

Jamila

Samira gave the word, so I was instantly on Rayna's head. Backhanding her in the mouth with one swift hit, I busted her lip, drawing blood instantly as she dropped to the floor. Grabbing her swelling mouth, she looked up at me cockeyed, caught by surprise that I'd actually knocked her pregnant ass to the ground. I didn't care that she was allegedly carrying King's baby. Rayna should've played her position, keeping her big belly at home. My advice had always been for her to stay clear of Samira, not trying to impose on her territory. But Rayna didn't want to listen, feeling he would automatically choose sides with her when the time presented itself. Samira had taken many "L's" when it came to King. My girl wasn't gonna lose him without a fight, and all day, every day, I'd have her back!

As the crowd inside of Flood's went crazy, I used that as my opportunity to drag Rayna out of the club to her car. Samira was too busy getting roughhoused by King to follow my moves. "Bitch, is you fucking crazy! Why'd you come here anyway?" I couldn't feel bad for her being pregnant because I was too busy feeling bad that my best friend had gotten publicly embarrassed again. This whole situation was so fucked up!

"This ain't between me and you, Jamila! Just 'cause we Instagram friends don't make us real-life friends. You should've kept your hands off of me. I ain't the one." For a pregnant girl, Rayna was sure acting tough, like she was ready to pop off on me for real.

"Girl, get the fuck on with all of that. I wasn't scared then, and I definitely ain't scared now to box your ass out!" Walking up behind her, I was daring Rayna to throw the first blow. I'd lay her out, leaving the paramedics to pick her rat ass up off the pavement if she wanted to bring it.

"Yeah, okay, whatever. You've been warned. You and that Samira bitch have been warned." She quickly opened her car door and slid in fast. She hit the lock button as soon as I reached for the handle to snatch her black ass back out. "See you later, boo!" She pulled off. I watched Rayna bend the corner probably headed back to her townhouse in the projects.

Chapter Two

Samira

"What made your crazy ass think you could keep putting your hands on me, Samira?" King went off as he drove my car through traffic like a bat out of hell. "If that fight gets more recognition than my man's album, me and you are gonna have more problems than you think."

I wanted to climb into King's lap and claw his eyes out. The only reason I didn't was because we all would have died. Instead, I held an ice pack close to my face, hoping K.P. hadn't split my jaw completely open.

"Come on now, K.P., you tripping, and you know you ain't got no real excuse for hitting her." Jamila came to my defense. She'd really proved to be a friend tonight, and this was the second time she'd had my back.

"Why don't you sit your crazy ass the fuck back? I'm not gonna tell you how wrong you are for busting Rayna in the face like that."

"Nigga, don't tell me for one minute that you think you're about to defend that bitch!" I yelled, feeling my face burn. "I wish Mila would've stomped that kid up out of her. You've got some nerve," I fought back, hitting him again. I wanted to haul off and punch him in the side of the head so bad, but I wasn't trying to walk around with an ice pack on each cheek.

"I don't blame you for feeling some type of way. But I swear to God, if you spit another word of venom on my seed, I'm gonna strangle some sense into your ass. You or your wild ass homegirl better not run up on her 'til my little one is here."

"Fuck you and Rayna, and I mean that from the bottom of my heart. You done got a hood rat pregnant before we had a chance to start a family. Nigga, drive this four-hundred-dollar-a-month whip faster. We about to box it out tonight. You ain't said nothing but a word." Feeling cocky, and feeling my anger rise, I started to have flashbacks of him yoking me up when the crowd went wild at us scrapping. Jamila had Rayna, grabbing her face within two seconds of me shouting to attack the obvious baby momma of my soon-to-be husband.

"That's on you, but I'm not about to be your punching bag. A nigga was wrong for raw dogging her, no doubt, but I slipped up. I made a mistake she didn't want to undo, so a nigga trying to do right."

"You can't call yourself doing that whore better than doing your soon-to-be wife." I threw my hand up, reminding him he'd put a ring on it. "I guess this was just a pacifier to shut my whiny ass up, huh? This shit is unbelievable." I was ready to spit in his face.

"A'ight, Mila, be cool." He swerved up to her house and hit the button to unlock the doors. "I'll holla at you in the morning."

"Call me if you need to, Samira." Being loyal to me, knowing King wouldn't take it personally, she let me know that even on the emotional roller coaster I was getting ready to go on, she'd be there too to hold me down.

"Thanks, sis, I love you."

"You already know I love you too." Climbing out, she saw Johnie pulling up behind us. She laughed, walking toward the car probably to ask him to do exactly what I thought.

I went against my word, physically fighting with King again, and I was pissed at myself. I didn't want to end up with more scars on my body, or even worse, in the emergency room having to make up a story about why I had bruises. I was sporting a vicious welt across my face that should have been across his cheek bone. The more I glanced in the sideview mirror, the more I drank out of Jamila's bottle of Cîroc. I was glad she had forgotten it.

"Why are you still here? Why don't you go over to where that bitch is breeding your family?" I snuck in a few word attacks, wanting him upset and in his feelings the same way I was. Drinking from the bottle of Cîroc Jamila left, I was getting tipsy 'cause I had nothing to be happy about. The night had been spoiled, even the few minutes of a fairy tale he'd managed to sell me.

"I suggest you keep trying to find the bottom of that bottle and stop pressing your luck with me, Samira. I ain't trying to hurt your feelings any more than I already have." King nonchalantly tried shutting me up.

"Don't stroke your ego, King. I ain't never necessarily felt lucky with you. You don't think that shit was hella foul for me to find out staring at her big belly? We both knew ya baby momma was gonna be there, but you couldn't forewarn me? Come on now! And to make seeing her knocked up worse, I instantly thought back to you telling me it was time for me to have your baby. I won't be first, King! I'll be second! And I'm supposed to be your first lady!" The emotional meltdown set in. All of the tears I'd been holding in came out in a whirlwind I couldn't control.

King aka K.P.: King the Producer

The last thing I wanted was to have conflict with the woman who helped make me. Me and Samira had an unbreakable bond. I could play in the streets all day and night, but when an ultimatum was on the table, I'd choose Mira in a heartbeat. She held me down when I was nothing but a struggling bum on the corner of Gratiot looking for a come-up. Everyone around the way knew she was the only reason why I actually made a name for myself. Samira kept a job, a hustle, and refund checks rolling in from being a scholar in nursing school to help fund me for studio time. If it weren't for her, I'd still be a lowlife.

I watched my childhood love go through a heartbreak I couldn't relate to. I'd never had my heart torn to shreds by her 'cause she loved me too much to do so. And by rule, I never caught feelings for a girl I was ramming on the side. When Rayna came to me, asking to take her to the clinic for a test, I knew shit was about to get seriously out of control. No girl takes you to the clinic on a dummy mission without already knowing the answer. On the low-key tip, she'd already been receiving prenatal care. Even though she kept it a secret, I still should've been smart enough to know the signs. I'd gotten rid of enough random babies to know better.

Samira had every reason to be on this emotional roller coaster, and I truly didn't blame her for attacking me at the club. A nigga was wrong for not putting my foot down to Ray coming out last night. What we did behind the studio walls was never supposed to pour out into the streets. But the pregnancy hormones had her flipping out about getting recognition. I couldn't win her battle of love and war. If my plan of getting Jamila to keep Samira occupied and drunk had worked, I wouldn't be in this bullshit of a mess now.

"Come here, baby. Damn, your man fucked up." I pulled her in closely. She fought back but still allowed me to hug her. I needed to console and comfort her since I'd created all the damage.

"Why did you tell me that shit earlier? Why her? Why not me? Am I not good enough to have your baby?" She was crying, soaking up my shirt. I couldn't bear causing this girl so much unhappiness. She'd held a nigga down at his worst time, being the backbone every nigga in America was out there praying for.

"I'm sorry, baby, I'm so fucking sorry." Dropping to my knees but not letting her go, I felt she was weak as I cried into her womb. I felt guilt rush through my body knowing I should've been put my seed deep into her gut. I still focused hard on pulling out whenever we sexed, but that wild, drunken night with Rayna had me busting multiple nuts without pulling back. *Yeah, I ain't shit. I can tell myself that.* Tugging at her panties, I wanted to start working hard on making things right.

"No, please stop. I'm so mad at you, King. I think I hate you!" I could hear the resentment, anger, rage, and truthfulness in her words, but I didn't want to. Samira was the type of chick you didn't want to let get away, so I had no plans on doing so. I didn't have any plans on being without Rayna. She was just gonna have to accept this child and the situation at hand.

"Shh! Please stop, honey love." I carefully made sure not to call her baby. "Let me try to make you feel a little better." I knew that she was already feeling the Cîroc, so cumming would put her straight to sleep and out of this nightmare. We could deal with this in the morning, unfortunately, but I was still happy the lie I'd been living with was finally out.

Able to get her panties down with her legs spread open wide enough for me to flick my tongue on her clit, I dove in, milking her quickly and loving every drop. She was panting, breathing hard, grabbing at my head. I continued to dine on my sweet lady's delight as she ground hard, teaching me a lesson for stepping out on her.

"Don't stop. Oh, shit. I'm about to cum!" Feeling her grip my head, I dove my tongue in deeper, willing to do anything to keep her from leaving my side. It was a lot to ask of her to hold me down in this situation too, but I was. With her being "Loyal Samira," she'd be willing to do it once she got over the shock of being second in line. Feeling her sweet cum squirt into my mouth, I bit down tenderly knowing exactly what to do to drive her beyond crazy.

"Get to the bed and let me finish. I need more." I pushed her toward the bed. She beat me there, spreading her legs, welcoming me home. I dropped my drawers. My dick was already hard enough to bang her wetness out. Sliding in with no problem, I dug into her as deep as I could go, hearing her scream and seeing her shake. "I'm so sorry. Damn, I'm so sorry." Feeling her legs wrap around my body as I transitioned from roughhousing her body to making intimate love with her, this was my way of making up for my doggish ways to her. Kissing every inch of her body, sucking on her fat nipples, I swirled my dick around in her milkshake, knowing my true intentions. Samira was going to carry my child too. "Take this nut, girl, every fucking drop." Grunting, shoving myself as deep as I could go, hoping my whole load reached her womb, I was sure that within four weeks I'd be expecting a second kid. I should've left my baby juice up in her. I'd been a fool but not anymore.

We cuddled up with one another as she cried herself to sleep. As I rubbed the side of her face, I instantly felt guilty all over again. Knowing I was temporarily dodging a bullet by her being asleep, I couldn't withhold the urge to make love to her still-whimpering body. I might've loved the curves of Rayna's body, but I lusted after my sweet Samira, no doubt. Moving upward, so her plump booty rested on my already-stiff manhood, I rubbed it up and down her slit, hoping she'd stir up, ready to take more of me. She was already wet, which was probably a mixture of both our nuts, and I was more than definitely getting ready to leave more off up in her. One of these fat ones was gonna give her what she wanted. I'd heard pleas for a mini me. I now wanted one more than her.

Samira

King might've been slick as a snake, but I wasn't a fool. By no means was I going to let Rayna be the only one out here with his baby. Hell to the naw! She might've been first, but I held way more seniority in his life. That's why he was here with me instead of nursing her probably broken nose. Jamila did me a huge favor, so for sure I'd get her on the comeback. We rolled like that, always looking out for one another, so this was just another notch on her belt. She hated that King couldn't do right by me, and it showed.

I knew King was trying to get me pregnant, but I was praying that he did so. Every time he went deep, I pulled him in deeper. And when his eyes flew to the back of his head, letting me know he was getting ready to cum, I wrapped my legs around him, playing it off like I was exploding too. The only thing turning me on though was the fact that I was getting the chance to make the playing field even with Rayna. I more than wanted his baby at this point. I needed it.

Feeling King sliding himself up and down my crack, I arched my back after a few seconds, letting him know he didn't have to wait any longer. I was gonna take every opportunity available at missing my next period. Call it what you want, but I'd worked far too hard at making King who he was, sacrificing family, friends, and my sanity. I'd be damned if I left another chick swoop in to take what was rightfully mine.

As he stroked and sexed me for the rest of the night, I was overflowing with his nut. King was most certainly trying to make sure that even if he was shooting blanks, one would be ever so lucky to knock me up. Holding my pee, refusing to piss any off his baby juice out, I held it in, and when he left to clean himself up, I lifted my legs into the air, helping the nut work itself into my womb. *Please, God, let me have this man's baby. Let us be a family.*

Chapter Three

Rayna

"So you ain't gonna file a police report on that bitch? Girl, bye!"

"I ain't trying to hear you right now, Tiana. Until King tells me what to do, I'm going to lie low." I pulled out my phone and dialed his number again, and for the fifteenth time, it went straight to voicemail. I knew he was with Samira, and I was pissed he wasn't here with me. For all he knew, I could've gone into shock from getting sneak attacked and was having his firstborn. Dirty-ass nigga was just over here eating my pussy, and now he had his phone off, kissing her ass. Slamming my phone down, I looked over at Tiana, daring her to say one more word. She could get the tongue-thrashing I couldn't give King 'cause he was dodging me.

"Okay, chill on me. My bad. I won't say another word. That's your drama!" My roommate stomped out of the room to tend to the dick waiting in her bed.

That's what got me in this situation in the first place, letting King's drunk ass in my bed after an all-night session at the studio. He'd been like a savage in my pussy, busting nuts like a shotgun, so now we were getting prepared to be proud parents. I looked around the room at the gifts he'd already started buying: clothes, the car seat/stroller combo, and even a teddy bear to congratulate me on the pregnancy. He was all into this, just like me. Fuck whatever lie he was over there feeding Samira for her sanity.

I took off the dress I'd worn to floss on him and his longtime girlfriend. I knew she'd see me and put two and two together. But I didn't care how she felt. I was the one almost seven months pregnant and feeling unloved. It was time for her to get caught up and in the know about what everyone around her already was privy to. Even her homegirl Jamila knew from lurking on my Instagram page that I was carrying her best friend's man's kid, but she'd kept it to herself too. I posted sonogram pictures, Textgrams about having cravings, and I'd even started following baby-related shopping sites to give them sneak-watching heffas something to look at. I didn't know why she called herself coming at me so hard or thought I wouldn't get back with her when the time was right. Family ain't never meant shit to me, believe that! So, of course, his meant even less.

Jamila

"I feel like shit for letting her come to a gun fight without even a knife." Puffing on the blunt Johnie refused to share, I was taking this straight to the head alone because I felt horrible. It was hard as ever trying to play it off like I didn't know about everything once K.P. got busted. But with Rayna threatening to put her hands on Samira, I had no choice but to pop off on her. I was just lucky that Rayna kept it a secret that I knew about her pregnancy.

"We all kept that secret 'cause it wasn't our story to tell." Johnie sipped from the ice-cold beer I'd tossed him from my fridge. "I ain't gonna say baby girl found out the right way, but shit, King a grown man and can handle the messiness he creates."

"Yeah, that's all big, man, but dealing in the girlfriend code, I fucked up big time. If she ever finds out I rolled with Rayna not telling her that he'd slipped a Mickey in ol' girl's belly, me and her are gonna fall out in the worst way."

"Damn, sounds like you need to stop playing the middle and start standing your ground." Johnie had an annoying way of keeping it real that I really wasn't trying to hear at the time. I knew he was right, hell, I was feeding him the information to make the judgment from, but no one wants to get kicked when they're down. "I don't know much about the girl code, but Samira should understand you didn't want to get mixed up in that craziness they call a relationship. She knows her man." For once he was starting to make sense.

"Yeah, King has been throwing daggers her way their whole relationship. Couldn't be me." Starting to feel a little bit at ease, I realized there was nothing I could do about what had already been done. Hell, I wasn't the one who was introducing an illegitimate seed to the family.

"My manz be on that tip one hundred grand, but I can't call it. If I had a down-ass chick like Samira, I wouldn't be caught dead banging no rats trying to get on. Every chick who comes through the studio doors ain't doing nothing but checking for a come-up."

Johnie continued to sip from his beer. He wasn't like most of the cats I'd seen K.P. bring around. He seemed like his head was more tightly screwed to his shoulders. The more he drank down the Budweiser, the more he schooled me on how he rolled. And you know what they say: "A drunken mouth speaks with an honest tongue." I was starting to feel his swag most because he seemed down to earth, real chill, and laid-back. Finishing the beer, he asked for another, so I took that as he was trying to pull a nightcap. No way was I turning down a vamp session with his fine ass.

"So where'd you and King meet?" I asked, sitting across from him Indian style on the leather sectional I'd just gotten on layaway. I was trying to give him a peek between my thighs. I was working with a fat monkey, but it had been experiencing a drought. I usually wasn't into fucking with random niggas with STD rates at an all-time high, but if he made a move on me, a compromise would be made. Once my ex dipped to the snow white side of the fence, I was left to lube up my toys on a regular.

"Through a mutual friend who does beats. I'm just try-ing to get my name out here, ma." Johnie was starting to get more comfortable, which made me feel more at ease too. I'd caught him peeking at my pussy imprint, which was almost dripping wet out of my panties, so I knew the chances of it getting some attention tonight were good. It had been a long time since a dude had been so close to me and smelling so good. I was still half dressed from the party, which was scanty off rip, but if things played out the way his eyes were dancing toward my voluptuous breasts, I'd be naked within the hour.

"Is that all you're trying to get here?" I couldn't help myself from flirting. I couldn't blame my bluntness on the beer and weed because that would be lying. Johnie was looking sexy to me.

"What's up, ma, you trying to put me in the game?" Licking his lips, trying to hold his grin in, he wasn't accustomed to cutting into girls, you could tell, but he was going to take full advantage of the easy opportunity. Before I could respond making myself seem like a fool, he burst out laughing loudly like a hyena. "Let me not even set you up for a downfall. I'm about to be out. Boss man just hit me up that we're about to hit the studio to lay down a few tracks."

"Boy, bye. Whatever, you'll be back." Even with egg on my face, I wasn't about to look crazy for thinking he wanted to get down.

"I know, so put your number in my phone so I can call when I'm on the way." He tossed his iPhone my way. I was now the one grinning. Pushing the numbers in then entering Jamila with a heart, I didn't care if I was doing too much. I was claiming his pretty ass.

Chapter Four

King

Me and Samira had gotten down like two freaks straight out of a porno. My dick was sore, while I knew her walls were weak from the hours of makeup sex we were having. At some point, she'd gone from fighting me off in tears to being the one riding the nut out of me. She knew what I was up to, but the way she threw her pussy back on me was confirmation enough that she was on board for at least giving our family a try.

Hearing her lightly snoring, I eased my arms from around her carefully, hoping she wouldn't wake up. Samira simply didn't deserve the hell I was getting ready to put her through. With the sheets and her full of my drunken cum, she would be too far in deep with me to leave. Like most girls' trap niggas, I'd set out to trap Samira. A nigga wasn't known to bust blanks, so she better hope I ain't knock triplets off into that wanting womb of hers. Fully out of bed and searching for my phone, I studied her innocence once again before grabbing a fresh pair of drawers from the dresser so I could go chill out in the man cave.

I powered on my PlayStation 4 and iPhone, and it only took moments for my notifications to start blowing up. Rayna was going hard in each text, not holding her verbal thrashes back on my voicemail, and threatening to even hold our unborn child from me once she dropped him or her onto this earth. Feeling my blood pressure rising, I wasn't in the mood to nurse her feelings or deal with another one of her threats. Rayna had gotten comfortable trying to control me with her threats, but tonight she was gonna strike out. Putting my phone on silent, I shot Johnie a text to come through here, then I set it down, picking up the controller instead. Killing a few chumps in *Black Ops* always put me at ease. My plan was to put Rayna on ice for a few days to make my home right. I'd never been 100 percent without my other half, Samira, so until she smiled without crying the next minute, I'd be posted right up under her.

Samira

If you'd ever woken up not knowing if you've truly just lived through a nightmare, then you could relate to the roller coaster I was on. Feeling I was in the bed alone, I dared to think where King was. If he wasn't somewhere in this house though, I was sure I was about to be the number one suspect in a breaking-news story for putting a bullet through his skull. I wanted to call Jamila for an all-out girls' venting session, but I wasn't in the mood to hear all of her "single woman" advice. She didn't understand the complexity of what was me and King sometimes, especially with her not having a man anymore.

I thought back on last night, and everything started to blur together. At first, me and my homegirl Mila were having a great time at King's album release celebration party. Then we were getting dragged out kicking and screaming by two guys in King's entourage. His right-hand man Johnie never left my side. As bad as King wanted to escort my wild, crazy, heel-hitting ass, he had to settle up with the owner on all of the tabs we'd racked up. After seeing him kissing all over Rayna, throwing the bottle, then seeing she was about to pop with a pregnancy from my fiancé, I'd lost track when he smacked me down in front of everyone at Flood's. What did I do to deserve this? Why me? Why couldn't he strap the fuck up or at least gun that bitch straight down to the clinic?

Already having a headache, which I contributed to, a hangover mixed with a broken heart, I tried not to think about anything more than the hopes King had gotten me pregnant too. At least with my own baby, I wouldn't be concentrating on the li'l bastard I had to secretly hate. It didn't matter what the circumstances were, that kid could be related to King all day long, it would never be kin to me. I wasn't into playing stepmomma for a child he conceived with a rat in the streets while we were together. Judge me if you want. I'll do me while you do you.

Getting enough strength to get up, I moved as quickly as I could to the bathroom. I'd been holding it in for hours, even in my sleep, so it was more than a wave of relief. Sticky from all of our cum, I took a quick ho bath in the sink, having to see where King had disappeared to. More than likely he was in the basement, but if he was cake baking on the phone trying to make shit cool between him and her, I'd be walking in swinging.

"A'ight, find King's slick ass." Speaking out loud, slipping his shirt over my head, I didn't bother putting on panties since I was in my own house. Creeping through the house like I myself was a stranger, I didn't want to alert him I was even up. From now on, he couldn't be trusted to even take a leak alone. Had I kept more of a tight leash on him, Little Miss Home-wrecker wouldn't be in the position to ruin the little family I'd work hard at keeping. Seeing the light on in the basement, I knew he'd be down there. That's the only place he could ever find total peace.

Our house was a three-story colonial, basement included, which King reserved for his man cave and studio. His setup was sweet, and I'd put in long hours at the hospital wiping asses to make sure he got the best HDTV Best Buy sold, the most comfortable leather sectional Art Van allowed me to finance, and a decked-out bar stocked with bottles of Rëmy VSOP, Hennessy, and even Amsterdam if he was trying to get totally lit with his crew. Our house sometimes turned into the Honeycomb Hideout with his artists hanging out laying verses down. I didn't mind putting in overtime to cash King out. Having him home meant I knew exactly where he was at all times.

Seeing him on the couch with the remote in his hand and head tilted took me back to the days when he'd first started trying to get recognized in Detroit. He'd go long and hard grinding, staying up days at a time going hard at his craft, then he would tap out just like this. Thought I wanted to go over, straddle his lap, and love all over him like I used to do, my heart couldn't let me give in. After I had a few winks of sleep and a moment to clear my head, the feelings of betrayal were starting to sit deep in the pit of my stomach. His phone began to light up beside him, which pissed me off even more. *Oh, yeah, Rayna, starting early huh? Naw, bitch, you ain't gonna ruin my day today. I'm gonna show your ass who got the better hand, believe that!*

I marched back upstairs, leaving King to sleep. With the sun starting to rise he'd be up soon enough. Going into the bathroom, I ran myself a hot bubble bath with Epsom salt so I could try to relieve my tense body. When I got done getting my body right, I'd pack for both me and him to hit I-75 to Toledo. He'd created this box he was in so today he'd have to man up. It was all or nothing. Either he could make me Mrs. Samira Wallace on demand or walk out of my life for good with the clothes on his back.

'Cause for damn sure straight he wasn't taking nothing I copped for his ass! Sliding into the tub of water, I felt my body melting into the heat. Yup, I liked the ring of that: Mr. and Mrs. Wallace.

Rayna

King had me all the way fucked up. I'd been calling and texting his phone all night since that bitch Jamila tried to see me at Flood's, but I guessed I wasn't as precious as Samira. Silly me for thinking this kid I was carrying meant the world to him. Flipping the visor down to make sure my lip hadn't started to swell again, I couldn't wait to give birth so I could square up with ol' girl for swinging on me. She was the fakest person out of all this, stunting hard on me like she didn't know what was up.

As the sun started to peek through the dusk-lit sky, I circled the block of where King and Samira stayed. I knew he didn't think I remembered where he'd taken me on one of the first few nights of us creeping, but I did. When Samira was at her study group session for her boards, I was getting all types of attention all through her crib. So here I was again. Nothing about my soul could rest not knowing where me and K.P. stood. Coming all the way around, then pulling up a few houses down from where they lived, I hoped I wouldn't stand out on this well-to-do block. Knowing the headlights would still run, I shut the ignition off then reclined my seat to lurk more comfortably. I wasn't leaving this house until he did, or at least until he answered my phone calls.

I rubbed my stomach. It was starting to grumble 'cause it was time for my early morning snack. I was glad I was about at the end of this pregnancy, because I was as big as a house. I didn't know if I'd ever get my pre-pregnancy body back. "Chill out, li'l one. After I catch your daddy up, I'll feed you." This baby might as well get used to not coming first in my life. I'd never been the one to want children, but I always knew I'd end up having one just to keep a nigga. That's how girls around my way played it. If a dude had money, the potential to get more money, or basically had a sponsor mentality, we'd work overtime hours wobbling on the dick to catch a seed. This baby was my way of making sure I'd never have to work for minimum wage on the line again.

Samira and King stayed near the University of Detroit area off of 7 Mile and Livernois in a house her parents left to her once they relocated down South. This area had been reserved for the more elite residents of Detroit who couldn't quite afford to stay inside of Rosedale Park or even Grosse Pointe but still worked and paid taxes in the city. It was a lot different from my cookie-cutter subsidized housing project. I looked around to see if any neighbors noticed my beat-up silver sedan. The neighborhood was still in fairly nice condition. Every home on the block was still standing, no houses had been left vacant to deteriorate, and even the birds in their community still chirped. What in the fuck was he slumming with me for? I ain't got no parents leaving me no houses! Not trying to dog myself out or nothing, but the two-bedroom townhouse I shared with my roommate Tiana could and rightfully should be considered a shack compared to how these two were living. Feeling a sting of jealousy spark inside of me, I wondered if my baby would ever have a green yard to play in, as opposed to just the few concrete steps right outside of my door.

Seeing his Lincoln truck tucked away in the driveway with her MKS right on his bumper, I felt tears start to build up in the corners of my eyes. I started my car back up, double-parking it directly in front of their house. If King wouldn't answer my calls, he'd for sure pay me some attention once I stepped foot on his territory. Hotfooting it up the walkway, I knew there was no turning back. The house was quiet and still, but that wasn't to say someone wasn't watching. With my pistol loaded right underneath my shirt, I dared Samira or her pit bull, Jamila, to run up again. This time I wouldn't be going down or away without a fight.

Ding-dong! Ding-dong!

King

"Shit, dog, that's my bad. I turned the phone off 'cause Rayna's crazy ass was calling back-to-back. I'd just gotten Samira to calm down, you feel me?" Explaining to Johnie why I hadn't been answering the phone, I sat up groggily, wiping the drool from my mouth. I needed about another good hour. Hearing my phone beep from call waiting, I held it back from my ear seeing it was Rayna calling again. Letting the call hang out there, I didn't want her to know she was intentionally being ignored.

"I ran up out of a hot one's crib to check in with your drunk-in-love, nutty ass, and you over there running from some shit you created? I'm about to shoot back through there 'cause I see you're tripping." Johnie intentionally left off that he was talking about Jamila not wanting his business put out there.

"A'ight, playboy. I heard that! What else did I miss last night?"

"Luckily that bottle Samira launched at your head. She straight shut the party down once she saw ol' girl." He laughed at my expense. I couldn't even blame Johnie for finding so much humor in it. All the fellas I'd rolled with warned me about trying to live a double life, but until the joke flipped on me, everything was fun. "Naw, but for real, I ain't even knocked her off yet. She's hot and ready for a nigga, though."

"You a wild boy, J! A wild motherfucking boy! I told you those soulful lovemaking tracks was gonna have the ladies wide open." I gave my manz his credit. Johnie was gonna have a flock of groupies jocking his every move once I produced him to be on my level. He was single with no kids plus could sing a woman out of her panties. Me and J were already making money together with plans laid out to make more. "Listen up, playboy, before you head back to tear some lucky chick off, swing through here to get these tracks I need you to lay down at the studio. I've gotta make things right with my lady, so I ain't gonna be making it in to work for the next few days." Standing up stretching, I was getting ready to make my way back upstairs to give Samira another dose of dick. I was on a baby-making spree.

"I'm bending the block now. Is shorty cooled down at least, K.P.? I ain't trying to walk into no war zone."

"It's quiet around these parts for now. That's why I'm trying to get you in and out. I'm about to open the door. One." Hanging my phone up, then turning everything off so I wouldn't hear Mira complain about the electricity bill, I hadn't reached the top of the staircase before the doorbell rang twice. "This nigga right here moves like lightning speed. I told him I'd open the door. Why'd the fuck he ring the bell?" Talking out loud, all the while running to the door, I didn't want Samira disturbed. I knew she wasn't going to wake up on the right side of the bed for all the right reasons, so I wasn't trying to get another red bottom heel to my dome for letting a nigga in her house at the wrong time.

"Nigga, I told you my lady was asleep, so why'd you—" Swinging the door open without looking through the peephole, I dropped my head in utter regret knowing my morning was starting right where my night had left off. I couldn't believe Rayna was staring back at me.

"Your lady huh, King? Fuck your lady right about now!" Raising her voice, Rayna was intentionally trying to start a scene. "Why haven't you been answering my calls? Why are you putting her before us?" Pointing to her growing stomach, she was really attempting to lay it on thick.

"Hey, lower your motherfucking voice, girl," I hushed her, walking out of the comfy house me and Samira shared and onto the porch, making sure to pull the door closed behind me. "You've got me fucked up if you think you're about to pop up here questioning me. Get the fuck on from my house." I didn't care about a single word Rayna was crying to me. She'd crossed the line by coming to where me and Samira laid our heads. She was nothing more than my baby momma, so she needed to act like it.

"You must be leaving here with me, King. 'Cause I ain't going nowhere without the father of my child as my escort." Rolling her eyes, giving me an ultimatum, she must've been snorting the highest priced crack-cocaine on the streets of Detroit to think I'd leave my security blanket for a Section 8 recipient.

"I ain't got no patience for this shit right now. I'll hit you up later, Rayna. Now real talk, for the last time, get the fuck from off my porch and block now!" All in her face, gritting my teeth trying not to raise my voice, I was gearing up to rip her head off.

"I'm not leaving!" she yelled as loud as she could.

"Bitch, please!" Within seconds my hands were wrapped tightly around her neck. "I keep telling your ass, Rayna, quit testing me!" Blinking out, only seeing red, I had her pregnant body bent over the banister with no remorse. The little punches she was landing on me were nothing compared to the weight I was putting on her. Slamming Rayna against the brick wall, I almost broke her back.

"Let go, oh, my God, please!" she begged through pants, which made my grip tighter.

"Don't bring your messy ass back around here! When I'm ready to be bothered with you and that bastard, I'll let you know." Whispering in her ear, I'd become ruthless. Rayna had overstepped her boundaries by coming to my home, so she had to suffer some consequences. Making sure she knew I meant business, I released my grip then shoved her as hard as I could. "King has spoken!"

"I can't believe you're doing me like this. Your momma ain't raise you to be worth shit, you old scumbag-ass nigga!" She talked cash shit, walking backward toward her car. I was everything but the son of God, plus I'd never see my kid. Once Johnie swooped into the driveway right on time, Rayna hurried her pace but not before picking up one of the LED outdoor lights placed along the walkway and launching it toward my car. Whop! The driver's side door was instantly dented, and my custom paint job was ruined. "You're gonna regret putting your hands on Rayna Robinson," she shrieked at the top of her lungs.

"Naw, you crazy bitch, I'm gonna put one through ya ass!" I ran off the porch toward her. Samira could be awake at this point for all I cared 'cause I was prepped to take Rayna's motherfucking head off! Johnie grabbed me before I could make it to her, giving her enough time to pull off. "Nigga, if I would've had my piece on me, I would've put one in that ratchet-acting-ass bitch!"

"Hey, K.P. manz, let that broad go. You've got bigger problems up top."

Getting a grip of myself, still fuming and ready to chase Rayna down on foot, I turned to see Samira standing in the door with her arms crossed, more pissed than a bitch.

"So if you never brought her here, how does that bitch know where we stay? Call her up, King. I've got more than a few words for that home-wrecker!" Draped in a towel, naked underneath, she was pacing back and forth and screaming louder than I'd ever heard her. I didn't dare run up on her like I did at Flood's though, 'cause in all actuality, she had every reason to be livid. Hell, I was outraged too. She went back inside to our bedroom, and I followed her.

"Listen, baby, I swear to Allah I've never brought her in our house." Lying, crossing my fingers so I wouldn't get struck down, I'd only fucked Rayna one time here, but I thought she was too drunk to remember. "She must've followed us here last night or something, 'cause bringing her to our home is most definitely crossing the line." Saying anything to cool her down, I knew the lies coming out of my mouth would only temporarily cool her down.

"Nigga, you better hope I don't find out otherwise." Now that she was in my face, I could tell she was itching to put her hands on me but was thinking twice about it. "I'm tired of these motherfucking surprises, King! You can't have your cake and eat it too with these trife-life tricks."

"I ain't invite her yamp ass over here, Samira. Matter of fact, you can check with these nosy-ass neighbors around here about how Rayna got handled."

"Oh, you name-dropping around this bitch now huh?" She picked up the television remote, flinging it at me, and I dodged to the left just in time before it had the chance to slap me in the face.

It took me one second to lunge across the room, grabbing her arms to restrain her. She was screaming, swinging, and kicking trying to get out of my grip, but she was no match for my size and strength. "Calm your ass down, Samira! I'll let you go but not to be throwing shit at me." I pushed her onto the bed lightly. That was my way of telling her to stay the fuck up off me. "I ain't gonna be walking on eggshells around here, Mira. Flat out, you know ol' girl ain't going anywhere because of the baby. But neither are you. I ain't about to be going through this shit every time I bring her name up. You're going to have to find a better way to deal."

"Find a better way to deal? She ain't going nowhere? You think I'm stuck? See, King, ain't shit wrong with me. I can find someone else to love on me, nigga. Just so you know, I ain't trapped in the game. You are. I'm here because I love you, so please believe that every time I hear that slut bitch Rayna's name, I'm going all the way in on you. It is what it is."

"Baby, please forgive and believe me. The shit ends here. It's me and you." I snuggled her body, feeling my dick start to wake up. That was the only way I knew how to make her feel better. It infuriated me thinking of her with another man, in every way imaginable.

"I want more than the dick, King. You're obviously out here giving girls enough of that. It ain't special no more." Letting out sobs and tears, Samira's voice was cracking, but she continued. "I want your last name, for you to make it official with me. She might be having your baby first, but I should be the one you vow 'til death do you part." The look in Samira's eyes let me know she was cutthroat serious. Baby girl wasn't prepared to back down, but I couldn't blame her 'cause she'd been working for the wife spot since I met her.

"That's nothing, ma. We can do that. I'm ready to do right by you. Fuck all these girls out here because ain't none of 'em held me down like you." I meant every last word I was speaking to Samira. She'd earned the stripes to be Mrs. King Wallace.

Rayna

"He did what, Rayna? Are you okay? I told you about that rap-a-lot-ass nigga. You need to chill out before you fuck my godchild up with that stress." Tiana swung open the door to our townhouse as I stumbled up the few stairs inside. I'd called her right as I sped off of K.P.'s block.

Plopping down on the couch, I was flat-out exhausted. For the first few miles of me leaving King's house, I was driving like a bat out of hell thinking he was chasing me. Breathing hard, rubbing at my sore neck, I was glad to be home. "Make sure the dead bolt is on and don't let his ass up in here if he does come knocking. I'm straight." It was foolish for me to think he was coming. My phone hadn't rung, and I was miles across town already.

"Girl, bye! You are far from straight. Those marks around your neck tell me he choked your ass out for real. And what type of nigga puts their hands on a pregnant woman, especially if the woman is carrying their child?" Tiana was angrier than me.

"That's the point, T. I ain't his woman. I went over there looking like the fool. I might have his dick on lock, if that, but Samira has his heart. That shit was more than evident." Feeling my back starting to cramp and pressure in my abdomen, I shifted in my seat, trying to ease the sudden tension.

"But you've got his baby, so that nigga should be respecting that if nothing else." Seeing that I was in pain, she rushed to my side, trying to see what exactly was wrong. "Don't tell me that fool done sent you into labor!"

"Naw, chill, T. I don't think so. It hurts right where he bent me backward over the banister, so that's probably just the bruise settling in. Can you grab me the heating pad?"

"Bitch, fuck a heating pad. We need to get to the hospital to make sure that baby ain't trying to come up out of you. I'm about to grab my purse!" Tiana was persistent, but with the amount of pain I was going through on account of these spasms, I was thankful that at least someone cared about me and my unborn child.

Chapter Five

Samira

I had King on the road pushing damn near eighty miles per hour heading toward Toledo, Ohio. He gave me the green light saying we could get married, so hell yeah, a bitch was chasing his last name. I'd be a fool not to. My whole life had been surrounded by King and his dream of being a songwriter/producer, so you better believe I was gonna ride this one all the way out. I didn't care if he was playing me. He was my family, damn it, and wasn't no hood rat about to ruin that. With Rayna about to pop at any minute, she'd be using that little bastard as bait against him for sure. The drama had already started, but this was my way of finishing it, or at least becoming more competitive in the game. Dressed in a simple white bubble dress that buttoned down my stomach then flared out right before my knees, I kept it cute and simple with a pair of studded sandals, accessorizing with diamonds.

"Are you sure you don't want to have a big wedding, Samira?" Turning down the Drake CD I had blasting, he questioned my decision, obviously ready to start another round of beef with me.

"Nigga, just drive. We can handle all of that later. You're about to do right by me today." I wasn't about to give King any extra time out here on the streets as a single man. "You already snuck a baby in on me. I'd be damned if I let a bitch sneak you to the alter, too!"

King couldn't help laughing at that before replying, "I'm just saying, though. This shit right here is cheating you out of the real thing. You deserve more. With the money I'm about to be bringing in with all these songs I've been writing, the bread will definitely be there for you to have the fairy-tale wedding you deserve and I know deep down you want." King was really laying it on thick, but I wasn't trying to hear it. Any reasoning he could've done with me was out the window when Rayna showed up to the house I owned.

"Are you serious with me right now? Let's just cut this conversation short. I ain't trying to argue with you on my wedding day, King. You and I both know what I deserve, and I'm tired of waiting." Smacking my lips and turning the music back up, I wasn't getting ready to entertain anything that didn't involve him becoming my husband on paper.

Jamila

"Samira is not answering my call. Oh, my God!" Rolling out of bed buck-naked, I slid on my robe, hitting the redial button relentlessly.

"King is not answering my calls either. He said him and Samira had to take some time away from the world, though. But fuck that. Keep calling back until she picks up. I'm about to swing back past their house to see if they're still scrapping it out," Johnie slid on his clothes, making a beeline for the door.

Pacing the room with the phone on speaker, I kept refreshing Rayna's Instagram page to see if she'd uploaded any new pictures. The last few posts had blown the sexual high Johnie wasted no time getting me on. Ol' ratchet Rayna was in labor.

Samira

We stopped at the jewelers along the way to grab him a simple wedding band. I was feeling waves of relief seeing King pushing forward and not backing down on his word to do me right. Once we arrived at the courthouse, butterflies danced in my stomach as we walked hand in hand inside as the last time as girlfriend and boyfriend.

"Listen, King." I grabbed his arm before he could get through the metal detector. "Don't take me in here to make no fool of me later. If you don't really want this, don't do this." With tears swelling up in my eyes, I didn't want to give him a choice, but I didn't want to feel like I was forcing him into marrying me either. I didn't think I could live with that hanging over my head.

"Can't nobody make me do shit I don't wanna do. Having a big wedding is for you. I've got all I need right here. Let's do this." Walking through the metal detectors, King didn't have to say no more, because from this point on I was strutting with total confidence.

I cried every step of the way, from filing our paperwork to signing our marriage certificate. *I can't believe this is real! Wait until that trick Rayna finds out I'm the real chosen one, the motherfucking wife!* King held my hand, kissed me adoringly, and tried his best to make any worries I had disappear. I respected his game 'cause I was more in love with him now than ever. Marrying us outside of the courthouse underneath a cherry blossom tree, Pastor Dinwiddie united me and King, making us officially husband and wife. As I looked up at the man who I'd spent seven long years of my life with, I sincerely thought this first kiss as newlyweds would be a new start to the rest of our lives.

King

Call it whatever you want, I'd made Samira my Mrs. Wallace. Maybe now she'd take me having a child by Rayna a little easier. Being real, I was gonna try to do right by my wife by not cheating, but what man can withhold the dick from their baby mom? Ya manz was gonna get an A for effort, but Rayna was a monster for what she wanted.

Laid-back on cruise control on our way back to the D, I was tuned into Samira calling out flight details about our getaway honeymoon to Miami. It was gonna be hella nice to get out of dodge for a while and maybe hook up with Turquoise while there. We'd both planned on making the big announcement together right before leaving, then having a large reception once back.

"Let's get a room 'til we leave, like a pre-honeymoon." I turned to Mira, hoping she'd say yes. This was also my way of keeping things calm with Rayna. I knew she was a headbanger who'd come back around the way, so us staying at a hotel room would be assurance I'd keep them separate until shit cooled down. My name was just starting to get big in the game. This foolishness could stop me from rising to the top, though.

"Hell yeah, babe, I'm with that." She winked devilishly. "Unzip your pants so I can give my husband a li'l taste of what he's gonna get tonight."

"Shit, you ain't gotta tell me twice, Mrs. Wallace!" I held the steering wheel with one hand while quickly unzipping the linen pants I was wearing with the other. Samira reached over into my lap like a vulture grabbing my still-soft penis. "Whoa, wife, you ain't playing!" I felt my meat instantly growing inside of her warm mouth. Samira was tickling my shaft licking up and down and going in vicious with her tongue. She'd never gone to town on my dick like this ever before. Kinda made me wish I would've wifed her long ago. I was almost getting ready to send my seed down her throat when the phone in my pocket vibrated. I ignored it, hoping Samira would too. Of course my luck had run out.

"Answer it!" She popped her head up, leaving my dick wet and dry. "I know that's ya girl."

"Be cool, don't stop." I was trying to push her head back down, and my only concern was releasing this nut.

"Boy, bye, you better answer that phone. You already know I'm pulling the wife card." Now sitting all the way over in her seat, she made it clear it was over for the ever-so-great impromptu head job.

Pulling the phone from my pocket, I knew that if I answered it would automatically come through my truck's speakers. And I couldn't have that. Tiana had been blowing me up for the past hour but had gone unnoticed. The first step on my agenda once in the room was to get my number changed. That chick could get an Obama throwaway phone number. "Oh, shit, you tripping, babe." I was relieved to read the caller ID. "This ain't nobody but Jamila's crazy ass." Pressing TALK quickly, I was about to hurriedly change the settings before she noticed what I was doing.

"Hey, Mila boo! 'We's married now!'" Samira sang out into the phone, quoting Shug Avery from *The Color Purple*.

"Bitch, what? Say, do I give a fuck? Where's ya wannabe husband at?"

The voice wasn't Jamila's. It was Tiana's. *Damn, sneaky trick must've got me with the spoof-number app.*

"Ay yo, ma, don't speak to my wife like that. Matter of fact, lose my number and tell ya girl the good news. I'll be in touch." Playing like a beast, I was insulted that Rayna was even allowing this behavior from her roommate.

"You better kiss my—"

Hanging up before she could get another word out, Samira was already on her phone calling Jamila to make sure this wasn't no shady best-friend shit.

"Get off that phone, Mrs. Wallace. We ain't entertaining nothing that don't concern me and you." Snatching the phone out of her hand and hanging up the call, I'd already powered my phone off then did the same to hers.

"Well, at least the word has been put out there." Not pressing the issue, she settled back but still looked uneasy. "I guess you're right."

I played her like putty, rubbing my hands across her thighs. "Of course I'm right. Don't let that ruin our day. Come on and get back to giving me a pre-honeymoon treat." At first, Samira gave me the side-eye, but within moments of my hand cupping her camel toe, my dick was back getting licked off.

Rayna

"Did he answer, Tiana? Is he on his way?" Concentrating on the beeping noises of the many machines I was hooked up to, I could barely focus on anything else knowing my baby was coming before he was done baking. This shit with King had really turned for the worse.

"Naw, that ho-ass nigga is not on his way. I didn't even get to tell him you were in labor!" Tiana was fuming as she pressed REDIAL, placing the phone back up to her ear. "Bad enough I had to download that spoof application putting in Jamila's number, with her fake ass, for him to answer."

"How'd you even get her number?" I had to question even though it wasn't an important detail.

"You already know I'm like the female Inspector Gadget of the dirty D. Plus she listed it on her Facebook page. Damn, I think King's ass turned his phone off now 'cause it's going straight to his voicemail."

"Just take a few more pictures for Instagram so Mila can go back and report on 'em. They can't hide from me and mine." Rubbing my belly as the nurse wheeled me to the room where I'd deliver my premature bundle of joy, I smiled as Tiana snapped and recorded away. "Hey, Insta! I'm getting ready to pop li'l King Jr. out. It's about to go down, but I must admit I'm a little scared. Help ya girl get prayed up, boos!"

"Oh, that's cute. They are gonna fall the fuck out 'cause I'm about to tag Jamila, King, and Samira. Private or not, she'll get the notification then won't be able to help but to lurk." Tiana was thinking on her toes just the way I needed her to. With me being hooked up to monitors and IVs, my motion was limited.

"Rayna Robinson, what are we doing here so early?" Dr. Wang walked in, grabbing my chart then coming to the side of my bed.

"Um, sir, let me excuse you two for one moment. Dr. Wang, can you take a look at this monitor please?" The nurse stepped in, stopping my explanation before it could get started. Truth be told, I didn't know what reason I would give my doctor for being in labor two months early.

"Rayna, I have a few concerns I must speak to you about," Dr. Wang cut into my thoughts with urgency. "Your son's heart rate keeps dropping."

Chapter Six

Samira

Back at home, I was running through the house like a madwoman trying to pack enough clothes for me and King to stay gone until Wednesday. He was downstairs getting him enough paraphernalia to get himself through. Plus he'd promised while down there we could celebrate with Johnie and Jamila. It was about to be bottles popped because I'd finally snatched my man up for good. Truth be told over it all, I was glad he'd suggested going to the room before leaving for Miami. He wasn't playing me into a trick bag. He was reading my mind. I didn't want no parts of ol' trick-ass Rayna either. For some reason, her roommate called on the tip, but since today was me and King's start on a new life, I wasn't turning that phone of mine back on.

"Come on, wife, let's be out!" King shouted upstairs.

Damn, I loved the sound of that! "Coming, baby!" Throwing my duffel bag over my shoulder then pulling out the handle to drag King's luggage out of the room, I did a double check around just to make sure nothing we needed was forgotten.

Ding-dong! Ding-dong! Ding-dong!

"Who the fuck is that, King? Don't tell me that bitch is at my house again!" Dropping my bags and running full speed out of the room down the stairs, I was getting ready to bust a bitch's ass this time for sure. "King, you heard me calling you!"

Seeing Johnie but no female with him, I stopped dead in my tracks. "Hey, J, what are you doing here? King? Why ain't y'all answering?" Something about the looks on their faces, not to mention the vibe in the air, told me whatever they were gawking at on Johnie's screen would ruin everything good about my wedding day.

"Baby, listen, look, um . . ." King couldn't stop himself from stuttering.

"Nigga, talk. What is going on? Don't sugarcoat shit with me right now." I was scalding hot, standing now with my arms crossed. Johnie couldn't do much but look down to the ground, shaking his head.

King stared at me head-on, trying not to blink, trying to read my mind. "Wife, I promise I'm sorry. Before these words even leave my mouth, I know they're gonna hurt you."

"Spare me all that malarkey. Spill it."

"Rayna is at the hospital giving birth to my son." He pushed Johnie's phone into my face. I smacked my lips, grimacing at each picture and video of my husband's baby momma.

"You shouldn't ever forget this date, King Wallace. You got your first wife and your first son on the same day. Not related."

King

"I ain't got time to nurse your feelings right now, Samira. I've been doing that shit all day. My son wasn't due until November, so some shit must be wrong." Brushing past her to grab my keys, seeing her face turned up with an attitude had me pissed. I'd already gone too far by putting my hands on Rayna to spare Samira from the cold, harsh truth. But that was what probably had my little one coming too early. No way in hell was I going further into the dog house letting her birth him alone. Everything had gotten out of hand. "Look, it's time for me to be a man about my shit and quit letting y'all puppet master me around. I married yo' ass, so please be happy about something!"

"I'll be happy when you grow up into a man, King. It ain't a day I ain't buying your ass an extra-value meal, a bag of weed, or even a fresh outfit to rock for these tricks like you're a real boss. Boy, I made you. The only reason why Rayna checked for your slimy-dick ass anyway was because of me, Samira Taylor." Throwing more than a few low blows, she was going for the jugular. I had to give her credit.

"Well, baby girl, be that as it may, you're Samira Wallace now. You made sure of that this morning. And since you're so good at raising boys, making their lives worthwhile, and being a saving grace, you surely won't mind changing Junior's diapers or making his bottles."

I left Johnie at the house to make sure Samira stayed put and calm while nursing her wounds. When I closed the door behind her cursing, screaming, and crying that she'd get me back, it was taking everything out of me not to run in to lay her ass out cold. I'd bent over backward trying to right my wrongs, even marrying her to prove she was the one I wanted to spend the rest of my life with. But right about now, even that wasn't good enough.

Lighting a freshly rolled blunt, trying to get high as a kite, I couldn't believe that after twenty-seven years of dodging bullets I was about to be a father. Rayna wasn't the ideal baby momma, but what was done couldn't be reversed. You couldn't have told me that Samira wasn't gonna be the mother to my firstborn, but the way I kept my dick swinging in the streets, this shouldn't have been a surprise.

Mira wasn't wrong about everything she'd done for me, no doubt. I'd taken her car for days, leaving her alone in the house, taken money from her account, and let the bailiff come to our last house when I lied about paying the rent. Naw, it wasn't like I'd always been a man in our relationship, but I'd been there with her ass every night dicking her down making sure she didn't have a day of pent-up juice. To me, we were serving each other's needs.

"Oh, look who decided to call back. You must be on your way," Tiana smartly answered the phone, reminding me of how much drama I was getting ready to deal with on their side of the game.

"What hospital are y'all at?" Being straightforward, I wasn't trying to feed into her attitude.

"Hutzel." Taking my hint, she was up front too.

"I'm in the car. Let her know I'm on the way, T." Hanging up the phone not wanting to hold a friendly conversation, I turned the radio back up and kept puffing on the blunt, trying to zone out.

Rayna

The palms of my hands were inflamed as I gripped the steel bars of the hospital bed. I was screaming to the high heavens, and my body was shaking in regret. Each time a contraction kicked in, my eyes rolled to the back of my head as this so-called premature baby was prepping to tear my vagina to shreds.

"Come on, baby, you can do this! You heard the doctor. You're doing wonderful!" Screaming over all other voices in the overcrowded city hospital, King burst into the delivery room like he owned the right to be calling shots in this motherfucker. "Come on, baby girl, do what the doctor tells you so you can deliver me a healthy boy."

Grabbing my hand from the bar, King tried to fall right into his role of what I wished he would act like 100 percent of the time to me: my man.

Cutting my eyes at him with the look of pure repugnance, I didn't want his slimy, cheating hands anywhere near me. Had it not been for him roughing me up on the porch, I wouldn't be in labor now.

"You can breathe easy now, babe. I'm here for you and my little soldier." King leaned down, kissing my sweaty forehead and having everyone immediately fooled. The nurses and even the four-eyed Asian doctor himself had the nerve to smile, approving of King's award-winning presentation of a nigga who really cares.

I tried playing the role too, happy that he'd gotten some sense finally putting me first, but his presence was disgusting me. King reeked of Samira's Beyoncé Heat perfume, and that band on his finger hadn't gone unnoticed. *This ain't the time, Rayna. Be cool just 'til this baby is out. You know what the doctor said.* Looking up at everyone smiling at us, happy that I was no longer solo dolo giving a high-risk birth infuriated me more. They didn't know my struggle, because this charade King was putting on was some straight bullshit!

"That's so wonderful that you made it, Mr. Robinson." The nurse smiled at King, in my eyes halfway flirting. "I wish more fathers were as supportive as you."

"That's what's up, thanks. But ain't no way in the world I'd leave her up in here to bring my junior into the world alone." He leaned down to kiss me again. I'd had enough, snatching my head back, letting him know I was done playing along. This nigga was dead-ass wrong for coming up in here with a band on his wedding finger after all that was said and done earlier like he was my number one supporter.

"Please quit punk faking for these bitches, K.P.! Give 'em room to fall back," I growled through my clenched teeth, fighting away the pain of another hard-hitting contraction. Going straight into it, I let out a tear-jerking cry because the pain was unbearable and I couldn't give King the ass whipping he deserved. Starting to spaz like the Tasmanian Devil, my body was losing control like in *The Exorcist:* shaking, shivering, and screaming. After the gruesome contraction was over, I fell back knowing another one would be hitting me soon. The Pitocin dripping through my IV had them suckers slamming back-to-back, but anything they could give me to get this baby out was well worth it.

The grin the nurse once couldn't wipe from her face had been replaced with a look of uncertainty. King still stood by my side, looking dumbfounded and not knowing what to say. As I panted hard trying to catch my breath, I pushed the few loose strands of hair in my face up into my ponytail. Biting my lip with anger, I was fed the fuck up. I was up in this bed going through the struggle with his kid while he was with her. That's some bullshit! He wasn't worried about her stanking ass while he was ramming this troublemaker up in me! "Get the fuck up off me, K.P.! I can't stand your stanking, trifling ass!"

"Chill with that shit, Rayna, and let a nigga be there for you. This ain't the time for all that!"

"I been blowing you up since I got here, King. I wasn't important then, so don't play me like I'm important now." Out of breath through my sentence, feeling another gush of pain nearing, I was tired of being his dedicated jump off while he played the streets like a boss. "Plus you hung up on Tiana when she called. This isn't the time for that. I ain't forgot about earlier!"

"Okay, Rayna, remember what we talked about earlier? The baby's heartbeat is starting to drop again because your pressure is rising, plus there are my other concerns. My team is prepping the O.R. for surgery," said the doctor.

Before I could blink, the nurse was shoving papers into my face for me to sign. I wasn't a fan of having a Cesarean section, but my options were bleak. The baby's heartbeat dropped drastically earlier, so the doctor warned me about his concerns for continuing with natural labor. Had I not wanted to give ol' jackass King more time to make it here, the doctor would've been cut me open.

"Whoa, Doc, and slow up signing those papers, Rayna. I need to know what conversation was had, then why the fuck an O.R. needs to be prepped. What concerns? Somebody better get to talking about my son!"

"Well, Mr. Wallace—" the doctor started to explain, but I cut him off straightaway.

"Naw, Dr. Wang, you don't have to explain nothing to Mr. Wallace." I rolled my eyes at King with hate. "And, King, had you not set me on my ass earlier for the so-called love of your life, you would be in the know about what was going on with our son. So don't come in here chin checking me or the doctor." Snatching the pen from the nurse, I signed my name quickly, feeling another contraction hitting. "Ahh!" Grabbing King's hand, I couldn't help but squeeze it hard enough to release my tension. He tried snatching it back, but my grip was too tight.

"Prep her now!" Dr. Wang commanded, grabbing the clipboard and turning to walk out of the room. Lying back on the pillow, I felt my contractions easing as the nurse slipped something into my IV.

"Hey, yo, Doc, what the fuck?" King yoked Dr. Wang up, slamming him against the wall. "Null and void on what that bitch said. You better tell me about my boy right goddamn now." Dr. Wang's glasses were cracked and smushed close up on his face. As the nurses hit the button for security, King kept shaking the small Asian doctor like a ragdoll, manhandling him as threats flew from his mouth. "You better start talking before I fuck you up! What's wrong with my son, Yang, Wang, whatever your name is?"

"Let him go, King! What, are you crazy? You're gonna go to jail, nigga, so stop!"

The monitors I was hooked up to started beeping loudly and quickly. "Oh, my God, her pressure, the baby's heart rate, Dr. Wang, um . . ." The nurse didn't know what to do. Running across the room, she tried pulling King's hands from around the speechless doctor's collar, but nothing was working.

I tried gripping the bars of the bed again, but any energy that I had once before was starting to slip from my body. As my eyes rolled into the back of my head, I tried whispering out for K.P., Dr. Wang, and the once-flirtatious nurse. I was starting to feel a stinging, burning sensation ripping open my vaginal walls, but I couldn't force out the words.

"What the fuck? King? What in the hell did I miss going to grab a Pepsi?" Tiana's voice was the last thing I heard before everything blacked out.

Chapter Seven

Samira

"Oh shit, yes, daddy! Oh, my God, you feel so good inside of these walls." Panting, screaming, not caring if my neighbors heard me begging for more of his long strokes, I was getting whipped on the dick, and that's exactly what I needed. As wrong as this was, I had to have this man. For King to have been cheating on me with Rayna, now off to console and hold her hand while bringing a kid I already despised into this world, I had to get mine in.

"How good?" He slammed his meat into me harder. I shrieked from a mixture of pleasure and pain. "Tell me how much you love this dick, ma!"

"It's the best. You're the best. I love it, I swear." My legs were spread wide as he dug deep into my guts. Each time I tried wrapping them around his waist to control his thrusts, he slammed my legs back down, refusing to give in.

"You feel better? Is this what you need?" He was grunting, thrusting, and breaking my back with each word. My pussy was taking the fierce pounding I needed. "Yeah, ma, here's your honeymoon dick!"

I felt his manhood swell inside of me. Johnie leaned down, kissing my neck then sucking on my enlarged nipples. The rougher he was with me, the more turned on I was. I hadn't had a different dick inside of me since the first week of me and King dating. That meant seven years of the same ol' stroke. "I'm about to cum, J," I purred.

"G'on and get that nut, girl. It'll really make you feel better." He stroked me deeper. I could feel him in my stomach. Shivering, losing complete control of my body, I let the orgasm take over, creaming all over him. Never once did he stop his stroke, which drove me even crazier.

"My turn." He grinned once I calmed down. He pulled back then slammed inside of me like a slingshot back-to-back. I felt his body tremble then watched his eyes roll to the back of his head.

"Pull out! Don't cum in me. I ain't on no pill, nigga, so pull out!" Those were the last words I said before I felt his semen fill me up. "Aaah, aaah!"

"No wonder my manz married ya ass!"

Damn, King just was busting like a fully loaded Uzi in me last night. Now Johnie. Fuck! Fuck! Fuck!

Stripping naked in the bathroom and climbing into the shower underneath a stream of hot water, I still had Johnie's cum dripping from my hot vagina. My thighs were sticky, my legs were weak and wobbling, and my mind couldn't come up with one reason to regret what just went down. It wasn't like we planned for him to slip into my coochie. Somewhere during the tantrum of me throwing things around the house to having a meltdown of tears I couldn't stop, Johnie's touch soothed my body, making me lust for even more of his coddling. King shouldn't have left him here in the first place. I tried rationalizing cheating on my newlywed husband, but the harder I tried to feel guilty, the more I remembered he was the one who'd created this dynamic in the first place. I was just a victim of playing by the rules King invented. He thought our love life was getting ready to be like some overdramatic R&B song he wrote, sang, and sold. *Naw, bro, over for that. Now you're the one gettin' played!*

Fresh out of the shower with the scent of sex washed from my body, I plopped down on the bed me and King shared, debating whether I should go back downstairs. The living room television was still blasting ESPN, so I figured Johnie was still sipping a brew on the couch. Part of me wanted seconds with his comrade because the dick was just that damn good. But part of me felt I'd taken it a little too far, especially in our house on the living room floor on our wedding day.

How can you honestly blame yourself when he started the confusion? He's the one who left that nigga to mend my broken heart while he chased for the next chick. Why am I tripping? Why am I going back and forth? I couldn't stop my mind from spinning. My heart ached while my pussy pounded. Digging my phone from my purse and powering it back on, I patiently waited for all the notifications to load up so I could call Jamila to have girl talk.

Jamila

Sipping on a glass of wine, with Johnie's soulful mixes playing through my home stereo speakers, I was cleaning my house in high heels, preparing for the new man who'd be spending more time around here. No man liked a dirty house or a woman too trifling to cook and clean, so I made sure Johnie would have a good impression this way. With a roast simmering in the Crock-Pot, fresh Kool-Aid in the fridge, and the CD player loaded with all of his underground mixes to show I was his supporter, I was willing to walk any avenue to get him back into my panties. I'd already gotten broken off with a few minutes of his good stroke, but just that quick I was sprung and wanted more. Not wanting to say it but feeling it for sure, I was glad King and Samira beefed last night, pushing me and Johnie together.

Ring, ring, ring.

Hearing my phone ring, thinking it was Johnie, I ran across the room full speed not wanting him to think I wasn't available. Seeing it wasn't him but just Mira, I still eagerly answered the phone because I hadn't talked to my girl since last night. And, boy, did I have some news to tell her! "Well, look who finally rose from the dead. Are you okay?" Deciding to see how my girl felt first, I knew she was dealing with a broken heart. Johnie had texted he'd gotten in touch with K.P. and they were at the hospital with Rayna. Since the messages and posts on Instagram stopped, I'd let the issue go, all the while waiting on my sister girl to reach out.

"Girl, no. I saw all of your messages, so my bad on that. My phone was on silent then King knocked it out of my hand, powering it completely off. It's a long story."

"I'm sure it is, but we can kick it, boo. I ain't got nothing but time if you need to talk. You already know I'm here for you." Sitting down on the edge of my bed, I pulled a bag of weed from my nightstand drawer then prepared to roll up. The cleaning was done, and Samira needed my attention, so I was about to blaze to chill, advise my bestie, and wait on my new boo.

"I appreciate you being here for me, Mila, I swear. But it ain't much to tell on me and King. Me and him drove to Toledo and eloped this morning after Rayna showed up on a nut." Samira was talking calmly, too calmly for the information she was dropping.

"Married? Wow, congratulations!" I screamed into the phone, sounding much happier than the bride herself. "Should I calm down? You don't sound so enthused. And what the fuck you mean Rayna showed up? Why didn't you call me sooner?"

"Again, it's a long story, but on the marriage tip, why? I mean, why should I be? You already know the second part of this equation. We're supposed to be checked into the Motor City Casino hotel as we speak. But naw, he's busy playing birthing partner to a girl I just found out about a few hours ago."

"Yeah, I could see how that would piss you off. I'd be feeling some type of way on that too." Having to let my girl wallow in pity before trying to pick her up, I had to admit I'd be far past hurt too.

"How am I supposed to accept his son? Am I immoral for wishing something to be wrong and that baby doesn't make it?" I knew Samira was hurt, but the words coming out of her mouth were mean and beyond cutthroat.

"Damn, Mira, that's a little harsh I think. Remind me not to get on your bad side," I joked but was keeping it real. I'd always known Samira to take her relationship with K.P. seriously, but to wish death on an infant was some graveyard love I'd never experienced. "I think with time you'll learn to accept his son, but in the meantime, you might want to keep your feelings to yourself. You know what King said about your slick tongue toward his kid," I reminded her, trying to be a good friend.

"I can't call it. Maybe you're right on that, or maybe you're way wrong. All I know is that she won't have to worry about me trying to play stepmomma. I don't want anything to do with his affair-affiliated kid."

"I think you're going to have to eventually have a relationship with his child, Mira. Come on now. Especially as his wife." I tried keeping it real with her, but I didn't know if she was in the mood to hear what I had to say.

"Let me tell you how everything played out first." As she proceeded to tell me about the oohs and aahs of their argument ending in him storming out and leaving Johnie there to console her. I wanted to hit pause in the conversation because that nigga J was supposed to be with King. Before I could pause her to be quiet, the last three words spat from Samira's mouth had me choking and coughing on the blunt harder than necessary. "Then we fucked."

"You and Johnie, King's artist, who took me to my car last night, just fucked?" Trying to make sure I'd heard her clearly, my attitude level was set to gear straight into go-hard if I'd heard correctly.

"Girl, yes! That's why I'm calling you. That nigga put it down and had my pussy squirting within thirty seconds. Am I wrong? Don't you think King deserves this for having a baby on me?" Every single word out of her mouth was being ignored as I pulled harder on the blunt, pacing the room, ready to explode. *This bitch right here gotta have 'em all!*

"Where is Johnie now?" Bypassing all of her questions, I knew the most important was the whereabouts of my dude. How could he fuck me a few hours ago then run up in her just like that? Naw, I wasn't about to be the one gettin' played around here!

"Downstairs watching ESPN. He's on babysitting duty until King gets back. So should I give him some more of this pussy or what?"

Hanging up on her without responding, I had to process what I'd just heard. Everything was beyond fucked up. Here I was feeling Johnie, thinking I was about to be having me one in the music game too, but Samira had to spread 'em wide for him not knowing that would leave me still out here single, lonely, and bitter. When I called Johnie's phone and was instantly greeted with the voicemail after two rings, my worries about just being a jump off were confirmed. "I need another blunt and maybe a drink to get me lifted off this bag of rocks my girl just hit me upside the head with."

Making it to the kitchen and pulling out the bottle of Cîroc I'd gotten for me and Johnie to turn up with later, I cracked it open, turning up by my lonesome, knowing that his ass was now off-limits to screw. *Damn, Mila, what now?* Samira had given up calling me back, since each time I shot her quicker to voicemail. When I read her texts asking what happened so suddenly, I lied saying the ex was over so I'd get back to her later. No sweat off her back, I was sure. She was probably getting comforted by Johnie again, to my dismay.

I was drowning my sorrows. The more liquor I drank, the more revenge I wanted to get. No one owed me anything, but with the games everyone was playing, I felt it was only right I got my fair share of playing time in too. Calling Johnie's phone then Samira's, both with no answer, I called the third number in my log, which was King's. He answered after the second ring.

Chapter Eight

King

"What up, Mila? I ain't in the mood for getting grilled over taking care of my responsibilities. So if Samira put you up to calling me, then you can hang up now." Standing in front of a hospital security guard who was making sure my temper stayed under control while Rayna underwent her C-section, I had nothing but time on my hands, but not for any additional drama.

"Slow down, King. I'm not calling you about your situation with Rayna at all. Is everything straight by the way?"

"Actually everything is fucked up, but that's a long story we can kick it on later. But what's up?" Seeing one of the two white security guards eyeing me for using profanity, I tried to straighten up, not wanting to be thrown out of this hospital altogether.

"Can you come by here right after you leave the hospital before going home? It's something extremely important I have to talk to you about." Jamila sounded frantic. Never before had she called me directly needing me for anything. Part of me felt like the whole thing was a setup, but I wasn't in the position to grill her like I needed to.

"Is everything good? Do you need me to send Johnie?" Double-checking to make sure she wasn't in immediate danger, I didn't want something else on my shoulders for Samira to fuss at if this was serious.

"Fuck Johnie if you don't mind me saying, with his weak-song-singing ass!"

"My manz must've dug you the wrong way," I laughed, getting more side looks from the same security officer. Cracker Jack Sam was gonna make me go ham on him next.

"Yeah, actually he has. And during the process, I found out he was plotting to do you wrong too. The information I have can't be shared over the phone, but I see you're trying to take me as a joke." Hearing the seriousness in Jamila's voice, I knew whatever piece of information she was withholding had to be weighing in heavy.

"No doubt. I'll be there once everything is okay here," I promised her, meaning every word.

"Okay, call me when you're on your way. Don't tell Samira or Johnie that you talked to me." She hung up the phone leaving me wondering why I couldn't communicate with my wife either. Jamila knew that I'd agree because the cloud of me wanting to know what scheme Johnie was plotting on me was brewing over my head. I'd been done shady a few times in this music business over cats stealing my beats or songs, but something told me this might've been more severe.

When the doors of the room we were waiting in opened, my heart froze for a moment. Seeing the itty-bitty Asian man still shaking from my attack, I wanted to apologize, but he had it coming for not respecting me as a man. Once it was whispered then finally announced to me that Rayna and the baby were doing fine in recovery, I counted my blessings and thanked God for giving me a chance to be a father.

"Congratulations, you lucky bastard." Tiana came in handing me a cigar. "I would talk some shit to you about getting married, but since this ain't the day to ruin Rayna's spirits, we can both hold off."

That was a temporary truce I could accept hastily. Tiana was relentless at getting what she wanted. "I'm down with that. I'd love to step out of these big, bad wolf shoes for a few hours."

"I can't call what demons you're fighting, but let's get escorted to see your son."

Chapter Nine

King

I'd always hated hospitals and today was no different. No matter how much disinfectant and antiseptic spray was used, the overpowering smell of germs and sickness kept my stomach twisted in knots. I would've much rather preferred to be stroking my newlywed wife in a five-star suite instead of welcoming into the world a bouncing baby boy by my side chick. But the consequences of me being a nut in the streets for groupie love had me in a tough spot with no way out.

Ring! Ring! Ring!

Samira was relentless when it came to getting in touch with me. Looking down at her smiling picture as it flashed across the screen, I felt horrible for taking her happiness away. In all of her extraordinary efforts to support my dream, I'd given her a nightmare in return.

"Hello," I calmly answered, hoping she'd return the same demeanor. The last exchange of words we had was of her yelling, crying, and trying to run up on me.

"Wow, I'm shocked you even picked up," she replied in a low tone. "Are you still with your other family?" The disdain in her voice was heard loud and clear.

"Come on now, Mira, let's not take it there." Hanging my head low while rubbing my forehead, I felt a headache coming on from hearing another round of her sarcastic comments and smart remarks.

"Why not? You took it there," she huffed, refusing to back down. "I don't know how you want me to react with you out here making babies and leaving your homeboy to nurse my wounds. Do you think that was the 'real man' type of move to make, King?"

The thin ice she was skating on was officially broken since she'd questioned my manhood. "Wife or not, Samira, you better watch your mouth. If I weren't a man, I wouldn't be out here busting nuts and making babies. Now quit fuckin' gunning to get your feelings hurt," I blasted her.

"Wow! It's like that? Well, husband or not, you better quit disrespecting me and running the streets like your messy ass can't be replaced. I'm not ugly, I've got my own cash, and just like I made you, I can make another!" Shouting into the phone, she was trying to play tough because her feelings were hurt. Then a second later, as I expected, she was crying through the phone. "Why don't you just come home and make this right? For years I've been your family. Why were you in a rush to change that?"

Unfortunately for Samira, I was more moved by her ranting words than her emotion-driven tears. Therefore, I swayed from being sentimental and let her have it. "Well you've made it quite obvious that you can hold your own, Samira, so do you. Don't let another one of my problems hold you back. My other family needs me. Once I see about my son, I'll see you when I get home if you're still there." Before she could respond, I hung up and refused to answer the following ten calls. A nigga might've been wrong, but she needed to put her attitude on freeze and play her position like the married woman she'd tricked me into making her.

As badly as I wanted to answer and confide in the one woman who'd made all my problems go away thus far, I knew for the first time in our relationship that Samira wasn't about to have my back. Who could blame her though? Out of the two women I'd been dividing my time with, she'd truly been the one gettin' played.

Taking a swig from a stale Pepsi I'd purchased from the vending machine, I hung my head into my lap and rocked back and forth anxiously. As a man, I was supposed to have better control over my emotions, but everything surrounding my love life was in limbo. And to make matters worse, I was missing the birth of my firstborn.

"Ay, me and you need to kick it one-on-one before going up in this room." Tiana grabbed my arm, pulling me to the side.

So caught up in my thoughts, I hadn't seen her come from the back. "What up, T? I thought we were straight." I shook my head, confused by her ripped expression. Today clearly wasn't my day with women.

"For the sake of what I'm about to tell you, K.P., I actually hope we stay on the up-and-up." She looked me deep in the eyes, letting me know she was on the serious tip. I put all of my judgments about her to the side so I could hear her all the way out.

"Damn, when you put it like that, what other choice do I have? Give it to me. What's up?"

She took a deep breath then began talking. "Rayna told me about you going haywire at ya crib then choking her up. I flew her here like a bat out of hell after she got home in pain trying to front like wasn't nothing wrong. They admitted her right away, and the rest is history."

"Real talk, it's not my bad on how things went down at my crib. Ray knows good and damn well it's a no-fly zone for her where me and Samira rest our heads. She brought that part of the drama on herself."

"Wow, K.P., you are more self-absorbed than I thought." She momentarily looked away disgusted. "Rayna might've been foolish enough to fall for ya sorry, singing ass, but y'all baby shouldn't suffer for his parents' stupidity."

This was why me and Tiana stayed at odds. She always found her place in my and Rayna's business. "You've got the game wrong if you think I'm about to stand around being berated by you. If I wanted to get burnt during a bitch session, I would've answered Samira's calls. I'm more concerned about my son, Tiana. Do you think you can update me about him?"

She snickered then twisted her lips while looking around like she couldn't believe I was addressing her so raw. No matter what she thought, I was tired of holding my hand for chicks who wanted to walk and talk like they had a dick like me.

"You're right." She took a cop then placed her hand on her hip. "The baby is really my main concern." She shook her head. I could tell she was trying to hold back the tongue-lashing she thought I deserved. "While you was marrying that cash-cow bitch of yours, the mother of your child was losing blood, cramping, and putting off delivering li'l man 'cause she wanted you here. The doctor you yoked up pushed for an emergency Cesarean long before you showed up because your son's umbilical cord was wrapped around his neck, causing his oxygen to be cut off. And you already know he's premature."

Tiana continued to go on about how Rayna lost a vast amount of blood, my son's current health condition, and how his future well-being could be jeopardized because of me manhandling Rayna. I felt my legs get limp as the responsibility and burden of bringing pain to my seed fell heavy onto my shoulders. "How's Rayna? Please tell me she's okay." I avoided direct eye contact.

"You already know how Rayna is. At this point, she's trying to be strong by putting up fronts like you haven't hurt her. I'm just asking that you support her and take whatever blows you've got coming like a man. Don't make shit worse by arguing back. The hospital is already doing a favor on her behalf by letting you remain on the premises."

It was obvious Tiana wasn't going to let me through the door leading to the back without agreeing to her terms. Whatever problems we had in the past were irrelevant at this point because she was telling me some real shit that deserved respect. I was regretful for not getting here sooner and definitely for spazzing out on Rayna when she showed up on my doorstep looking for my love. Everything was on me, and it was all the way fucked up.

"You have my word on that, 'T'. I done fucked up enough for my li'l one already." How could my life be going so great and so terrible at the same time? I need to get faded to stomach this craziness! It was hard keeping my balance and my head high while walking what seemed to be the green mile toward Rayna's room.

"We can blow a blunt in the car after you handle ya business if you need to," she said, reading my mind. "But be cool. Li'l man is the most precious baby I've ever laid eyes on." She smiled.

If only you could always be this pleasant to be around. I nodded and returned the smile. It was refreshing to have a dose of her lighthearted personality. I just wished it wasn't under these circumstances.

"Congratulations, K.P." Turning around and opening the door, Tiana walked in, holding it open for me to finally meet King Wallace and to hopefully make amends with his mother.

Rayna

They say the person you loved to hate most during your pregnancy is the one your child will come out looking like. Caught up staring at my and K.P.'s creation,

I saw that King Wallace Jr. looked just like his father at only a few hours old. All of this seemed so surreal. I was a mother and King was a father. For the first time, we both were parents.

"I love you K.J.," I spoke softly, kissing my son on the forehead. I'd been practicing being peaceful, calm, and serene so my vibes could pass to him. According to the midwife, babies can nurture and thrive off a mother's good spirit.

When his tiny eyes drooped low and closed, I gently laid him in the hospital's bassinette then rolled over to get a few winks of rest myself. My body was exhausted and still heavily doped up from the draining delivery, which scared me half to death. It would be a cold day in hell before I bred again.

My head snapped toward the door when my roommate and baby daddy walked in. "Really, Tiana? Are you serious? I told you to get rid of his ass, not have him trailing behind you looking like the pathetic piece of shit that he is."

"Come on now, Rayna, don't trip on me. I'm just trying to be helpful. That's li'l man's daddy. He got the right to at least meet him. King's coming back in peace, so at least offer him the same platform," Tiana fronted me off, then took a seat in one of the visitor chairs.

K.P. thanked Tiana for speaking up for him, which pissed me off even more. King was the last person who needed another ally, especially when the chosen one was my best friend. In girl world, Tiana knew the rules were designed for her to ride with me.

"So clue me in." I looked at each of them, dumbfounded. "Since when did y'all become cool enough to come in here tag-teaming me? Did ten minutes of solo time make y'all official comrades? I'm so confused."

King threw his hands up defeated while Tiana continued to do the talking. "Calm down, sis, damn. You're blowing everything out of proportion. Me and King are both trying to be here for you. Don't play me short, and try giving King a little credit. At least he did show up."

Tiana was making me feel more than a little betrayed. Just a few hours ago, she was the main advocate in the "Hate King" campaign. Now it seemed to be she'd fully crossed over to his side. That was phony of her to me, but my friend pool was too scarce to be picky.

"I'm the one who needed a blood transfusion for losing so much on that table, and he's the one who is only five pounds, underdeveloped, and lost a lot of oxygen to his brain." My emotions poured out. "Neither of you went through shit, so don't tell me to calm down."

Tiana looked to the floor, biting her lip, meaning she had something smart brewing inside but was holding it back. King stood speechless. What could he say? If T hadn't spilled the beans already about what drove me into labor early, he should've been smart enough to put the pieces together by now.

"So now nobody has anything to say?"

"Okay, let me think about it. No. What can either one of us say to you that won't get us ridiculed?" Tiana spoke up first, finally leaning back in the chair, crossing her legs. "I guess you're the boss to call the shots. You've earned the right." She made the "matter of fact" face. I could tell she wanted to say something clever but knew this wasn't the time or the place.

"Listen, Ray, don't be mad at Tiana. She's only trying to help me right my wrongs—" King started to speak, yet I threw my hand up quickly, cutting him off.

"You're gonna need Jesus Christ Himself to jump off of the cross and counsel you twenty-four hours a day to right your wrongs, King. I was supposed to mean more to you. Your son was supposed to mean more to you." Sniffling and trying to hold it together, I was two seconds from putting him out of my room. As inevitable as it seemed, I didn't want to emotionally go back on the roller coaster K.P. kept me on.

A volunteering minister at the hospital offered prayer over me and K.J., motivated me with an inspirational pep talk, and left me with a lot of reading material to help lessen my fears and woes. Still feeling empowered, I wished to be a strong single mother. And everything about King the Producer made me weak.

"Come on now, Rayna, you know I meant every word of love and affection. I'm sorry for what went down. Shit got crazy, and I'm man enough to say today I didn't know how to deal with it. But I ain't trying to keep fucking up your and li'l man's world. That's my word. Let me hold him. Let me be his daddy please."

Walking toward me, no longer waiting at my mercy for an invitation, King knew I didn't want to turn him away. I'd been nagging him about being a family with me since day one. He was wrong as it was to walk in two left shoes for putting both me and Junior in this situation. However, if he was willing to put our relationship in a better place, I was willing to let him.

"You can't do him like you've gotten so comfortable doing me. He's your son, your DNA," I spoke dramatically.

I was trying to make sure King understood how serious his bond to this child truly was. In return, I knew, he'd automatically be linked to me. K.J., as I nicknamed him already, meant a lifetime for King Wallace and Rayna Robinson. In time, I'd share the same last name as my son. Trust that!

"I got you, Ray. I got my bloodline, too." He reached down, picking his son up from the bassinette. I noticed a look of contentment on his face. In just a split second, King was locked in and in love. I'd never seen him look so calm, happy, and peaceful in all of the months of us messing around.

King had me glowing with stars in my eyes. Not one single day of my pregnancy did I think he'd be coddling or accepting our baby as much as he was doing now.

As he walked around the room whispering to K.J. about being sorry and promising to right his wrongs, I detected Tiana discreetly taking videos and pictures with her phone. I had the slickest bestie ever! When she noticed I'd caught her red-handed, she winked and smiled. "Thank you," I mouthed to her. If it hadn't been for Tiana going against my initial wishes to get rid of King, I wouldn't have this chance at a family and a one-up on Samira. Yes, even after birthing a premature child with major complications, ol' stank ass Mira was still on my mind.

"Time for a feeding." The nurse walked with a bottle in her hand, all the while giving King the side-eye. She'd struggled with him first-hand in trying to get his paws from around Dr. Wang's throat. "Mom or Dad? Which one of you will do the honors?"

I nodded my head toward King, who didn't look like he was gonna give K.J. to me anyway. "Dad can do the honors. Mom will try to get a little rest. I've got a feeling he's in good hands." Smiling from ear to ear watching King sit in the rocking chair next to the bed, the nurse helped him hold K.J. the right way, then put another blanket over him for extra warmth. "You're off to a good start King, a real good start." I wasn't above giving him credit for a good beginning, even though it was hard acting like Samira's fragrance wasn't still banging off his clothes.

"Yeah, King, what Rayna said. A real good start. Now smile for the picture." Tiana brought her camera phone out of hiding.

King surprisingly grinned real hard for the picture while holding the small bottle of milk to K.J.'s eager mouth. My son might've been a preemie, but he was definitely latching on. And his dad was dropping my jaw in awe by being such a stand-up guy. Life was good, at least for now.

"Send me a copy of all the pictures you've been snapping, T. You haven't been slick. My son just isn't a secret." King never looked up but gave Tiana a half but genuine smile.

The nurse sat in the far side of the room in the corner, making sure everything continued to go smoothly. Dr. Wang agreed to give King a pass but not for a second occurrence. As she watched the little makeshift family I'd created bond with one another, even her smug, unconvinced expression started to lighten seeing King so overwhelmed with the son we shared.

Taking a few glances back and forth between Tiana and King, I thanked God for delivering K.J. and then closed my eyes to rest up for the game ahead of me to be played. Something told me things were about to get hella real.

Chapter Ten

Samira

Sprint must've had Jamila's phone tripping. As of late, they'd been notorious for having the worst service in metro Detroit. After calling back a few times and not getting an answer, I rolled over on the bed, staring at the ceiling with a mind full of thoughts. Once she texted back that her ex had popped up, I knew the vent session I needed to have would have to wait even longer.

How did my world go from sugar to shit so fast? What bullshit did I put out in the world to deserve this karma after being so good to King? I'd been that man's fucking lifeline. I guessed my loyalty to him had been in vain.

Shifting my wedding ring around in circles on my finger, I began to feel more vindictive than ever. Running a mental tally up in my mind, I'd been digging deep in my pocket for years to keep his ass fresh to death on these Detroit streets. Sneakers, loafers, fitted caps, custom outfits, jewels, King had it all to floss because of me. I'd made that nigga into the man Rayna had her teeth sunken into. Rolling over and snatching my phone back up, I scrolled down my call log to his name, hitting SEND.

King's got the game fucked up for real if he thinks I'm ever gonna play stepmomma. Let me be sure to make myself perfectly fucking clear.

King

"Hey, lil' man, Daddy loves you. No matter what happens in this world or goes down with me and your mommy, I need you to know that Daddy loves you."

I held my son close to my body like the nurse directed. Already he was getting spoiled because I hadn't put him down. I couldn't. He weighed only five pounds eight ounces and was thirteen inches long. Tiny but a slugger no doubt, he was breathing on his own, eating on his own, and was projected to stay in the hospital for only a few days longer to make sure his vitals remained normal. I'd witnessed blessings before to recognize that God was working in my child's favor. Rayna had taken a beating but still managed to deliver a tough kid. He was definitely a Wallace.

Ring. Ring. Ring.

Feeling my phone vibrate in my pocket, I hurriedly moved to snatch it out, hoping not to disturb K.J. too much. I already knew it was Samira calling or messaging again, with every right to. Silencing the vibrating, I thought twice about answering. Jamila's words from her suspicious phone call earlier clouded my judgment because all I could hear was her begging me to speak with her first. *Damn, how should I play this? Mira is my wife, so don't I owe her some loyalty? How are we ever gonna be right if I keep doing her wrong?*

Rayna was fast asleep, and Tiana was gone to the car for the smoke session I no longer needed. Besides K.J.'s virgin ears, there was no one around to hear my conversation. "Hey, what's up?" My whispers hadn't fully left my mouth before my mind registered that this was a bad idea.

"Are you serious about greeting me like 'hey, what's up?' What the fuck is that about?" Samira was screaming at the top of her lungs. Even K.J. squirmed in my arms. "And why haven't you been answering my calls and texts? Don't make me feel froggish enough to leap my ass down to the hospital," she warned.

"Chill out screaming, Mira. I'm sitting here with the baby." I tried remaining cool. "This ain't the time or place to be beefing with you, so I thought it was best to let you cool down. I don't mean to keep pissing you off, but I'm doing the best I can. I'll be home in a few." Samira deserved comforting, so I was trying to give her just that. But like Rayna was giving me credit for coming through, Samira should've been extending the same olive branch.

"It ain't never the right time for you to leave your wife out in the cold, King. That's some bullshit you selling and I'm not interested in buying it! You've always had me by your side." She sounded heartbroken.

I was still talking low and trying to rock K.J. at the same time. Samira wouldn't take a break long enough from calling me every name but the child of God to hear me begging her to settle down. "Mira, can you stop two seconds to listen?" *Where is Johnie? Why did this nigga text me that Mira had been pacified for her to call me turning up? This shit is wild! I ain't gonna keep fooling with this convo.*

Li'l man was squirming with a balled-up face. My discomfort was rubbing off on him, and with his health risks, I wasn't having that.

"Naw, I can't stop two seconds to listen to whatever sorry excuse you're gonna try running. If you only want to talk about that bastard baby of yours—" Samira's harsh words had crossed the line.

Hanging up in her face, turning the ringer down to silent, I wasn't about to give Mira's scorned ass any extra energy. She was entitled to be upset with both me and Rayna. However, K.J. was off-limits for her and any other bitch jealous of my seed. If they couldn't accept him, they couldn't have access to me.

"Don't let that ho catch the business speaking ill about my son." Rayna's eyes were wide open, staring straight at me. "You've got some nerve answering the phone to her up in here in the first place."

"Settle down and be cool, Ray. That's the last thing you'll have to worry about, so take yo' fiery ass back to sleep."

Johnie

My and King's mixtape was getting major hits on internet soundboards. As a lover, King might've been the messiest man I knew. But as a businessman, he had his record company rising in the rankings. K.P. was making a name for himself around Detroit as the hardest working hit-maker close to the greatness of J. Dilla. My skills as an artist made us a powerful combo, but my greed behind the scenes was much more forceful. No one did their research on me. Being the quiet, pretty boy was my superpower in the game we all were playing.

People loved our style and were steadily downloading our songs, which was money in the bank for both of us. I'd been waiting on an opportunity to be bigger than the game for years. Now that everything was falling into place just right, my swag felt like a boss.

Geeked about the positive feedback new and old fans were hitting our website with, I sent King a screenshot so he could celebrate our success. With all the drama going down, I knew the mere mention of getting more bread would lighten his burden. Besides, K.P. was gonna need to capitalize off me for as long as he could. Once shit hit the fan about me and Mira, which it would, bridges would be burned and never rebuilt.

You've got to be kidding me. She can't be serious right now with all this thick dick I just shoved up her juicy behind. Samira's piercing, loud voice interrupted me checking my social feeds and contacting DJs on the solo tip for interviews. I might've been blowing up because of K.P.'s skills when it came down to producing, but I was gonna surpass him by far by staying on my grind.

Jumping up and pushing the vertical blinds to the side, I checked to make sure K.P. hadn't gotten back then jetted up the stairs two at a time headed for their bedroom. Me and King were already sharing profits, so we might as well share pussies, too. I'd been wanting to stroke Samira's fat kitty ever since seeing her tenderness hugged up around King anyway. My dick was a happy boy. He'd knocked two pretty bitches down in less than two hours.

Samira

"Hello, hello, King?" Pulling the phone back from my face, seeing the call duration timer blinking, I tossed it across the room out of anger. "Damn it to hell, fuck him and that illegitimate child," I shouted into our bedroom I sat in alone.

Once again, my feelings were put on the back burner while Rayna and that entrapment baby I was bitter over got put on a pedestal. No matter how many times I tried coming to grips with my reality, King's disrespect kept hitting me in the head. This wasn't an ordinary situation for me to adjust to. So it was even more frustrating that King was backing me into a corner to respond with compassion. He truly deserved something more heart-wrenching than me banging his boy to prove a point. Nevertheless, I was too whipped in love to put him out and change the locks.

Beep. Beep!

Recognizing the Facebook notification alert, I went from zero to one hundred quicker than Drake. King had big balls to be posting status updates when there was a conversation to be had with me. For a moment, I fell back and watched my phone light up from across the room. In my mind, I was trying to prepare myself for what I was about to see.

Waves of relief shot through my body when I saw it was just Johnie tagging King in music links. He was more than holding his right-hand manz down on the promotion tip when it came to hyping their songs up, but him hitting me raw let me know his intentions came with shade. On every level of K.P.'s life, his rising-star artist was taking the lead. If my husband weren't so consumed with hiding bitches and babies, maybe he could've seen the power shifting in their business relationship.

Like the redundant Kermit meme jokes flooding every social network nowadays said, it wasn't my business. I was gonna sip my tea and watch the bullshit unfold. Me making sure King stayed taken care of was what enabled him to dip off in the first place. Every time I gave him cash toward building his dream, I was really giving him a crutch to stay off his own two feet. I wasn't gonna be the fool to put myself in the same position twice. *Keep telling yourself that Mira. Put that shit on repeat.*

The more I scrolled through King's feed, the wider my eyes popped open. Pictures of him and that baby were tagged on his page with punch lines like "Daddy and Junior," and "A Music-made Family." The last caption got under my skin since I knew King's side life started in the studio. Out of everyone involved, I faulted myself for cleaning him up and catering to his ego. My investments were the ones that helped turn him into a music mogul in the underground world. He was a Samira-made man, if the bitch Tiana really wanted to know.

Revenge was about to be more than sweet around this way, believe that. If King wanted to have his groupie with a family on the side, it was only fair that I had my secret squirrel life too. He could choke on a fat one for trying to play daddy to Rayna's son, especially without a DNA test. I was tired of playing the fool to this man over and over again.

Knock. Knock. Knock.

Hearing soft taps coming from the other side of my door, I knew without asking it was Johnie. "Come in." I didn't hesitate to invite him within the confines of my and King's bedroom. As wrong as this might've been, King was more than responsible for pushing me away.

Like a little kid looking for trouble, Johnie entered with a sly smile on his face. He was more attractive to me now than he was before we banged. "You straight, ma? I heard you going ham on my manz all the way from downstairs." His mouth was doing the talking, but his eyes were locked on my curvaceous body, right where they needed to be.

"Yeah, he's still at the hospital playing family man. I'm so tired of playing the fool for that nigga. You just don't know the half of it."

"I might not know it all, but I roll with K.P. enough to know the half of it," he dry-snitched on his supposed right-hand man.

Johnie's smirk turned into a grin as he stood with an erection at the foot of my bed, waiting on my reaction. If the mask hadn't been dropped before about him being disloyal to King, he was shining bright as an opportunist now. Here and now though, I didn't have room to judge.

"Naw, maybe not. What I do know is that you should start tending to your own needs." Coming all the way into the room, closing the door behind him, Johnie stood less than ten paces from me with a bulge in his pants. Neither of us needed to say what was obvious. He wanted a round two just as badly as I needed him to take the edge off again.

Nothing about our flirting was subtle. Johnie's eyes roamed my body as I allowed the towel to drop to the floor. *Fuck it! I might as well get down while I can, 'cause if this shit ever hits the fan King will kill us both.*

"You might as well get busy with what you came up here for. I'm not stupid. I know this pussy's got that cum back." Sitting down then sliding back onto the bed, I spread my legs open so he could see my already-wet slit.

"That it does, ma, and I see it's purring for me. Let me see how you taste." Sliding down his denim Mek jeans then pulling his white T off and tossing it to the side, Johnie lifted my legs into the air then disappeared between my thighs.

I couldn't stop wiggling, inevitably fighting back the strongest orgasm of my life. He was tongue-fucking me better than King ever had, making my body experience pure nirvana with my mind totally blanking out. I felt warm sensations from head to toe, and the blood flow in my body rushed to my vagina as my legs locked in preparation for an orgasm.

"Cum in my mouth, Mira. Don't you fucking move." Johnie's words were muffled.

"Oh, shit, daddy! Kin . . . Johnie, work me out!" Rightfully losing my mind, I accidentally was about to call Johnie by my husband's name. If I was gonna be cheating, I fa'sho needed to get my game straight.

Chapter Eleven

King

The studio was cloudy with thick smoke as I bobbed my head, trying to zone out to Johnie's raps laid over T.I.'s "No Mediocre" track. Two fat Swisher Sweets in, and I still hadn't figured out my game plan or mixed the beat properly. Today defined me as a man but ran together like a blur.

For the first time since I stepped out on Samira, her reactions proved I couldn't have my cake and eat it, too. In the near future, I saw myself having to choose a permanent home team between Rayna and Samira. And truth be told, it was gonna be hard.

Once I laid eyes on King Wallace Jr., I knew he was created in the likeness of me. His tiny nose, the shape of his lips, and even the roundness of his head were all miniature features of me. He was my son, my firstborn, and my responsibility to protect from the cruelty of this world. Rayna had my word that she'd have my support and I'd have her back when it came to raising him. There was no way in hell I could live without him, even for just one day.

I now had a family with Rayna, and from the numerous amount of death wishes coming to my phone from Samira, she wasn't supporting the idea. Sneaky-ass Tiana uploaded the pictures of me holding K.J. to Facebook, and the rest is history. Samira could roll with it or roll on. I wasn't abandoning my son.

Frustration was setting in because the turmoil within my love life had me slipping when it came to my moves with music. If I didn't get a handle on the drama going on with me, Samira, Rayna, but ultimately Junior, my comparable status to a legend would be downgraded to that of an amateur. I'd put in too much hard work and hustled too many dollars from Samira to lose rank.

Shit, this might be part of the problem. After taking a long hit that had me choking, I put the blunt out. As much as I wanted the buds to soothe my nerves, it was probably responsible for stunting my creativity. "A'ight, music makes money, and you're gonna need it for li'l man." I gave myself an out-loud pep talk then slid my headphones back over my ears. Focusing on getting my paper up always motivated me to grind hard.

Back listening to Johnie's next single to be released, I knew his singing voice would bring more attention to the brand I was trying to build. It didn't take but a few bars to know I'd gotten over by signing him. Switching from his love songs to my hip-hop tracks, I played the few I'd just recorded to see if any were worth me passing off to the radio station to increase our website play. I'd gotten Johnie's text earlier and was feeling myself at my hard work, blowing up and getting the credit it deserved. I was mad serious about my career and was ready to monopolize on every opportunity possible.

Buzz!

I looked up to Johnie coming into the studio. With more swag in his walk than yesterday, his ego was making growth.

"Since you're here, I take it everything went well at the hospital." Johnie gave me dap.

"Yeah, her and my li'l man are doing one hundred." I left out the potential health scares. Me and Rayna would cross that bridge when we got there if need be. "He's tiny but tough, ya feel me?" Like any proud father would, I pulled my phone out to show him the few photos I'd snapped plus the ones Tiana sent me.

"That's what's up, man, congrats! Your bloodline is looking good. I saw all the uploaded pictures on Facebook. I don't know what the world is getting ready to be like with a little King running through this bitch!"

"Who you telling? That's getting ready to be my li'l homie right there." Johnie gave me another dap of congratulations. It felt good having someone on my team happy about my son's arrival.

I felt a sense of pride. With all the drama and craziness Rayna put me through, she'd actually made me a father. Next to hearing my track on the radio, having Junior nestled in my arms was my happiest moment. As wrong as everything seemed to be, my son was the peace I needed to at least try to make things right.

"I commend you for being so cool when Samira is lighting firecrackers with her attitude at home." Johnie threw salt into my parade.

"I've been avoiding her every call and text," I admitted to him. "She's been blowing me up, but I ain't trying to hear all that 'whomp-whomp' nagging. I wouldn't be surprised if she's got my clothes on the curb by now." I swung around in the chair.

"Y'all two are a mess," Johnie laughed, not debating the probability of Samira clowning on me so hard. "She was up in the bedroom when I left so I can't call what her intentions were." He was the last one with her, so he should've had more information to give. That's what I deserved though for trusting another man to clean up my mess.

That's when Jamila's words came ringing back to me loud and clear. I was supposed to be looking at Johnie sideways and questioning his motives, not confiding in him like he'd been a decades-long family friend. Hell, even then trustworthiness couldn't be counted on. Family would fuck you too. Anything else regarding my women that needed discussion was set on the back burner. It was time to get down to business.

"Let's get busy with a few of these tracks. You already know getting to work is the only way I clear my mind," I played it off.

"A'ight, bro, I'm game. I think the D might be finally ready for the beats we bang out." Johnie was ten times more eager about getting to work. "My YouTube page has been doing numbers since that gig down at Flood's, plus our website has gotten over a thousand hits. We're out in these streets heavy."

Johnie thought he was putting me up on game or clueing me in on something I didn't know. I followed the charts, our site, blogs, and soundboards for reviews closer than I followed my health and heartbeat. Samira could get gone if she wanted to give me a compromise to music. This game I was achieving in was much more than a hobby. It was my passion.

"Like I told you when we inked that contract, we're about to come up in a helluva way. Just this week, we've got a photo shoot for the new album, more studio time to lay some tracks, and an interview with this underground hip-hop magazine that's looking to feature new artists. We in this bitch, baby boy." I gave him dap. "Trust ya manz."

"Whoa, I see in between mackin' that messy-ass life of yours, you've still been making boss moves for the brand." Johnie's response showed he was surprised. "That's what's up."

"No doubt. Real talk, man-to-man, all this drama ain't did nothing but motivate me to step my game up even more. When it's all said and done, I've got a mouth to feed, and that little boy is not going to want for anything. Ya feel me?

"Word up. I can dig it. I don't know what your plans are when it comes to Samira or Rayna, but I wish you the best of luck." He gave me a brotherly hug then cut out into the soundproof room.

"Sound check one, two. Let's make this cash."

Johnie

I wasn't mad at King for sticking to the promises he'd made when inking our deal to significantly increase my name recognition. All I saw was dollar signs and my portfolio growing. The number of gigs he'd lined up for us would for sure send my career skyrocketing off.

We stayed locked down in the studio for hours making track after track. Unlike all the other days of us putting in work, it was bone dry of pussy in here. From the looks of it, he was trying to make moves with his brain instead of with his dick. But it was too late. I'd already made moves on what I was interested in.

"Let's take five so I can check in on Rayna and li'l man." K.P. finally came out of his all-work zone.

"A'ight, no problem." I slid the headphones off then tapped the mic. It was a little ritual I did to thank the musical instrument for loving me so much. Corny I know, but every artist has a quirk. "We've been flying through those tracks. I think yo' ass gonna fuck around and have our next mixtape by tonight," I said, giving him props.

"You saying that jokingly, but we just might. Ain't no rest gonna be had at the crib with Samira on a rampage, so I might camp out here and throw myself into the music."

"We cool and all that, bro, but I'm not about to have a two-man slumber party. After I lay this next verse, I'ma cut back out to Jamila's crib." I wanted another piece of K.P.'s wife, but the snake in me wouldn't let me drop the ball that I was now banging her.

"Oh, yeah, with all my mess going on, I forgot you was smashing that," he chuckled with an odd expression on his face.

"Well, pay better attention." I snuck a gut shot in without him knowing. "You ain't the only one gettin' pussy out here."

Buzzing myself out to give King some privacy to check on Rayna, I called Samira to see if she'd cooled down. Real bad boys moved in silence right in front of your face.

Rayna

"Well, kiddo, if ya daddy pulls a slick move disappearing on us, it'll just be me and you. Regardless of his actions, however, I promise to be the best mommy to you I possibly can be." My son wasn't a day old but already strapped with abnormalities. He'd come from the womb a warrior and deserved a mother who was just as strong a fighter.

King was gone, but I kept him up to date via text messaging with all of our son's progress. No matter how in depth my messages were, his responses remained short and sweet: "Okay, tell him Daddy loves him," and "Thanks, kiss him for me." My heart wouldn't let me complain, for it was too overjoyed that he was including us in his life. It felt good to no longer feel regret for purposely getting pregnant.

"Hey, boo, how's my nephew doing? Let me get some auntie time in." Tiana held her hands out.

I passed him over with a smile. There wasn't a chick in the world I wouldn't ride harder for. Tiana might as well have shared my bloodline, because no matter what, she couldn't do no wrong from here on out. "Thanks for everything. He wouldn't even be here without you, T. Can you take the honor of being his godmother?"

"Aw, I'm flattered." She rubbed Junior's fingers. "I'll be like your fairy godmother, K.J.," she spoke to him in a baby voice. "And it ain't nothing, sis. You already know how I get down. No one I love suffers, and li'l man right here is always gonna be straight."

"I swear you and King better not be on no bullshit when it comes to holding him down. Both of you have promised not to abandon him."

"Well, since you brought him up and made me god-mother, let me give you my opinion." Still cuddling up to my and King's son, Tiana didn't hold anything back when it came to telling me what she thought about the only man I truly loved. "You already know how I feel about how you and him get down. However, if he's gonna do right by Junior, it ain't much I can do but support him. I just need both of y'all to realize this is much bigger than some quick dick, nut, and fuckin' shit that y'all got accustomed to doing at the studio. King Jr. deserves a real mom and dad."

"You ain't telling me nothing I don't already know, sis. Trust and believe that I'm not going back down the same path. He can either do right by me and Junior or get gone." Fumbling with the bag Tiana brought with my clothes to go home in, even I didn't believe the words rolling off my tongue.

"Naw, Rayna, listen up good. I think, as a friend, I should tell you something you might not want to hear." She looked up at me, seeming like she was slightly afraid to say what she was thinking. I swallowed my pride, knowing her words were about to hurt. "Real talk, boo, you know I love you like we're flesh and blood, so don't take this the wrong way," she tried prepping me.

"G'on and spit it out." I looked her straight in the eye. "I respect whatever it is you must say. You've been down with me since day one."

"Cool, because I ain't trying to cut into you. I'm trying to save you from the bullshit I know his daddy is known to pull. If he stay with that trick Samira but still do for his kid, Ray, fall back. Don't be that type of baby momma niggas love to hate."

I wanted to buck at Tiana and say I was more than just a groupie chick. But the truth had been on the floor since the first day I fucked him at the studio. King kept our relationship behind closed doors but paraded Samira to the world. The jealousy that brewed inside of me each time he put her before me was what sparked my sneak pregnancy attempts in the first place. Now that my secret weapon was here, it was time to claim my man. Little K.J. was gonna aid as my crowbar to help pry King and Samira apart.

Chapter Twelve

Jamila

I paced my small bungalow home feeling some sort of way. I thought King would've been here by now to hear the information I was holding on reserve. Not only was he in the wind, but Rayna's best friend's Facebook feed had dried up, too.

A few hours ago, Tiana kept posting picture after picture of K.P. and his new baby, and I could tell from his smile he was in love. Since I was bitter about Samira fucking my potential nigga, I purposely liked the photo so it would show up in her feed. My intentions weren't good. I wanted Samira's feelings driven into the ground even further. It was about time someone joined me at the bottom.

With all the love I had to give, I always ended up alone. I'd been around long enough to know life isn't fair, but when it came to my love life, that department seemed considerably unreasonable. Even home-wrecking-ass Rayna found a way to hold on to a man. If I ever got the chance to trap a nigga, trust that in a flash I would. Samira kept calling, but I didn't have it in me to play the whole "hang up" thing off because I was saltier than ever. When was it going to be my chance at love?

When my alarm went off that my show was about to come on, I popped a bag of butter lover's popcorn then curled up with my throw blanket on the couch. *Love &*

Hip Hop's new season was getting ready to air within the next week, so VH1 was playing a marathon of the previous season. I couldn't wait to get caught up in their drama since I didn't have a man in my world to have any with. I lived vicariously through Stevie J and Joseline, and if I got five minutes of fame, I'd pay my fare and hop on the bus, too.

During the commercial, I checked my phone and saw no one, not even slick-ass Johnie, had called. It was really bothering me that King hadn't reached out, so I shot him a text with the word "Congrats." That way, if he did forget about my call and plea to him earlier, his memory would be triggered. It was the oldest move in the book, but one I hoped would work.

I couldn't wait to drop the bomb on him that Samira was cheating. The type of nigga he was, I knew fa'sho he'd be in my panties quicker than I could slide them off. Getting a taste of what his groupies have been getting stroked with has always been a wishful pleasure of mine. It might've not been fair to the friendship I had with Samira, but neither was her hitting off his recording artist. From the way everyone was playing it, wasn't nothing fair about love, money, and sex. So why should I adhere to the rules?

Maybe I'd finally get what I truly deserved: some real happiness. What female doesn't want longevity and a man to come home to every night? Even in my man-hating stages, I ain't never been down with that team-single garbage. I was tired of being second runner-up and not having a companion. No matter how ignorant their love life might've been, Mira should've continued to hold him down like she'd been doing. Despite it all, K.P. was a good man.

Ding-dong! Ding-dong!

I checked my phone, but there were no missed calls. Hopefully, it was King so I could finally blow the spot up. I peeked out of the blinds only to see Johnie's car. What in the fuck did this nigga want? Since I wasn't supposed to know about him and Samira getting down, I tried to get my mind right as much as I could within the little time that I had.

Ding-dong! Ding-dong!

"Hold up! I'm coming, damn!" There was no need for me to be friendly or act like I wasn't pissed off. I was temporarily holding water about all the sketchy shit going down, but Johnie had it coming for standing me up. I swung the door open then rolled my eyes. I didn't know what agitated me more: the sight of him or that he was holding a bouquet of roses in his hand.

"Damn, girl, I see you ain't the one for sweet gestures. You gonna invite a nigga in or what?"

"I don't see why I should." The flowers were nice. Yet and still, I wanted something much more than some crap from the ground I couldn't keep alive for more than three days.

"My bad about not swinging back through here earlier. After shit popped off at King's crib between him and Samira, I sat with her for a while as a favor to him until she calmed down. It was wrong for me not to call, but I figured you knew what was up."

"If it was all good, you don't owe me an apology," I said through gritted teeth then tried closing the door in his face. "I was busy so I'll holla at you later."

"Slow the fuck up, Jamila. What's your problem?"

"Whoa, why are you so persistent all of a sudden? You weren't thinking about me a few hours ago, real talk. I ain't mad or nothing, but I really ain't too keen on being a second thought."

"I swear, y'all chicks riding the fuck out of that emotional roller coaster today. You know you don't want me to leave, so quit playing games," he said, calling my bluff.

I knew he'd just fucked my homegirl, but she had a man. In lieu of getting stuck in my feelings, I moved to the side and allowed Johnie inside. "Thanks for the flowers." I snatched them from his hand. "I'll put these in some water. Want a beer or something?"

"Naw, I'll take something a little stronger," he said, then slid off his shoes.

Before I could find a vase to put my flowers in, I heard the television tune into ESPN. *Thank you, God. Please let him stay for a while!* I fixed Johnie the strongest drink I could then powered my phone off to prevent any distractions. I needed to snag me a man and put it on him better than Samira had.

King

"Hey, you've reached Jamila. I'm not available to take your call right now . . ."

Frustrated that she hadn't answered, I hung up from the voicemail recording, figuring Johnie was already at her house. Otherwise, I couldn't see a reason for her not picking up. She'd sent me a message earlier saying congrats, but I knew that was just a play for her to stay on my mind. I guessed whatever news she needed to tell me would either disappear or escalate after Johnie left. The whole hookup between them was out of the blue. That coupled with Jamila's random phone call about me needing to speak with her urgently had me wondering what was really up.

Jamila was Samira's best friend but my homegirl through association. Samira kicked it with me so much about Mila's business that I could run down her problems like the first and fifteenth. Something told me that in the long run, I'd be part of her monthly.

Several tracks were finished, plus I'd burned a few dozen discs to pass out as free promotion of our new mixtape. Despite everything going on outside of the studio, I was in rare form when it came to producing. Not having a room full of eager sexy ladies probably helped with the creative process, too.

After touching base with the photographer and club owner trying to plan our next gig, I sent a few disc jockeys direct messages of links to our site. My plans were to stop by a few stations personally, but in the meantime, I had to keep the name K.P. relevant and on their minds.

In the midst of my social networking and uploading a few more pics of K.J. that Rayna messaged me, Samira called again. Although I was tempted to pick up, I figured she'd just seen the photos and wanted to clown. Instead of getting into a word-for-word brawl while I was on the clock with studio hours, I sent her to voicemail with the intention of heading home later. I didn't know if it would be impossible, but I was gonna start grooming her for our new life as a split family.

Samira

"Get a grip on yourself," I grunted. Shaking my head out of frustration, I hit the END button on my phone once again and was just about ready to throw it through the wall. I'd called King over twenty times within the last hour. Nonetheless, each time he sent me straight to his voicemail. I really didn't know why I was still calling. With a belly full of nut and a sore vagina from my husband's recording artist, trying to check him about the mistress he reproduced with was starting to seem slightly irrational.

I'd been sitting in the house for hours, pitying myself over not being able to keep King happy and satisfied within our relationship. The same problems we had as boyfriend and girlfriend were now escalating as husband and wife. Shame on me for thinking a ring or some vows to God meant a change in K.P.'s behavior. I'd rushed him down the highway to marry me in vain for everything to blow up in my face.

King wasn't answering any of my calls, and surprisingly, neither was my homegirl Jamila. I was out here with a confused mind and no best friend to share my woes with. It was time to make a move up out of this stuffy house. When *Love & Hip Hop* went off, I slipped on my rainbow-colored Adidas fitted shirt and leggings with a fresh pair of matching sneakers. Even on a relaxed day and with a broken heart I wouldn't be caught off my A game. Making sure my hair was wand-curled perfectly, I flew out of the door to get rejuvenated from some fresh air.

The first and only stop was at the liquor store on the corner of Jamila's block. I purchased three bottles of white Zinfandel plus some snacks to get us through the impromptu girl talk discussion I was popping up on her doorstep with. I needed to get drunk in love to handle all of the weight on my shoulders. And even though she hadn't said it, any time her ex came around Jamila drank like a drunk. From my standpoint, I was doing both of us a favor by coming over unannounced.

As I eased up to Jamila's house, I slammed on my brakes in the middle of the street and threw my hands into the air. "You've gotta be fucking kidding me," I shouted, almost busting my own eardrum. My eyes must've been playing tricks on me. *Is Johnie's car in Jamila's driveway? Are they fucking around? Is that why she hung up on me and is playing missing in action?*

All the pieces of her behavior today started to make sense. Jamila was bitter at me for banging ol' boy, but I had no idea they were even getting down. I felt like a straight sucker. If no one else knew, Johnie did. And he was the only one winning out of our whole crew. Little did he know, he'd just played himself.

Ring. Ring. Ring!

Startled when I heard the phone ringing, I looked around to see if Mila or Johnie spotted me. When I saw it was King calling, I started to leave him dangling the same way he'd done me. But I was too afraid he'd not fight as hard for me as I was fighting for him.

"Hello," I answered in a nonchalant voice, playing a role. I was relieved to still be on his mind.

"Hey, can you talk?"

"I've always had time for you, King." I was being sarcastic as I pulled over and parked, still on Jamila's street.

"I really don't need you trying to come for me, Samira. I know as a woman you're hurting and all, but real talk, I've gotta be a responsible man."

"It's a fine time for you to decide doing that." I took my shot at the sneak diss he walked right into. I didn't care how he was feeling.

"I'm trying to have a conversation with my wife, not get badgered. How many times are you gonna go hard about some shit you can't change? I'm sick of hearing you throw it up in my face. I ignored your ass earlier, and you're asking for the same treatment again."

"Well, you know what? By all means, nigga, do you." This time, I was the one to hang up in King's face. He and his boy could officially kiss my ass.

I sat inside my empty car, screaming until my throat hurt. When I realized my assumption was right and King's fight was minimal because he hadn't called back, I cracked open one of the three bottles of white Zinfandel, taking it straight to the head.

My whole world was spinning around me, and I wasn't the one in control. My nigga really wasn't my nigga. My best friend really wasn't my best friend. And the dude I'd just fucked a few times so I could feel good was playing me for his own benefit, too. I had too much style and class to not be winning.

As I took another gulp of the wine with 12 percent ABV, I felt myself catching a slight buzz and knew that's exactly where I needed to be. I couldn't take these blows with a sober mind and heart. Naw, not at all. Not only was it time for me to start dealing with the cycle of bullshit King presented, but it was time for me to start showing the fuck out.

I drove around Jamila's block then parked on the side street nearest her house. Needing to be incognito, I threw on my oversized beauty-supply shades and the hooded jacket I kept in my car for when it got cool, and then I grabbed the other bottle of wine to serve a more vindictive purpose.

I hopped out with purpose and ran down the alley full speed, hopping over old tires, broken glass, and a few dead rodents before reaching the back entrance to her house. I opened the gate quietly then leaned down in front of Mila's car, waiting to see if I'd been peeped. Knowing Johnie though, I was sure he had her more than occupied. After a few seconds went past, I duck-walked to the passenger side of her car, opened the gas tank, and poured as much of the wine into it as I could.

Before running off, I made sure to swipe her already-crappy paint job with my car key. A few creative slashes in, I was satisfied enough to call it quits on a job well done. Within ninety seconds flat, I was back in the comfort of my car, fleeing the scene. "I won't be needing this anymore." I tossed the wine bottle from my window. Hearing the bottle shatter against the concrete, I turned on the radio, feeling complete gratification.

Chapter Thirteen

King

Samira's outbursts and mood swings were becoming unpredictable. Of course, I expected her continued tyrants. However, I was getting tired of hearing my own voice apologize. With Rayna upgrading from a secret side chick to the mother of my child, Samira felt misused and unloved. I could tell that from every whimper, yell, and volatile word that left her mouth. The control I had over her and our relationship was obviously slipping.

Sitting on the living room couch, I'd only been home a few minutes and was ready to go. The whole reason for me coming home in the first place was for her and me to have a face-to-face conversation, but she was too irate to even hear me out.

There's only so much rope I could give Samira to hang herself. She'd already put it on the table that she'd leave me, downgraded my status as a man, and disrespected my innocent son. If she wanted to talk tough, I'd have to love her the same way. Honestly, I couldn't work on grooming her into the best stepmom in the world if she wasn't willing to accept my li'l man.

Since I didn't know her whereabouts or how long she'd be gone, I swiftly moved through the house, packing enough clothes, shoes, and travel-size equipment I needed to make music with for at least a week. I didn't want to leave Samira, but I couldn't live in a war zone. Yet given her attitude, I thought we were both prepared to go the long haul. The Comfort Suites would be my home away from home until the madness cooled off.

"What up? This is K.P. Speak to me," I picked up my ringing cell while climbing into the car.

"Nothing much but these charts." The call I'd been waiting for finally came through. "The manager down here at the station is putting together a showcase of Detroit's musical talent. I dropped your and Johnie's names of course. Y'all down or what?"

Hard work did pay off. "Hell yeah, no doubt. You already know I'm trying to capitalize on any and every avenue that can lead me to having constant fame." I kept it real with the disc jockey.

"Cool. One hundred and then some. I'll send the details over in a second. In the meantime, keep grinding, K.P. Dudes out in the streets are imitating your style heavy."

"No doubt and good looking, bro." I thanked him for the heads-up. "If my head's not in a pair of headphones, it's definitely to the streets." I relayed the personal message with every intention of protecting my throne.

"I feel that. A'ight, K.P., keep in touch."

Samira

My adrenaline was still pumping from attempting to tear up Jamila's car. We'd been cool for so long that I couldn't understand why she just hadn't kept it real with me about her kicking it with Johnie. Instead of her checking me about how wrong it was for me to wish death on K.P.'s bastard kid, she should've been on my head about sleeping with her side man. I didn't know why she was keeping secrets and lying all of a sudden.

Me and Jamila were supposed to be comrades, best friends, and accomplices if need be. Just like I'd called to run my personal business down to her about me and King, Johnie, or whatever struggle I was going through, she did the same with me. We could've laughed it off like the aces we were then moved right back to our normal lives. It wasn't like I didn't have a marriage to fix with King anyhow. We were sisters to the core without even sharing the same blood, or at least I thought. *Damn, Jamila, now it'll never be the same between us.* If only she knew my thoughts.

The more I thought about how everything was unraveling, the more upset and regretful I became over sleeping with Johnie in the first place. Then the blame shifted to King for starting this whole domino effect of negative bullshit. Had he not been pulling several stunts with that Rayna bitch, I would've never fucked his friend or lost my best friend in the process.

Until my sorrows were drowned in two whole bottles of wine, I drove in circles around Detroit. There was nothing for me at home but boredom and memories of King. I loved him more than I loved myself and would've given him a house full of kids if given the opportunity.

I was drunk in love, hurt to the core, and bitter beyond belief. Yet and still, I needed to reconcile with King. The wine had my eyes fluttering and heavy as it slowly crept through my bloodstream, taking over my body. I went from feeling tipsy to drunk all in one second.

King's scent greeted me when I walked into the front door. Looking back over my shoulder to make sure I hadn't gone crazy by missing his car when I drove up, I slammed the door pissed off when I realized I'd missed his sneaky run home. My heart fluttered with each step I took up the stairs toward our bedroom. Like I smelled his cologne lingering, I hoped he hadn't picked up on my and Johnie's after-scent of sex. I'd sprayed Febreze plus lit candles, but now I wasn't sure if that had been enough.

Closing my eyes, I pulled his nightstand drawer open then slammed it shut in rage. The lamp that sat on top fell to the floor, shattering into a million pieces. But that was the least of my worries. King's music journal was gone. That meant he was gone too.

I knocked a photograph of us off the dresser, and my emotions flew up and down the spectrum ranging from hurt to anger to animosity. My hands were shaking trying to dial his number. If King was trying to leave me for good, my whole world was about to crumble.

Jamila

Sure, each time Johnie stroked my needy cat I thought about him stroking Samira, but that wasn't enough to turn me off. Matter of fact, it turned me on even more knowing that he'd slammed her yet still needed me for satisfaction. Each time he pulled my hair, I arched my back. Each time he choked me roughly, I clenched down on my pussy muscles. And each time he told me to tell him he was the man in bed, I shouted it so the neighbors could hear. Truth be told, he was fucking me hella right.

When he'd first gotten settled in earlier, I cooked him a feast to prove I was more than just a fuck. Every man liked a woman who knew her way around the kitchen. In every move I made, I was campaigning to be somebody's woman.

It didn't take long for us to start back up conversing like before. Johnie's plans to be the man in music were far more extensive than I thought. The more we drank, the more he talked. And like a trained woman knew to do, I absorbed every word that left his mouth.

Chapter Fourteen

Rayna

Having a newborn baby wasn't the hardest thing I'd done. Matter of fact, I was starting to like the feel of being a mother. King Jr. gave me purpose. Until I gave birth, the only thing that consumed my time was chasing up behind no-good niggas who didn't think I was worth more than the few dollars they offered to trick with me. Now that I was blessed with a son, there was more of a reason to get my life together.

Tiana pulled the car around to the front door of the hospital while I said, "See you later," to my son. The doctors assured both me and King he'd be in the hospital only for an extra week, if that, but I was released to go home. It was a deflated feeling to know I'd be walking out the doors empty-handed. Since I didn't have nearly close to what I needed to bring him home, I was planning to use the extra time as my opportunity to set my bedroom up the right way.

"Okay, Mommy's baby, I'll be back in a few hours to check on you. I've gotta go out into this world to get you some presents."

I gave him a kiss before the nurse placed K.J. back into the crib. All the tears of me being worried about him being healthy were already cried out. Now it was time for me to be strong enough to handle everything he'd need to grow up without any further complications.

"We'll take good care of him, Ms. Robinson. Go home and get some rest." The nursing staff had been more than helpful during the birth and my short recuperation time. Although they were just doing their jobs, I still felt special.

"Thank you, ladies, so much. And despite me leaving here without him, I'll try." I was honest as I walked out of the hospital's nursery.

"Have you talked to King?" Tiana asked, sliding into the passenger seat of her car.

"Yeah, we've been texting back and forth. He hasn't responded to me getting out of the hospital yet, though."

"And so it starts." Tiana rolled her neck then turned the radio up. "If I gotta go upside K.J.'s daddy's head for going against his promise to me, I will."

"I be wishing upon a star I could be as gangsta as you," I laughed, then took a hit of the joint she was puffing on. That's the main reason I wasn't planning to breast feed. It was time to jump back on the drug like Puff the Smoking Dragon.

"Congratulations, bitch, you're a mom." Tiana smiled as I choked from my first hit.

"I know, right! It still feels bizarre." I gazed out the window all the way to the hood.

I didn't feel elated, because my son wasn't in the back seat. But since I still needed a car seat, I guessed everything happened for a reason. I pulled out my phone, saw King hadn't responded yet, and then sent him another text letting him know I needed to hold a few bucks for the baby.

Once we made it back to the projects, there was a get-together going down at the house of one of my other homegirls, Cameron. She and Tiana put it together as a surprise celebration for me giving birth. I couldn't have been happier. I didn't know if I was going through postpartum depression or still experiencing pregnancy hormones, but tears gathered in my eyes as soon as I saw the blue and yellow balloons tied up everywhere. Living in the hood had its harsh days, but it for sure had its perks, too. Everyone around here acted more like family than low-budget neighbors.

There was liquor flowing, blunts in rotation, and people celebrating in and out of Cameron's small duplex. They even put together a donation box so I'd be able to get K.J. a few things before he came home. I was more than grateful 'cause I didn't have nothing more than a few Walmart bags of clothes. This was just what I needed to help get my mind off of everything surrounding K.J., King, and unfortunately Samira too.

"Let me see some pictures of the baby boy." Cameron pulled me in for a hug. "Can you drink or smoke? You know I'm ready to get you all the way fucked up," she laughed.

"Yeah, I'm not going to breastfeed so pass the blunt. You already know I need my weed." I eagerly reached for her Swisher Sweet.

"That's my girl! Them doctors always wanna talk about our babies being deficient 'cause they ain't been breastfed, but I'ma call bullshit! All three of them little nappy fucks running around out there can't get me a check and ain't haven't one of 'em drank one bit of the titty milk."

"Girl, you crazy." I almost choked on the smoke, laughing at Cameron being ghetto and funny.

"Naw, I'm just keeping it real. I gotta go check on the food, so let me know if you need something. Party up today, because once li'l man gets home, it's lights out for yo' ass for a while."

Cameron walked away while I kept showing off pictures of K.J. when he didn't have tubes running from his nose, arm, and mouth. The more photos I swiped through, the more tears gathered within my eyes. My heart, mind, and soul missed my baby. I wanted to know his vitals, how he was progressing, and more than anything I wanted to touch his little toes.

The nurses all collaboratively said it was best for me to go home, get some rest, and get prepared for motherhood. It seemed like an unscrupulous thing to do with feeling the emotional connection that I did. Seeing that King was K.J.'s parent too, I wondered if he felt the same way. Digging my phone out my purse, I went to send him an emotional text then lit up when seeing he'd responded from earlier. I instantly felt butterflies in my stomach reading he'd be coming through.

"Excuse me, y'all." I pardoned myself from the smoke rotation then went outside. It was time to freshen up for my baby daddy.

"Damn, you're smiling wild as hell." Tiana looked up from kicking it with her dude Deon. Their relationship together began like mine with King's: off and on. For some reason though, he'd been coming around more often nowadays than ever before.

"King is coming through later with some stuff for his son." I did a little dance, not embarrassed to show how happy I was. "So I'm going home to get myself together."

"Girl, bye! Me and Cameron went through a lot to make sure yo' ass came home to some shit to make you smile, and you gonna diss us for that nigga?" This was the second time I instantly felt shaded by Tiana.

"Dang, T, I thought you were all for him playing daddy. What's with the shade? It ain't like I don't appreciate y'all."

"Nothing. G'on and do you." She shooed me away then picked up her conversation with Deon. "When that nigga play you on some more dumb shit, don't expect me to coddle you."

I took each gut blow Tiana hit me with like a champ without wavering. My curiosity was far past piqued, to the point of aggravation. She was crossing too many lines with me. It was one thing to kick it with me "real" one-on-one, yet putting me on blast in front of a lame-duck-ass nigga was doing a little bit too much.

"Damn, that's fucked up. I thought if one cried, we both cried together." I nodded with my bottom lip turned down. "Well like you said, let me get to doing me." Flipping my hair over my shoulder, I turned around with much attitude, leaving in my dust her and the flunky bum she considered something worth belittling me over.

King

Ring! Ring! Ring!
Deep in a sleep, I heard my phone's text notification going off, making me sit straight up. I looked around the room, remembering where I was, then finally got up to find my phone. After checking into the hotel, I'd blown through an eighth of Kush and drunk myself into a stupor. I knew I was in a bad spot emotionally because I couldn't even write songs to clear my head. Though the ringing stopped, I managed to find my phone and saw it was Rayna texting.

I need to hold a few dollars to get K.J. right. He ain't even got a car seat to come home in.

Junior gonna be straight. I'll get you right in a few, I responded, then sprung up to take a shower. Never once did I plan on leaving her out to dry.

Just in case a quick nut presented itself, I had to be fresh, clean, and prepared. Until now, the thought of banging Rayna never crossed my mind. It must've been a male/dog thing 'cause with money involved my dick took over thinking for my brain. Hell, when I thought long enough, a quick nut was probably just what I needed to clear my mind.

Fresh to death in a pair of True Religion denim jeans, a pumpkin orange "Detroit versus Everybody" T-shirt, and the matching orange Nike LeBron 11s, I walked flat-footed so my sneakers wouldn't bend. Flossing in the mirror, I knew my style was fly, yet it had to be since I stayed in the public eye.

After spraying on some cologne, brushing my waves until they rolled perfectly to make a nigga sick, and then sliding my wedding ring off into my pocket, it was time to hit the streets. Being a married man, this was a more dangerous game I was playing. Two steps from walking out of the hotel to meet up with Rayna, my phone rang. I knew it was Samira.

Samira

"Hey, Mira," King answered the phone dryly.

"Hi," I responded in the same tone. *How dare he throw me shade with his cheating ass? And he better not be with her either.* "What's up for today, K.P.?"

"Music and making some moves to get K.J. straight." Once again he thought I cared about his son.

"Oh, okay." I shrugged my shoulders, brushing his comment off. I didn't want to be rude and tell him fuck his kid, so I changed the subject abruptly to what I was really concerned about. "So, about you not coming home, are you serious?" I was frozen still in the center of our bedroom, and my heart was pounding as I waited on King to say some more shit I didn't want to hear.

"I ain't really trying to get started with you, Mira. That's part of the reason I need to stay away for a few days, to clear my mind."

"Hell naw, you don't take a vacation from your wife to go clear your mind and sort things out. We handle everything from the inside out 'cause we're family. I can't believe this shit, King!" Storming through the house, I couldn't get downstairs to his personal bar in the basement fast enough. King's undercuts were knocking the life from me.

"Where was all that 'we're a family' talk earlier, Mira? You backed me into the corner with all that slick shit you've been spitting, so don't play the innocent card now. It's a little too late for that," King said, throwing my words back at me.

"What? Are you fuckin' serious with me right now?"

"Unfortunately so, Samira. I'm dead serious."

There was awkward silence on the phone as I tried absorbing the fact that my husband was temporarily leaving me. No matter what I'd done with Johnie, King kept leaving me alone to ice my broken heart. "I feel like you're pushing me away." I lowered my tone, showing I was weak. This wasn't the time to play rough. Acting out of character, being hardcore, had made matters worse.

"I ain't trying to hurt or push you away, girl. I ain't never trying to hurt you. Damn." His voice drifted off. "You don't think it was hard not sleeping next to you? You don't think I want my lucky charm back around my neck, preferably by my side? You're the most important lady in my life. It don't seem like it, but I hate hurting you." He broke down.

"Then why do you keep doing it? Just come home. It'll hurt me more if you don't." I knew I couldn't live without King. I needed to know he felt the same about me.

"I'm sorry, boo. I can't." His words surprised me. I thought we were making a breakthrough. "Look, the more I say, the more I'm gonna hurt you. I'm just gonna take a few days to get shit straight on my mind, and on my money, then we'll work on our marriage. That's my word, Samira. I promise."

"Your promises don't mean shit to me, King. How can I respect a promise if you can't respect a vow?"

"See, that's some more corner-backing shit. All I need is a few days to get right, yet you're too selfish to understand that. I never said I wasn't coming home. Why can't that be enough? Why do you always have to have things your way?"

Before I could respond, King continued with his rant then hung up before I could find out where he was temporarily staying.

Chapter Fifteen

Rayna

It didn't matter what type of hating Tiana wanted to do. King answered my text without much delay and was here within a matter of hours to cash me out for our son. My smile couldn't have spread wider when he swerved up and leaped out. The whole community of project heads turned in disbelief that even after me giving birth, King was still around. In my neck of the woods, keeping a man after sneaking them with a kid was unheard of. With that engraved into my mental, of course, I felt like I was winning.

"Will this be enough to get li'l man straight to come home?" Peeling off five hundred-dollar bills, K.P. handed them over but kept his knot out just in case I wanted more. He's always been on the generous side when it came to giving me money, but never so freely.

"Hell yeah." I snatched the bills from his hand then put them in my dresser drawer. "Why don't we ride out to the mall together? It'll be nice to have your opinion on what he should wear, sleep in, and get strolled around in." I crossed my fingers behind my back. If K.P. wanted to make my day, he'd agree to playing daddy.

"That'll be cool. We can take care of that after we leave the hospital from checking on him."

My feet couldn't move fast enough. I was sliding off my clothes, preparing to get dressed in something more appropriate to floss in the streets with my baby daddy.

"Whoa, slow down, Ray." He noticed my enthusiasm. "I've gotta take care of some business down at the studio first and foremost. I just needed to make sure you had some cash on hand."

"Oh, okay." I was deflated. "How long will you be at the studio? Should I just drive myself back down to the hospital?" King and I both knew what went down at the studio. Real talk, that's probably where K.J. was created. He could disappear behind those closed doors for hours, making it time-out for the rest of the world. I wasn't trying to miss visiting hours waiting like a sitting duck on him to show back up.

"Naw, you good. I'll be back within the next couple of hours for sure." He stood up over me. "Quit doubting me, Ray. Until I give you a reason to think I'm going to abandon you and K.J., chill out and trust ya manz. I'm trying to hold you down. Let a nigga do it without all the worries."

When I looked in K.P.'s eyes, I could tell his heart was heavy. For the first time since our relationship and this pregnancy unraveled, I put my feelings on the back burner to think about how it all was affecting him. I had to give King props. He was doing better than most men in his predicament would. He wasn't hiding me from his wife, shading his son, or making plans to disappear that I knew of.

Being a woman, I knew his decisions weren't being taken lightly by Samira. There wasn't a female on this green earth who wanted to share her man, let alone with another woman who had his child. I felt her pain as being valid and real. Yet and still, I couldn't fight the desire to come up from it.

Something deep inside of me was telling me to leave this man alone. I just couldn't. The way he smelled, the way he tongued me down, and the way he carried himself had me stuck like glue. Even if K.J. weren't a factor, I would've been nursing this nigga's nut sac, refusing to find me a new life. King had become my world. And as pathetic as it sounds, I wasn't sure I'd have the strength to move on.

Dropping to my knees, I knew the best way to make his problems seem like dust. Once my mouth swallowed his limp dick whole, I got on my grind trying to work him over. I knew my slobber job couldn't be denied. That's what got me here in the first place. Grinding slowly into my mouth, he grunted loudly then sighed in relief each time his mushroom tip hit my tonsils.

My and King's sexual attraction to one another was wild and raunchy. Matter of fact, every time we got down was like a porno waiting to go viral. His moans and my slurping could be heard over the loud festivities going on outside my window. I was sucking the meat off King's dick, and when he nutted down my throat, I sucked him back hard and bobbed for another thirst-quencher. In my eyes, King deserved a master head job for showing up and, so far, showing out.

King

I dropped another hundred into Rayna's hand after pulling up my denim jeans. The two nuts I'd just let loose down her throat relaxed every tense nerve in my body. My marriage, my music, and not even my son crossed my mind as she slurped down to my nut sac. Rayna wasn't slobbering for fun. She was bobbing to get kept.

Too bad my intentions weren't to offer her more than an upgrade in status. She and I could never be a family no matter how hard it would be for her to accept. If I ever fell off in the music world, she'd trick with the next chart-topper in a heartbeat. At least that would be an unnerving worry.

As I looked around the boxed room that was already too cramped with her queen-sized bed, dresser short one drawer, and broken-up blinds, I couldn't imagine how K.J. would fit in here let along his belongings. And truth be told, I didn't want my son living like I did in the slums. Rayna didn't have a choice. She was gonna have to do better. Her being bold meant my son would be bold, and it was my word to God I couldn't have that.

I was already plotting on how to make things better. If the next mixtape Johnie and I released skyrocketed, I was gonna move her up out of the projects into a nice, suburban apartment K.J. would be safer in. I owed my son a fair shot similar to the one Samira afforded me. I knew my parents weren't shit, which meant I was gonna try ten times harder not to mimic their ways.

Rayna snapped her fingers in front of my face to get me out of deep thought. Mira was instantly on my mind heavy because she deserved a little more love for getting me off rocks in the first place. It didn't matter how many years back she saved me from off craps, I was indebted to her and owed her respect. She's never treated me less than worthy.

"You got time to smoke one or want me to fix you a plate? Cam and Tiana threw me a surprise party for the baby," she proudly announced.

"Naw, I'm good. And since you brought it up, I don't want you or your ghetto-ass friends getting blazed in front of Junior." It didn't matter how much of a weed habit Rayna kept similar to mine. She was gonna have to curb that shit immediately in order to keep problems down with me. Before, she was just my side piece, so I didn't have any rules, regulations, or aspirations for her to reach for. Now that she was the mother of my child, my expectations were raised.

"Hold up, Negro, you can't come around here calling no shots. I won't smoke with him in the room, but I'm gonna fa'damn sure blaze my trees." Rayna reminded me why I kept her playing in the backfield.

"Don't think for one minute I won't go upside your head over K.J., Rayna. Whatever you do you better make sure it's well received on my end." I finished making sure my outfit was back crisp so I could leave. This conversation was dead, plus my appointment with Johnie was in a few.

"Whatever, K.P." She popped her gum, pulling a half-smoked blunt from the ashtray. "I might as well smoke up while li'l man ain't here, since I'll be in jail in my own residence once he's well enough to come home." Her words sounded spiteful.

It was in both of our best interests that I got up out of there as fast as possible. If only Rayna kept her mouth full of dick instead of words we wouldn't have constant problems. Her mothering my child was gonna have to stay monitored.

"What up, bro? I'm about to drop a few singles off at the radio station. What time do you wanna meet up at the studio?" Pulling out of Rayna's projects, I hit Johnie on his cell to make sure he wouldn't be late. We hadn't touched bases with each other since he left to visit Jamila.

"I see you're up making moves for that dough," he groggily spoke.

"Big things need to happen with our next mixtape, so every day gotta be close to a twenty-four-seven grind."

"I can dig it." Johnie yawned. "I've been locked down since last night with Jamila, so it's gonna be at least an hour before I'm up and out."

"No problem, you good." I scratched my head, remembering Jamila and I had to talk. "Make it tonight at eight.

That'll give me enough time to take care of everything with Rayna and Junior."

"A'ight, bet. I'll make sure to pump the promotions up on my end. Everything straight on the home front with Samira and Rayna?"

"Hell naw," I replied, exasperated. "Low-key, I think shit has gotten worse. I was so caught up in trying to do the right thing for my son's sake that I fucked around and forgot how rat-acting Rayna can be. I should've never shaded Samira for that girl." My reservations about Johnie might've been piqued because of Jamila's call, but I needed someone to vent to. Besides, if he was on some fake shit, he already knew too much of my dirt for this epiphany to matter. There was no reason to hide my hand. All the cards I'd been holding were played.

"Damn, chief, that's fucked up. You better hope ya wife can forgive your faults and welcome your sorry ass back home." His words gave me little hope.

"Samira's been holding me down for a long time, so I can't see her stopping now." I held on to the past.

"That don't mean she's about to continue playing a fool." He crossed the line.

Perhaps there was more validity and background behind Rayna's warnings than I gave her credit for. "Just maybe." I cut the conversation short. "I'm pulling up at the station so I'll get at you in a few." From this point on, my dialogue with Johnie was gonna be strictly contractual.

Before going into the station, I called Rayna, informing her of the change in plans and that I'd be back within the next twenty minutes. She yelped, giddy with joy, then hung up, promising to be ready. I couldn't tell if she was more excited about seeing our son or shopping in plain sight with me. Nonetheless, I had obligations to fulfill. I opened the door to 107.5. The more I moved up in the music game, the further apart Samira and I grew.

Jamila

I'd just stepped fresh and clean out of the shower when I heard Johnie talking on the phone. At first, I thought he was talking to another girl, maybe even Samira. Then I heard him speaking on business and figured it was King. Listening to them kick it about Rayna and Samira had me feeling some sort of way.

I held on to my towel as I lurked near my bedroom door. The more words of wisdom Johnie called himself sharing, the sicker I became to my stomach. Unbeknownst to King, he was getting mocked.

Johnie sounded like a hater. He wasn't cheering King on when it came to him making things right with his wife. In my opinion, he sounded like he wanted King out of the picture so he could make more moves with Samira. That left me as the runner-up again.

After putting it on him four or five times like a seasoned porn star, I still wasn't topping his charts as the woman to be with. Johnie wasn't shit but an opportunist, and I foresaw all of us gettin' played if we kept him within the circle. Maybe he and Samira were better for one another than I initially thought.

"Damn, girl, whip that towel off and climb your caramel ass back in this bed." Johnie pulled the covers back eagerly.

Had I not heard and formed my own opinion from his conversation, I would've leaped in headfirst. But I was on to something new. "Boy, bye. You've put enough miles on my pussy without paying a bill, taking me on a shopping spree, or at least out on a date. There are plenty of dudes checking for a chick of my caliber." I tried my hand at doubling my worth.

Throwing my hand on my hip, I shifted my weight to the side while waiting on his response. The only way I'd deviate from kicking him out was if he came with something better than hard dick.

Johnie

"Well naw, this ain't that." I leaped from her bed and into my clothes. "I'm sorry if you got things misconstrued, Jamila, but I wasn't trying to make you my woman or no shit like that. I thought we were just having a little fun."

"A little fun? You've got to be kidding me." She sounded shocked and embarrassed. "What were the flowers for then? Why'd you even bother?" She was steaming hot with anger.

"All women love flowers. I figured it was a nice gesture to butter you up for playing you to the left." I kept it real at her expense. I didn't care about sparing her feelings. There was no reason to.

Jamila flew out of her bedroom without saying a word. I was too busy into my phone trying to see what hot-tail I could get into next to notice her come back with the vase and flowers in hand.

"Get the fuck out of my house, you dirty-dick bastard motherfucker!" She hurled the vase in my direction, and it crashed against my shoulder right after all the flowers and water splashed against my face. "Butter that up, bitch." She didn't flinch.

"Bitch, I oughta split your head to the white meat." I balled up my fists, feeling heat pumping through my veins.

"It's nothing. I'm sure your little music blogs would love to hear about your little love-song-singing ass being a woman beater." She deviously smiled.

Raising my hands, I surrendered to her initial request. "We good, Jamila. You ain't even gotta take it that far, 'cause I'm good as gone."

"Well hurry up and get gone quicker." She had to have the final word.

I knew what time it was. Jamila definitely wasn't the type of chick you could trick with from time to time. Whatever nigga she caught slipping would for sure regret raw-dogging in her. I labeled types like her entrapments. You'd catch a kid, a case, or a concussion dealing with they assess.

Hearing her threats, I wasn't willing to risk losing everything I'd worked hard for plus was trying to steal from underneath King's nose because of her tired-pussy ass. She could view me like a punk if she wanted to. I was bowing out gracefully, right on out of her house.

Chapter Sixteen

Samira

Running through Target, I stocked my buggy with all types of items I could find for King and Rayna's baby. None of this was part of my plan in teaching him a lesson about stepping out on me. Nevertheless, I needed to give him a reason to come home.

He'd sneaked in, packing at least a week's worth of clothes while I was gone, so I knew he was serious about needing a break. What type of newlywed husband needed a break so soon from his marriage? I thought we might've been two steps from an annulment. True to my inner being, I was upset about him having a baby on me, but not enough to give him up to Rayna, especially when it was down to divorce.

Checking all of the items off of her registry plus some, I'd gotten King Jr. one of damn near everything they had on sale for newborns. As badly as I didn't want to, I was aiming for stepmother of the year. If King saw my efforts and that I'd at least played the game, he'd remember that my loyalty and love ran deep.

Ring! Ring! Ring!

Holding the cashier up, I answered my phone showing Johnie's number. I wondered why he was calling. Even if he and Rayna put two and two together that I was the one who tampered with her car, he shouldn't have been the one to reach out.

"Hello," I answered casually.

"Hey, beautiful, I was just calling to check in on you." Johnie sounded convincingly concerned.

"Oh, you don't have to do that. I'm good," I spoke with the least bit of emotion. If I thought I was feeling Johnie before, I was turned off and repulsed by him now. He was fuckin' my girl, and I didn't play sloppy seconds, believe that!

"You're good? How so? You found another one of King's artists to stroke that kitty?"

I almost dropped my shopping bags hearing Johnie put me on blast. "No." I brought my voice down low. "And I think we should keep those few times I let you hit it between you and me. Things can get messy if it gets out we fucked," I whispered. The sexual acts might've been done with ease, but I was still paranoid about King finding out.

"Oh, it's too late for all that second-guessing now that the deed has been done," Johnie chuckled. "If you ain't talking about giving me that ass on demand, it might slip out during a studio session that you're just as much of a freak as Rayna."

"You wouldn't," I dared him, even though his words sounded clear-cut and definite. "There's too much on the line with your music career if King finds out." I continued pulling his card.

"I'm my own entity, baby girl. Your man, if that's what you wanna call him, ain't nothing but a stepping stone in my career. I'm gonna be gravy with or without his ass. Now back to us. What's up with giving me that wetness?"

"You can try it if you want to. King won't believe your half-singing ass over me. So whatever card you wanna play, Johnie, drop it on the table."

Johnie didn't finish our conversation. He ended the call after loudly cackling. I was left trying to figure out what move he was about to make. I couldn't dwell for long, though. I still had one in motion myself.

Rayna

Having King's son was already turning out to be beneficial for me. Purposely getting knocked up by a nigga for security was older than the invention of hot, buttered popcorn, so I was glad that for me it hadn't played out. Not even home from the hospital yet, and K.J. was already responsible for copping his momma 500 fat ones. Ain't no telling what I could come up on by the time he turned eighteen.

"Hey, Ray." I heard Tiana screaming my name from outside.

"What up?" I poked my head out of the window.

"Now that K.P. is gone, are ya bringing ya ass back out here? Me and Cam didn't spend the majority of our food stamps to feed the hood just because we felt like being good Samaritans," Tiana huffed.

"I'll come out to chill until he gets back. But we're going shopping for K.J. in a few. He just went on a run." I couldn't wait to throw it up in her face. No matter who thought King wasn't gonna do right by this one was sure getting shown otherwise, even me.

"Oh, okay. Well, I can't even throw salt on baby K.J." She turned her drink up. "Make sure you take those few dollars we collected from everyone to get him something nice. We'll be here partying when you get back." She turned around, walking back to Cameron's unit.

Rather than trying to figure out Tiana's hot-and-cold attitude, I got back to getting ready for King to pull back up. There was always a party going down in the projects, so there was no reason for me to rush to chill with the same folks shooting the same shit.

Whether or not I acted cocky or brazen when King tried checking me earlier about being on the same immature tip I'd been on pretty much my whole life, my common sense knew better. Junior deserved better, and as his mother, my job was to give him that. King, however, could save his "run your actions through me" bullshit for his son when it would be needed.

Samira

Bumping Jhené Aiko's "The Worst," I was caught up in the lyrics as I sped to Rayna's project housing development. I knew her little broke ass didn't have much of nothing, and even though I was trying to make peace with King, this was a grand way to stunt hard in her face. It was like killing two birds with one stone.

Anxiety was building up within me. I couldn't wait to pull up on her home-wrecking ass with a trunk load of baby stuff she couldn't afford to get her own child. She might've had the baby, but I was the wife. It was time for me to play my trump card like a real woman as opposed to playing word games like a child.

The GPS system told me to make a right within a half mile. Not wanting to get seen without looking flawless, I pulled over to make sure my makeup and hair was laid perfectly. Once that was done, I slipped a blade underneath my tongue like I used to do back in the day. Me and my blade used to cut shit up despite people underestimating my gangster. Trust, it was nothing for me to relive my youth! If Rayna wanted to get buck on some silly shit, she could get cut on some relentless shit.

The ghetto was turned up as expected. There were ratchet folks by the truck full sitting on their cars, lounging in the middle of the street, and leaning by the mailboxes shooting multiple games of dice. Nothing in this one-entrance/exit death trap was pleasant or inviting. Twinges of anger shot through my body as I thought of King over here slumming. *He better hope he ain't brought home no type of disease, roaches, or bedbugs fucking around in this filth.* Even with my windows rolled up and my Flowerbomb perfume lingering strongly underneath my nose, I still felt like I could smell their offensiveness coming through my car's vents. King was wrong as fuck for going from sugar with me to shit with Rayna.

Unmoved by the amount of people swarming around and eyeballing my car like I was some type of movie star, I kept pushing toward the address I'd gotten off Google. Nowadays, it's nothing to find out where a chick or trick lays their head. Finally pulling up at the supposed townhouse C-318, I didn't think twice before leaping out and knocking on the screen door. The main door was wide open, and I heard music pumping out loudly, so I knew someone was inside. My presence screamed "stranger," so of course all eyes remained focused on me.

"Who is you? Can I help you with something?"

The ghetto-sounding voice made me turn around. I looked up to see a brown-skinned woman with cheap-looking clothes trotting toward me. And here started the bullshit. Jamila would have really been an asset right about now. "Yeah, if you know where Rayna Robinson is." I made sure not to stutter. Alone or not, I had my blade, and it could be whatever.

"Damn, they must've raised the pay for social workers." Another girl walked up behind the first ghetto travesty who spoke. "Are they hiring for a receptionist or housekeepers at the hospital yet? I've been trying to get a job. Put me on!"

"Fall back, Cameron." The first girl threw her hand up. "I don't think this bitch is no social worker, and I fa'damn sure don't think she's here to spread no good deeds throughout the projects." I watched her grim me from head to toe as the other girl folded her arms and fell in line as a follower.

I didn't know if they could see my eyes rolling through my lightly tinted shades. I wasn't fazed by the little low-life union they shared. Rats were known to run in packs, and I didn't need a troop of followers. I felt my finger twitch, which meant my intuition was telling me strong that Thing One and Thing Two wanted to catch what I was carrying. "Bitch or not, this is not your business. I'm looking for Rayna Robinson."

"That's my girl, and you're on my porch, so anything coming up out of your mouth is my business." She refused to back down.

"Oh, okay, well, pull Rayna up out of your pocket since you're her keeper and shit." I turned and dropped my hand low with a balled-up fist, letting her know I wasn't opposed to getting it popping.

"Say the word, Tiana, and I'ma pull what I got in my pocket out for her slick-mouth ass." The initial nice girl added her two cents in.

My first thought was to keep quiet until my common sense kicked in. Dressed in a pair of skin-tight booty shorts, ain't no way in hell she was packing more than a yeast infection. And even if she thought she was gonna come from the left on me first, I would've sliced and diced her before she blinked. While they were busy getting grim with me, I'd peeped the center of attention slowly pulling up. The broken-down version of Lilo and Stitch were no longer factors and low-key, and neither was Rayna.

"Samira? Have you lost your fucking mind?" Rolling the window down, King stared me dead in the face as I nodded my head like a boss.

"Yeah, nigga, as a matter of fact, I have."

Before I could mutter another ill word, the woman I came over here looking for flew out of the door, swinging.

Rayna

Imagine my surprise when I heard the commotion going on outside of my window that involved my name. Like a trained veteran of the projects, I surveyed the scene for a few seconds before coming out, so I knew it was Samira on the porch. My intent was to let Tiana and Cameron handle my lightweight since I was still stitched up. But when King pulled up, I ran out ready to bust a bitch's ass.

"You should've told this uppity bitch about me," I yelled, landing one swift blow to the back of Samira's head.

She turned around, moving with the quickness. From the club, I should've known not to underestimate her. Before I could blink, she backed up a few paces to gain her composure then whipped out her weapon. "Yeah, ho, so you want it huh?"

I could hear the blade going against the wind as she swung it wildly at me. I'd never been the type of female to be intimidated by a broad, but I knew I couldn't handle her with my stomach freshly stitched up. Had I not just dropped a load though, it would've been over for Samira, no questions asked. Backing up into the house, I locked the screen door just in case she wanted to run in, then ran to grab my own weapon.

"Mira! What in the hell are you doing over here? Get your ass in that damn car and burn rubber out of here," I heard King yell. "Ay yo, Tiana, take ol' girl, whoever the fuck she is, and bounce. I got this and y'all ain't about to jump my wife."

The words went through my ears then hit my heart. His wife? Was King serious? All that talk about holding me and K.J. down couldn't be nothing more than bullshit if he was married to Samira.

"Fuck you and yo' wife, nigga. She gonna learn today about bringing her mutt-face ass around here." Tiana got crunk.

"Oh, if that ain't the funniest shit I've heard all day." Samira laughed loudly like a hyena. "Even on the first of the month, you can't fuck with me. I pity ugly hoes like you."

"Hey, Rayna! Bring yo' ass out here! I'm about to do you one last favor," I heard Tiana shout.

Then I began hearing Cameron calling for her clique to bring up the back. Even a blind man could see Mira wasn't leaving up out of here without a fight.

I couldn't throw shade at ol' girl. She was holding her own. Unfortunately, she didn't know how we got down in PJ's. Ignoring all the pain surging through my body, I clutched my steel bat then flew back down the stairs, running out the door full speed.

"Rayna, aw hell naw," I heard King yell as my bat flew toward Samira's head.

"Yeah, Ray, tag that ass," I heard Tiana and Cameron cheering me on.

She ducked just in time as King jumped in between us, almost catching a slug to the midsection. My feelings were hurt so I was out for mass destruction.

"Give me that damn bat, Rayna." King snatched it from my hand. My palms were burning.

"Tame that wild, mangy bitch, King," Samira shouted. "If she hits me, I swear to God you better put a bullet in that ho."

"Is you crazy? He ain't busting caps at the mother of his child. Fuck that ring and whatever title you trying to claim." I went hard on Samira, dismissing her grandiose notion of K.P. blasting me for her.

She tried reaching around King to swing on me like she snuck me in the club, and surprisingly caught a quick two piece from Tiana to the jaw.

Whap! Whap!

"Keep ya hands to ya'self, homie." Tiana followed up her hits with a verbal warning.

All hell broke loose as King tried keeping the mob of us project girls off his wife. Tiana was pulling Samira down to the ground by a wrapped handful of hair. Cameron was karate-chopping her in the stomach. And I was taking every clear shot I could at her pretty face King loved to adore. It was total mayhem going down in the small yard my son would soon play ball in.

All three of us ghetto-born girls were giving this prissy chick a whopping she'd remember for the rest of her life. Not because me and her were sleeping with and gettin' played by the same man, but because she'd come here unprepared.

"Where's ya girl at now?" I couldn't help but mock his wife as she shielded our blows as best she could.

Samira was a bright girl, so there was no reason why she shouldn't have felt any of our meetings wouldn't result in an altercation, especially when my crew was there to back me up. No matter how hard King tried, he couldn't stop the three-on-one girl brawl.

King

Despite my wants and beliefs, once the squad of girls began getting the best of Samira, I began laying down my hand. I didn't hold back an ounce of strength tossing them onto the concrete, one girl after the last, not caring if I broke their backs. Rayna felt my wrath too. I just snatched her off and held her back in a bear hug.

"Get up off of me, King! You know I'm sore from having your baby." Rayna tried fighting me off like I was hurting her.

"Calm the fuck down, Ray." I turned her away from Samira as she peeled herself off the ground. "Even if I were hurting you, yo' ass did way more damage coming out here like Rambo."

Rayna whimpered, kept trying to fight me off, then squealed in pain when Samira slit her left side with a blade. My heart momentarily stopped, and so did my reflexes. By the time I shook off the surprise of what Samira had done, she was already sliding into her car and turning over the ignition.

What in the hell just happened? This is all bad. I bent down to Rayna's side as Tiana and her girl finally got off the ground and started running toward Samira's car.

"Fuck all y'all. And fuck you most, King, for tending to that bitch." Samira tossed a Target bag full of baby stuff from the window then sped off, almost hitting groups of people who were standing around.

I felt even worse because she'd been shopping for my little one. And knowing her, she'd set him up straight for months to come. Samira didn't show up here to beef. However, none of this madness could be undone.

Rayna cringed on the ground in pain, crying that her incision was sliced back open. In spite of me wanting to scoop Rayna up, nurse her wounds, or take her to the hospital myself, I wanted to chase after Samira because she was the real one wounded. I'd been able to keep them apart at Flood's, but I'd failed today horribly.

"Pull the car around, Cameron, so we can get her to the hospital." Tiana panicked at the sight of her best friend bleeding out. "Rayna, girl, hold on. You're gonna be straight, and I'm on that heffa's head fa'sho."

Kneeling down by her friend's side, Tiana glanced up at me with a menacing stare like this was all my fault. How was I supposed to know Samira was going to show up here? I went from being concerned and pissed about how things were playing out to being on guard. The more people snickered, voiced their opinion, and encouraged Tiana to hold her girl down, the more motivated I was to make a move after my wife.

Ring. Ring!

Figuring it was Samira calling to continue cursing me out, I dug in my pocket to fish the phone out. I deserved to hear what she needed to say. More importantly, I needed to know her whereabouts. From the way it sounded, Tiana, Cam, and a few other girls in their wrecking crew from the PJ's were about to be on her head. When I saw it was Jamila, I answered anyway, thinking that Samira must've called her girl.

Chapter Seventeen

Jamila

It felt good stunting on Johnie and putting him up and out of my house. I was still thrown back and disgusted by his nerve to belittle and mock me. Sure I might've been thirsty for a man, but he was misleading me as a woman.

My broken ego and devastated pride wouldn't let me allow him the peace of walking out of my house without consequences for playing me. To be honest, he deserved worse than getting hit with a vase and flowers. There was something brewing in my retaliation Rolodex for Johnie though, and I was already making my move.

I couldn't wait to get in touch with King so we could link up. Time might've passed, but I still had bombs to drop in his lap. I hoped things played out with us better than they did with Johnie and me.

On my computer, checking Facebook for any recent updates or pictures of King's baby, I waited for him to answer my call. It was already on the fifth ring, but I was gonna let it go to voicemail before hanging up. If he was with Samira by slight chance, I would just play it off like I'd called her too but didn't get an answer. That was the most overused lie in the land with the invention of smartphones. Whether or not it was believed this time wasn't my real concern.

"Hey, Jamila, what's up?" King sounded out of breath, and his background sounded wild.

"I know this motherfucka didn't answer the phone instead of helping his baby momma. He's got life fucked up! Where's Deon at? I need my nigga front and center for this wimp-ass wannabe Drake," a woman's voice shouted out.

"Um, nothing much this way. Is everything good with you? Is it a bad time?" There were women screaming, cursing, and even directing a few disses at him.

Listening in, I didn't know what K.P. was in the middle of. Never hanging up the phone, he went back just as hard on the random lady plus called whoever this Deon cat was out to a brawl. I held the phone with my eyes bucked open and silent as a church mouse, not wanting to miss a word of the drama unfolding.

After a few minutes, King finally spoke back into the phone, answering me, more out of breath than he was when he first answered the call. This time the screaming in the background was gone.

"Shit is all bad, Mila! Where's Samira? Is she okay?"

"Huh? Is she okay about the baby? About yesterday? I don't know what you're talking about, King. What's going on?" My attention was fully focused on waiting for his reply. I thought I was calling to throw him off guard, yet I was thrown for a few loops myself.

"You don't know? She hasn't called you? This is all bad." His voice drifted off. "Ya girl showed up to Rayna's house for whatever reason and ended up getting jumped. They managed to hold her on the ground for a good minute before I threw them off."

"What? Are you serious?"

Part of me was giddy that Samira got what she had coming for going to ol' girl's house in the first place and doing the shady deed K.P. knew nothing about. On the other hand, Samira always rode with me when I fought my battles, so I felt semi-responsible for letting her down.

If I'd just been honest about Johnie in the first place instead of chasing behind his dick, some of this drama could've been prevented. Too bad I wasn't bigger than the game.

I tuned back into King going on and on about everything that'd been transpiring between him and Samira. When the opportune time presented itself, I offered my friendship, a blunt, and a drink, with the hopes of our crash session ending in more. I even made the empty promise to try talking to Samira. After I reassured him girl power could probably help ease the situation, he agreed, falling right into my plan.

"Yeah, I'll meet you in an hour. I'm gonna shoot past the hospital to pay my son a visit, and then you can meet me at my room. I've been at the Comfort Inn, giving Mira her space."

"Cool. Text me the information, and I'll be there." I turned the computer off so I could get ready.

"Oh, what did you have to tell me the other day? With all that's gone down, we haven't gotten a chance to talk." K.P. changed the subject.

"It can wait until we link up in a few. You deserve to see your son without more burdens on your shoulders." My words were half true. I wanted to see his reaction with my own two eyes when I told him Samira and Johnie were fucking.

"That's like telling a nigga his death date in advance." He lightly chuckled. "Whatever the case, thanks for trying to be considerate. I'll see you in a few."

Right after I made sure the phone hung up, I moved through my contacts to call Samira. Not because of the promise I made to King about trying to smooth things over, but because I needed to know her location before making a move to go fuck her man. It was too late, and we were too grown for that "BFF" bullshit. I wanted a man, and she had one who was dangling.

The thoughts of me settling for Johnie went out the door when I realized he was just settling for me too. It was time-out for all that runner-up crap. I wanted who I wanted, and that was King.

Samira

If King thought we were gonna bounce back from this, he had another think coming. My head ached more at each flashback of him holding Rayna back. He should've been putting her on ice for beating me down. I was literally dragged onto the concrete and mangled. My well-being should've been more of his concern. Disgust was an understatement to describe my feelings toward King. I'd been officially thrown from the pedestal I sat on beside him. Whether I was the wife or not, Rayna seemed to be "the one."

In addition to my body aching, the pounding in my head wouldn't go away. Putting my hand to my face, I found it was swollen and sensitive to touch. When I finally came to a red light, I flipped the visor down and was instantly distraught at the torn-up and battered reflection looking back. My hair was all over my head, there was a cut right underneath my eye, and my neck was red from all the karate chops I took to the throat.

Rayna and her posse of girls more than ganged up on me. They pounced hard and tapped my ass. However, the blood on my hands was a clear indication that I'd left the scene with one up. If I could've sliced Rayna's side again, I would have. If I was lucky, home-wrecker bled out.

Ring. Ring! Ring!

My eyes rolled to the back of my head when I saw Jamila's name flashing on the screen. I might've gotten away with a few scratches and bruises from fighting

Rayna and them, but me and Jamila were more personal with one another. We were bound to emotionally scar one another. Regardless of me wanting to answer, I didn't want her to think I was ducking or dodging or the one responsible for her car.

"Hey, girlie," I greeted her like nothing was different.

"Heyyy, booo," she sang into the phone. "I'm sorry about being missing in action, but you know how my ex can last for hours," she lied through her teeth.

Instead of calling her out, I listened intently for what lie she'd tell next.

"Anyway, what are you off into? Are you and King back on good terms? I see ol' girl's Facebook feed has dried up."

Judging by her demeanor, I could tell that Jamila couldn't have known about her car or that I knew she was banging Johnie. Therefore, I kept my hand close and was careful not to spill the beans. "Girl, bye, ain't nothing changed. He's still out here playing daddy, and I'm still out here chasing my tail like a foolish dog."

"Well, girl, quit moping and start living until King decides to fall his ass in line. We should meet up for a girl session or go out partying tonight. That will keep your mind off King, plus you'll feel better."

"Naw, I'm straight. I'm too drained for partying, Mila." I didn't need to tell her about the fight. "I just made reservations down at Immerse Spa, so maybe tomorrow." I blew her off, knowing that tomorrow wasn't an option either.

"Dang, why are you being so dry? Why didn't you invite me to the spa? We can sip wine and have girl talk." Jamila had the nerve to sound surprised.

"You're not worried about sitting around with me when it's dick to be had." I rolled my eyes, tired of the conversation. "I'm not upset or anything, but do you. I'm about to walk in the door so I'll holla at you later." I ended the call then powered the phone off. I was done with the outside world until my inner being was nursed back to health.

Stretched across the deluxe comfort bed and snuggled in the hotel's robe, I felt a little better having been in the spa's Jacuzzi, gotten a massage, and soaked in the elliptical pool. I focused hard on meditating the entire time strictly on me and how I needed to proceed from here. I had a life to live, a job to work, and issues with Johnie I had to work out that I hoped stayed undercover. I was tired of my and King's worlds intertwining if he only meant a struggle for me.

The only good thing about me working so much overtime at the hospital to afford taking care of King the Producer was that I'd accrued enough time to take a few paid days off. After letting my supervisor know from the hotel's phone that I'd be doing just that, I doctored my wounds again with their first-aid kit and popped a Norco for the lingering pain. I was smart enough to know my first and last visit to the projects was today. Crawling under the cover, I pulled it over my head while squeezing my eyes shut. My only goal for the rest of today was to sleep it off.

King

My and Samira's house looked quiet, the driveway was empty, and the delivered mail was still in the doorway. There was no reason for me to stop because it was obvious Samira wasn't home.

In spite of me trusting Jamila to sprinkle her girl power over the situation, I rang Samira's phone back-to-back, hoping her line was tied up and the phone wasn't powered off. Slamming my hand on the steering wheel, I was furious with frustration realizing there was no way to reach her.

"Hi, this is Samira. You've reached me at a bad time, but please leave your name and number so I can return your call," her voicemail greeting played.

"I know I'm the last nigga you wanna talk to, baby, but please call me back. I don't know why you were there or how things got to that point. All the same, I need to know you're all right." After a few seconds of not knowing what else to say in such little time, I rushed out what I felt needed to be said before the timer beeped. "And despite contrary belief, the only woman I want to be with is you. I just need your unconditional acceptance and love of my son."

"If you're satisfied with your message, please press one."

I followed the prompts, making sure the voicemail was marked urgent and sent, then hung up. The ball was now in her court. All I needed was a positive response from her saying I could return home, and I'd be there on bended knee begging for forgiveness. Until then, I'd be between the hospital, the hotel, and the studio. For her health, I prayed everything was okay.

"It's good seeing you here," the same nurse who'd helped Rayna deliver K.J. greeted me as I walked into the nursery. "Your son has been doing wonderfully. His vitals are up, he's drinking almost an ounce more of formula, and the doctor doesn't think it'll be a whole week before he's released from here."

"Wow, my little slugger, you've got the fight of your momma in you," I joked, rubbing his tiny hands. I could've sworn he smirked. Having spent nine months brewing inside of Rayna, he knew better than the both of us just how nutty she was and how she operated.

The peaceful and serene feeling I'd been missing since leaving K.J. was returned as soon as I sat in the rocker with him in my arms. I watched him with love. I was proud of him being strong and resilient already at such a young age. As he chugged down the bottle I was feeding him, he was looking up like he recognized me as his dad. I found a new motivation to work things out with Samira. I wanted to give K.J. a little sister or brother to grow up with, bond with, and have as a partner in this world like me and Samira didn't have. I wanted all of us to be a family.

"Wow, you've got some nerve to have ya black ass up in here after you left his moms bleeding on the pavement." Tiana came into the nursery, disturbing my visiting time. If she was here, that meant Rayna was here, which meant hella drama for me.

"Not here and not now," I cut her off. "If you think I'm about to argue with you over my son, you've got the game twisted." I rudely dismissed her then gave my attention back to Junior.

After sticking up her middle finger and mouthing the words "Fuck you," she stormed out of the nursery just as quickly as she'd come in. That was just the calm before the storm.

Thus far, Rayna hadn't pulled her baby momma card on me. However, after what went down earlier with Samira, I knew she'd be trying to trump me as soon as the doctor got done stitching her up. Once I finished coddling K.J. until he dozed back off to sleep, I placed him back in the crib then snuck out. It might've been a punk move, but I wasn't trying to get into any more escalated incidents at the hospital.

Rayna

Once again, had it not been for Tiana coming to the rescue over some shit that involved King, I would've been up shit's creek without a paddle. The doctor said the slit to my incision didn't do much damage but would extend my healing process after giving birth. It didn't take Dr. Wang long to disinfect the area, stitch me again where I was sliced, and chew me out for not following the after-care directions.

I took Dr. Wang's words with a golf ball stuck in my throat. It was true I should've been preparing for K.J. coming home instead of fighting Samira, but if she came back for round two, I'd be willing and waiting to swing. Samira and I were officially enemies.

"Girl . . ." Tiana frantically burst through the door then covered her mouth. "Oh, my bad, I didn't know you were in here, Doctor." She fell back but kept her eyes locked with mine.

With Tiana shaking like she had a nervous condition, it was hard focusing on Dr. Wang thoroughly going over the same suggestions for a healthy recovery that I ignored the first time. After he asked me if I needed to speak to a social worker and I declined, I was willing to play whatever positive role he needed me to play to not be caught up in the system. I wasn't trying to have K.J. taken from me by someone snooping around my crib like I was unfit.

"All of this extra nonsense because King's wife can't accept his real family," I blurted out, making Dr. Wang's brow rise.

Once he wrote my scripts for some additional antibiotics and pain meds, he walked out to get me a referral list for some psychiatrists he thought would be beneficial for me to see. I didn't have a chance to react to the hurdles I'd have to jump through before Tiana exploded.

"Yo' punk-ass baby daddy is in the nursery with K.J., Rayna. Get up so you can get down there to check his ass." She rushed to my side in an effort to help me up.

"I can't, Tiana. You heard what the doctor said." I fell back, gripping her hand with anger. "But trust and believe him and ol' girl are gonna feel it hard when I heal."

I wanted to react. Matter of fact, I was itching, too. The hotter I got, the more flushed red I became. My temper was flared to the point of my skin burning. King had me all the way fucked up, him and his wannabe wife who had one coming.

"I can't blame you for that, and I support you for making sure li'l man can come home." She fell back from giving me a hard time. "However, I'm on their head like a savage before you heal. I don't like how that uppity bitch showed up trying to stunt or how that ho-ass, beat-bopping flop artist left you on the pavement. You know how we roll in the PJ's when an insider tries to get tough in our territory. Them two ain't did nothing but up the ante in our revenge," she spoke sweetly, exposing her hot-and-cold personality.

Caught between a rock and a hard place, I couldn't pop off the way I wanted to on King. He deserved to feel my wrath in the worst way, but I was already under the microscope in the hospital. Any false move I made that presented an unsafe environment for K.J. was only a lose-lose situation for me.

Nonetheless, just like Samira was gonna catch her payback in the streets because my law wasn't the same law as the cops, King was added to my list too. The quickest way to hurt a nigga's heart was to consistently dig his pockets raw. He could play Daddy all day long as long as my checks rolled in. As soon as I could, I'd be down to Michigan's child support office, Friend of the Court.

"Right now, Tiana, can you just help me down the hall to my son?"

Chapter Eighteen

King

My luck must've been looking up, because I escaped the hospital without having a run-in with Rayna. I knew without a doubt our relationship was about to take a negative spiral downward, especially with Tiana's hateful ass running the show. If I could still wrap Rayna around my finger long enough, my plan was still to move her up out of the hood, more so now than ever. I still desired to be the type of father Junior could count on, no matter how many times I failed these chicks on the streets.

I checked my phone and saw Samira hadn't returned any of my calls, and then I tried hitting her back once again. After getting her voicemail before it had a chance to ring, I knew it was still off, and wherever she was, she didn't want to be bothered. To lay it on thicker for my case, I left another message dedicating my love. In time, if she hadn't already, she'd receive my messages and call back.

Turning the radio up, I rode back through the streets of Detroit and past my house to see if the scenery had changed. Everything was the same, which meant Samira hadn't been home. The uneasy feeling had me wrecked. So much so that I barely recognized a beat I'd made playing through the speakers.

Simultaneously, my phone began blowing up with notifications that another K.P.-made track was on 107.5.

The DJ made good on his word, so all I needed was for the public to receive it well, therefore blowing it up.

When I pulled up to the room, I sent Jamila a text message of where I was staying and then went in to blow a blunt and wind down. Too much shit was heavy on my mind to wait on her to arrive before starting. That's when my day got even worse. Not only was our record live on the radio, but so was Johnie behind my back.

Johnie

"What motivates you to write? What hits are in the making for you and King the Producer?"

Ignoring the vibration coming from the phone on my hip, I stayed mentally focused on taking care of business. "It's nothing but fire coming from our camp." I leaned up to the mic. "We've been putting in hours at the studio working on a few love tracks to help the fellas get the ladies wet," I spoke like a true debonair pimp. I used whatever tactics at my disposal to sell records, make fans, and leave lasting impressions.

"Ahh, so are you saying the brothers around the city are falling short? Come on, man, kick it to me. Spit a verse to teach a lesson and make the ladies weak right quick." The disc jockey signaled for me to sing a rhyme.

I wasn't here to be a show piece. I was here because King said he was dropping off a few tracks for 107.5 to play. The snake in me, of course, wanted to jump on the opportunity to get some solo shine time.

Not long after me and King hung up, Jamila played me to the left, and Samira fell back foolish in love. I made my way to the station to try my luck for a spur-of-the-moment interview. It didn't take much persuasion. Not only was the host a fan of our work, but he also respected our grind as artists, having been one himself.

I sang a few verses during the show, took a few calls, and even answered a few questions for the host. All in all, it was a hella good look for me, and even my personal Instagram page friend requests went up. Of course, I made sure to speak about K.P. and our plans as a group to do it big. Looking like a snake out in the open could ruin me. Yet and still, promoting myself and the talent I had to offer a major record company was my first, last, and unspoken goal.

K.P. could keep his pussy problems to himself, including Samira's confused ass. I had fun hitting her, no doubt, and I even thought we had a good thing going for more sessions of fucking for fun. But since that was a no-go, I had to fuck him out of something he loved just as much if not more: music. The game was on, much hotter than before.

King

I was in a complete trance. 107.5 was blasting through the speakers as I listened to Johnie's interview. Every word that he said stuck to my membrane like glue. I was in complete disbelief that he was doing an interview without my knowledge. Yeah, he name-dropped a few times and spoke on us as a team, but any real nigga, especially me, saw that Johnie's hand was exposed. Not wanting the disc jockey to sense sloppiness on my end, I stuck to calling Johnie's personal phone instead of the radio station, but I didn't get an answer. As far as I was concerned, bad milk was officially spilled between us.

When the interview finally closed out and the show went to commercial, I finally shut the car off and made my way into the hotel. Johnie couldn't continue being an artist under contract with me if he was gonna be making underhanded moves. It wasn't wrong for him to want to do publicity or represent himself more at venues. The suspicious flag was that we'd kicked it earlier, I'd mentioned the station, but I couldn't recall hearing him say he had an interview scheduled.

The more I thought about the questions and answers spat back and forth between him and the disc jockey, the more blurred my judgment became. Popping the cork on my personal bottle of Patrón, I guzzled almost a fourth of the bottle down before taking a breather. I was breaking bread with a dude I barely knew and breeding kids with a chick I'd just begun banging.

Samira grounded me, and I needed a dose of her badly to get right. She'd help me put things in perspective while helping me clean up the mess I'd allowed to spiral out of control. Before I could get lost in my thoughts about Samira, taps on the door disturbed me. I swung it open to see Jamila standing with a bag in her hand and a slight grin on her face.

"I hope you're ready to unwind. I came with goodies."

"That's what's up. Did you get in touch with Samira?" Jamila didn't get a chance to get through the door good before I bombarded her with questions. I didn't care about her li'l stash. I was already turned-up tipsy.

"Yeah, we spoke for a hot second right after we hung up. She ran some shit down about needing some space to think." She pulled another bottle of Patrón from the bag. "My suggestion is that you quit worrying about her, though. Take a drink and start celebrating all your hard work. I heard Johnie on the way over."

I was already holding on by a thin thread, and something inside of me snapped. "Fuck some goodies. Did you know that grime-ball-ass nigga Johnie was up to that slick shit? Huh? You better start talking, and I want the truth." Not only was she banging Johnie, but she'd called me with alleged news only days before the interview. I was tired of her holding out on shit she knew. If another thing blew up in my face, I was sure I'd ice a nigga.

"Um, naw, I didn't know about the interview, but I did know his ass was shady." Jamila began dropping the ball.

"How so? Elaborate." Clutching my bottle, I swigged a few more sips then took a few steps toward her. "I ain't got time to get played on my music, Jamila. So whatever you know you better spit it out."

She fumbled with the cork to her bottle of Patrón, popped it open, then guzzled down damn near a fourth just as I'd done earlier. Watching her sudden moves to get drunk, I knew the news she was about to drop wasn't favorable to me.

"When he was at my house earlier, I went through his phone and saw a bunch of inbox messages to people in the industry. From what I read, he's been trying to get a solo career jumping. All he needed was a better portfolio, which you helped him with."

"Damn." I shook my head in disbelief. "So I'm not going crazy? This nigga is using my brand to come up." It's not like I didn't know the game could be disloyal and grimy. Cats jump ship all the time to different labels for different perks. Yet and still, me and Johnie were supposed to be on another level and more like friends.

"That's not the only thing he's doing right up under your nose, K.P." She dropped a not-so-subtle hint that she was hiding something. "I guess you've been too caught up with the drama that is your love life."

"Cut the introduction to whatever it is you've been itching to tell me already, Mila." I got tired of the cat-and-mouse game. "A nigga has had a real long last couple of days, as you already know. So trying to figure out your riddles is only gonna piss me off further." I couldn't continue to beg for her one-up on Johnie.

"Fine, fuck it! There's no nice way to tell you about your first hit artist smashing your newlywed wife." She spat a sentence of words out that crushed my heart.

"What in the fuck did you say? Say the exact same motherfucking thing you said, but this time, enunciate every damn syllable. I need to be sure I heard you right." I was seconds away from exploding. No matter how much dirt I'd done in the streets, my manhood wasn't allowing me to believe I'd been gettin' played by Johnie and Samira.

"You heard me, King. Samira and Johnie got down." This time Jamila spoke confidently. "Matter of fact, I'll give you a few more details so you can confront them face-to-face and read the truth. When you went to see K.J. be born, they fucked on your living room floor. Your little wifey called me afterward bragging and shit."

I looked up between Jamila and the floor. Then Jamila and the door. Then Jamila and my dick. A million thoughts raced through my mind as I tried to remember either Mira or Johnie giving off clues that they'd been attracted to one another. It was messing me up mentally that I couldn't remember one solitary time of Samira even giving his joker ass a second glance. And now Jamila was staring me boldly in the face saying I'd been betrayed. Damn, I couldn't believe Samira had that shit in her.

The more I tried to put things into perspective and/ or discredit Jamila, Samira's words from earlier of "not making a man move" and her "finding another nigga" played back. I thought back on the moment in time, wondering if she was parading her trophy right under my nose. If Jamila's story checked out, by the time I'd conversed with Samira she'd already made the ultimate move by banging my boy. So now was she investing in Johnie like she'd done me? Was that who he got the bright idea from to go behind my back? Nothing was making sense.

"Hey, K.P., snap out of it." Jamila snapped her fingers in front of my face.

I was hot. I didn't want to snap out of it. I wanted to snap a nigga's neck, preferably Johnie's. He'd come to the studio after banging my bitch, grinning all in my face about being brothers. This motherfucker used my connects and probably had Samira dangling on the sideline juicing his ego.

"King, hello! Damn, if I'd known you were gonna go all traumatic and shit into a mute, I wouldn't have said anything at all." Her words were only background noise to the voices in my head.

In my living room? While my son was struggling to get into this world? While I was going through the worst moments of my life? I thought of him licking, sticking, and pounding Samira with the intentions of filling my shoes. I knew she wasn't shit to him but a trophy and a flag for him to wave in my face. I didn't know what he was to her, but I was hoping Samira only used him as a pawn.

The more Jamila tried getting my attention, the more I focused on what her role in the game could be. "Yo, why in the fuck are you here anyway? What do you get from snitching on ya best friend?"

"The real question is, how much do you appreciate my honesty and loyalty to you?"

When she saw the confused expression on my face, coupled with my hesitation in answering, she continued. "I mean, come on, King. Don't play foolish now that the cards on the table. I kept the secret about Rayna being pregnant between us when I could've blown your spot up when the trick first posted it on Instagram, but I didn't. Then when your women crossed paths at Flood's, I dragged your side chick up out of there without a second blink. I didn't do that for Samira's benefit. I did it for yours. It's been all about you in my mind for a while now." Jamila confirmed what I'd been wondering off and on for a while.

I tried warning Samira about keeping female friends too close to her happiness, fortune, and success. As I watched Jamila bite at her bottom lip, trying to read what I was thinking, I thought back to when I told Samira about keeping her around in the first place. Being a dude, I peeped the pettiness that erupted between women. Jamila couldn't dog Samira enough back in the day for getting with a broke nigga who required cleanup. But her negative judgments tuned into praises the more my music popped off. Samira was too wrapped up in having a friend to cut the strings with the slithering snake. If only I could've read my own situation so clear.

"I think it's about time I give you exactly what you came here looking for." I pushed her down onto the bed.

Her face lit up as she watched me pull my dick from my pants. Before I could attempt to, she ripped her own clothes off then began fingering her coochie. It was a bit too hairy for me to lick, but I fa'damn sure was about to stick it. If Samira wanted to go around fucking my friends, I was gonna fuck hers too. And as an added cherry to place on top of the sundae, she was officially Johnie's groupie, too.

"Ahh, yes, King. This is where you belong," Jamila screamed and moaned when I slipped inside of her raw.

Right then I knew I'd made another ill-bred move, but I had a point to prove and a nut to bust. Samira shouldn't have fucked with a friend.

Chapter Nineteen

Rayna

Someone from around the way figured I needed the baby clothes and items Samira tossed from her car window, so they left them on our porch. I'd been going through the bag, torn between wanting to hate her or appreciate her for getting my son so many nice things. There were sleepers, outfits, pacifiers, bottles, and even a few rattles that said, "I love Daddy." From the looks of it, she was really trying to be the bigger person. I saw through that fluff, though.

Samira wanted to impress King. I knew the game well since I majored in Ratchet Thinking. She was smart enough to know that she'd lose him to me if she didn't accept his son. So she was going out of her way to prove she'd accepted him. Since K.P. wasn't here nursing my wounds, she'd obviously won this round.

"So is that nigga answering ya calls or not? Cameron and her cousins are downstairs ready to make a move." Tiana stood in my bedroom doorway.

"Naw, he's not answering. I don't know where he's at, but we can at least ride past to scope the place out." I checked my side, making sure blood wasn't leaking through my bandage.

"Fuck a scope-out, Rayna. You're either all the way in to retaliate, or you can stay home and nurse your wounds. Either way, me and the crew are about to ride out." She bent down to lace up her knock-off Air Forces. "Ol' girl tried jumping you at the club, came through our neck of the woods knowing you were fresh from the hospital, plus she's the reason K.J. won't have a full-time dad. You're more of a sucker for love than I thought if you ain't talking about causing no baby-momma drama."

Me, Tiana, Cameron, and two of her cousins from the east side rode piled up on each other in her four-door Neon. A blunt was in rotation, but I wasn't taking my turn. I'd only taken two puffs and was feeling like I'd made the wrong choice. The last time I showed up at K.P.'s, things didn't end up so good.

I'd have given anything for it to go back to the good ol' days when me, King, and Johnie would sit up in the studio for hours getting bent. You couldn't tell me I wasn't K.P.'s girl. Tiana tried to tell me I was just the main groupie, but when he and I clicked, I felt like it was love.

Every time he signed in to mix or sample a song, I was right there on his lap, dancing. Every time he brought a potential music group in to showboat, I'd be the one walking away in heels and cutoff booty shorts to entice them to sign. And each and every time he told me to drop and suck him until his creative juices flowed properly, I motivated him like any good woman would. Samira might've been the money behind the man, but I was his stimulus. Shiiiit, in my mind I was that nigga's power.

"Please don't tell me you're back there on some regretful shit, Rayna." Tiana turned around from the passenger seat, addressing me.

"Girl, bye. Like you said earlier, it's about time for me to start stirring up some baby-momma drama." I twisted my lips, knowing she'd like my response.

"That's my girl." Her smile went a mile long. She reached back to give me a play. I swore she loved getting revenge more than me. Tiana had always been the feistiest of us two. "Okay, here's the plan once we pull up . . ."

We all listened as Tiana instructed each of us on how things would go down once we arrived at Samira and King's. From the sound of it, she'd had this mapped out since finding out I was banging another woman's man.

It was too late to turn back if I wanted to. Everyone was eager and in agreement to tear shit up with no remorse. Checking my phone, seeing K.P. still hadn't called to see how I was doing, my uncertainty turned into bitterness. "Make another right. It's the eighth house on the right-hand side. It's painted a reddish color. The address is 15763."

Everyone in the car turned in my direction with twisted faces and side-eyes. The cousins even chuckled.

"Damn, girl, I'ma take that private-eye description you just ran down to me as a sign that you've been over here a few times." Cameron burst out laughing. "That musical dick must sing all up in yo' coochie."

Cameron had the car tilting over in laughter. The joke was on me, yet I didn't care. There was no reason to get upset, so I joined in on the laughter. "Yup, you're damn right I've been over here stalking. Unfortunately, from the sound of Tiana's plans, that'll all be coming to an end."

"Yup, yup, yup. I'm ready to huff, puff, and blow their little castle down." Tiana peered out the window with a menacing smile in her eyes.

Jamila

All the makeup I'd packed on for tonight's escapade was now smeared all over my face. As soon as I slid into the comfort of my own car, I let out all the tears I'd been holding in.

At first, he was stroking me to sleep each time he dug into my guts. Then he flipped and turned against me like I wasn't shit. My tears drenched the pillow as his cum drenched my back. I thought K.P. was won over with me after I dropped the bomb about Samira and Johnie, but the joke was on me. He put me out of his room just as quickly as he nutted. I couldn't help contemplate if any of this was worth it.

"Come on, Mila, get a grip." I fumbled with the key, trying to slide it in the ignition. The last thing I wanted was for King to come out of the room while I was still parked outside. He'd already called me a thirsty broad. To be lingering would make me look like a dehydrated wolf.

The car acted like it didn't want to turn over, so much so that I almost flooded my engine making it. Right afterward, it sputtered then shut back off. My flushed nerves turned to panic. *Oh, my God, this can't be happening. I'm so tired of piling money into this piece of crap!*

When I finally got it started again, I threw it into reverse without checking behind me then floored the gas pedal, making it speed out of the parking spot before it could cut back off. I went through this routine of having the car sputter, choke, and cut off on me three times within a three-mile radius of the hotel.

I guessed karma was kicking my ass already. I couldn't help but feel this was God's way of teaching me a lesson for sleeping with my best friend's husband. Picking up my phone, I couldn't even call and reach out for Samira's help. Instead, I pushed SEND after scrolling to Johnie's name then waited for him to pick up.

"What up? Speak to me," he answered, sounding on top of the world.

"I know I'm the last person you expected to hear from, but I didn't have anyone else to call. I need your help," I said, cutting to the chase.

"Oh, really? Well, damn, I thought you said a chick of your caliber can have any nigga she wants. Where are any of them at now? Why are you calling me for help?"

He was rubbing my words in my face, and I didn't have a choice but to take each syllable with a grain of salt. "Please, Johnie, I'm stranded on the side of the road. Do you think you could come help me out? I don't know what's wrong with my car."

When I didn't hear him respond or even laugh, I pulled the phone from my face and saw he'd disconnected the call. Leaning my head back against the headrest in frustration, I let out a bloodcurdling scream then took a deep breath, trying to start the car again. Unfortunately, it still didn't rev up. Karma was truly a bitch. When I got myself together, I was gonna start serving portions out.

Johnie

The way Jamila clowned and came for my head earlier was unforgivable and unforgettable. She could miss me with any conversation, contact, or common courtesy. If she saw me in the studio or around the way because of King and Samira, her ass better play the background role. Jamila was bad news.

Setting my phone in the cup holder, I laughed at her audacity and nerve to even ring my phone after earlier, especially for a favor. She was sicker in the head than I thought. I would've never pegged her for the psychotic type when Samira first brought her to the studio, but it was obvious I'd been fooled. It was a good thing she was in the dark about me and Samira having sex.

The more I thought about it, the more I worried about what information I actually did give her while we were talking and drinking. In my attempt to hit her skins, I could've slipped and said too much.

I tilted my fitted cap like a boss. My interview with the radio station had me feeling myself. I could see myself blowing up sooner rather than later. Knowing that, I couldn't keep giving major thought to a small-time figure in my come-up. Jamila could only be calculated with my downfall, and I wasn't having that.

Rolling the windows down to catch a fresh breeze, I also needed the wind to keep me up because I was like a dead man walking. I'd been fucking like the Energizer Bunny, making hit songs in the studio, plus doing interviews and promoting behind K.P.'s back. It was a shocker I hadn't passed out yet from exhaustion.

Ring. Ring! Ring!

Instead of answering Jamila, I powered my phone off then floored the gas pedal home. I was in dire need of some long, uninterrupted sleep.

Chapter Twenty

Samira

"Yes, that'll be three locks I need changed. Okay, see you when you get here."

I hung up the phone from the locksmith then took another glance out of the blinds. If King thought he was gonna play family man with that bastard baby and Rayna, he could do it all the way up out of here. Fuck giving him the option to come and go like he pleased and like his name was on some bills.

I got his voicemail message. Needless to say, I wasn't impressed. If that's all he could come up after letting Rayna stomp all over my ass, I was wasting my time fighting for love. King couldn't have wanted to truly reconcile.

When I woke up at the hotel with dried tears all over my face from crying in my sleep, I knew that my heart was broken and would bleed out if it could. If I was fighting with his baby momma today, I'd be fighting with her for a lifetime. My eyes were wide open. I couldn't go the long haul with King's luggage on my back. I went through every spectrum of emotion before finally coming to the decision to kick him out.

Once I was done grandstanding and setting King free, I'd be going back into the rented-out cave to set my emotions free. King was a heavy weight I needed lifted. I was about to make the move I should've made instead rushing his ass to Toledo. The decision wasn't final whether I wanted an annulment, but I was choking on the chunk of bullshit I'd bitten off.

This wasn't our household to share. It was mine and mine alone. My parents left it in my name only because they knew about simple niggas like King. They might've allowed their daughter to make dumb decisions, but they still provided me a safety net for just-in-case purposes. I guessed for bullshit like this.

While I continued to wait, I grabbed a few of the boxes I'd picked up from Home Depot on the way home and threw them down the basement stairs. It was time to get King up out of my life once and for all. Once I was done packing his stuff, I tossed the boxes on the curb and sent a text to his phone about it being there. Verbal conversation wasn't needed.

With one swoop, I cleared off a whole shelf, which included his DVD, CD, and video game collection. I tossed them into the boxes carelessly, not caring if the discs got scratched up. And I dared him to bump his gums at me recklessly like this wasn't my cash I was fuckin' up. For years, I'd let King dig deep into my pockets for his big-boy toys, but the sun had set on those dreary days in my life. I'd be the biggest fool on this planet if I continued to let him play me like my worth didn't matter.

My moves were swift as I tore the basement down the same way I built it up: one gift at a time. His PlayStation 4 went flying across the room then shattered into several pieces against the wall. I didn't give a fuck. I secretly wished it was his head. The precious studio equipment I financed, which was what led to all the heffas and hoes like Rayna, I stomped until all the buttons popped out.

"Yeah, nigga! Fuck me? Naw, fuck you! And I'ma fuck ya homeboy again. Believe that."

With a heart of heavy emotions, I was crying, scream-ing, and melting down, all because I was in love. All I wanted was my man and my happy home.

Crash! Crash! Boom!

I heard glass shatter, followed by a loud explosion, and my heart and stomach dropped as I fell to the ground, covering my ears. The sounds seemed so close. Panicked and unsure of what was going on, I flew up the basement stairs then damn near passed out once I hit the kitchen. Smoke was thick in the air as my living room was burning to a crisp. Someone must've set my house on fire.

The only way out was the side door. I'd already con-templated and canceled out the chances of me running through there for my purse, keys, phone, or any belong-ings. The fire wasn't staying contained within the living room. Making sure I got out alive, I was empty-handed as I ran down the driveway into the middle of the street. Tears streamed down my face as I watched everything I owned go up in flames.

"Oh, my goodness, child. I hope you have insurance. This is horrible." One of my nosy neighbors added her two cents while pointing her camera phone at my house. She had more than big balls and nerve to be filming my house burning down with me standing right next to her.

"Spare me your opinion, lady. And run that fuckin' cell." I snatched her iPhone from her hand. "You're rude as hell."

"Are you crazy? Give that back." She tried snatching it back, but I moved too quickly.

"Chill out. You can have your phone back after I make this quick call. From the looks of it, you weren't doing anything but being entertained by my misfortune." I rolled my neck then threw my hand up. That meant for her to fall back, which she did.

I didn't expect King to answer from this random num-ber, but I was hoping he would. This was a 911 emergency.

"Speak to me. This is K.P.," King answered.

"King! Oh, my God! King!" I screamed into the phone. My heart skipped a few beats when I heard his voice.

"Hello? Who is this?" His voice was slurred, and he sounded confused.

"Samira! I'm calling you from the neighbor's phone because the house is on fire," I blurted out.

"What? You've got to be fucking kidding me, man." King's voice cleared up. It was obvious he was high and drunk. "Is it contained? How'd it happen? Have fire trucks been dispatched? Did you grab any of my music equipment?"

"Your music equipment? I'm telling you our house is on fire and you're asking about some replaceable-ass equipment? I swear you don't care about nothing but music, that baby, and Rayna," I shouted for the whole block to hear.

Everyone out watching the show darted their eyes from my house to me as I screamed over the phone. I went from being panicked and nervous over the fire to irate at King for being such an asshole and so inconsiderate.

"You can cut out all the bullshit and theatrics, Samira. I'm up and on my way. And when I get there, please spare me the long, drawn-out speech about someone caring about you when you've fucked my manz Johnie." He snickered into the phone then hung up.

Pulling the phone from my face, I couldn't believe what I'd heard.

"Now give me my damn phone back." My neighbor snatched her phone from my hand.

The blaring sirens of fire trucks coming were drowned out by King's words playing over and over in my head. No matter how much dirt he'd done to cause me heartache and grief, my dirty deed was much more personal. I just wondered which demon spilled the secret: Jamila or Johnie.

Despite me worrying about how things would play out with us from here on out, I couldn't help but wonder how he felt finally being the one to get played. The beat don't stop. The game is always reinvented.

I sat on the curb with elbows on my thighs and my face perched on my fists. The red and yellow flames danced in my eyesight as I waited on King to arrive. And that's when I saw my precious car torn all the way up. All the windows were broken out, the tires were flattened, and the paint job seemed to have scratches all over it. *Payback is a bitch. Jamila must know I fucked with her car . . . or . . .*

Rayna

"Yeah, baby! We bombed that bitch." Tiana high-fived Cameron, more hype than me about throwing the Molotov cocktails into King and Samira's front window.

Our first intention was to break in, tear some shit up, and then light the house on fire. That plan quickly changed once we saw Samira's whip pull into the driveway. I had K.J. to worry about, Cam was fighting a welfare case, and her cousins had warrants. Tiana was the only one unconcerned about the police coming, and she still wanted to run in on Samira. We were able to pacify her by tearing up the car. She did most of the destruction alone.

I couldn't get the sound of glass shattering out of my mind as I threw the first of two bricks into the picture window. And when Tiana tossed in the cocktail, my ears damn near fell off from hearing the loud explosion. The home King loved to leave mine for in the middle of the night was no longer a motherfucking factor.

Ring. Ring! Ring!

Right on time, K.P. was finally calling my phone. "Hello," I answered indifferently.

Everyone in the car held in their giggles. Tiana turned and stared at me with a grin, egging me on.

"Have you been to my crib, Rayna? And don't fucking lie," he screamed into the phone. He was so loud I had to pull it away from my ear.

"Fuck you, King. I'm done gettin' played. The beat stops here. I'll see yo' ass down at court for my child support." I hung up and high-fived Tiana.

Ring. Ring!

My text notification went off, and it was, of course, him.

K.P.: Naw, the beat don't stop.

Chapter Twenty-one

Rayna

Unable to break my eyes from reading the text message from King over and over again, I was shaking from worry in my jogging pants. This was not how things were supposed to end up between him and me. We were supposed to be at the hospital playing the position of happy first-time parents, holding hands and nursing our son to good health, not fighting battles against one another. Sure, Samira invaded my territory and slashed me like a bitch, but I should've gotten back at her in a more clever way. If she went to the police and the dominoes fell, I could lose custody of K.J. quicker than I'd filled out the birth certificate. Damn!

My whole life was becoming a nightmare that I couldn't stir myself awake from. With every emotion in my heart and all the common sense in my mind, I knew things could never be the same between me and King. If I could rewind time back to only an hour ago, I would've stayed locked in my bedroom, sorting through all the baby items Samira purchased, and never guided my clique to his house in the first place. *How could you be so stupid? Why didn't you think about all of this earlier?* Hitting myself in the head, I couldn't believe I played the game so stupidly.

My girls were in the liquor store buying it out. According to them, we'd won the war, so it was time to celebrate our victory. I, however, wasn't feeling on top of the world. Setting Samira and King's home on fire didn't move me paces ahead in the game. Matter of fact, it forced me ten paces back. I deeply regretted not following my first mind. It was my life we'd acted so recklessly on. And in my opinion, the move was ratchet even for us and completely amateur on my part alone. It screamed, "These are the consequences of having a baby by a bitter bitch."

The more turmoil I realized I'd caused for myself, the more I wanted in on the liquor my girls were getting. I wanted to get faded and buzzed so my mind wouldn't explode from thought. My son was still in the hospital, I was even further from having a man than I was a few weeks ago, and my future included arson charges if anyone saw us bomb the house. Clearly, I wouldn't get the family I'd been desperately fighting for.

Twiddling my fingers, I looked down at the text message again, trying to think of the perfect way to respond. It needed to be something witty, something that made me seem more like the victim than the aggressor, and something that reminded him of our son. I'd always been able to woo him back to me, so there was a little hope in my heart that I'd be able to in this situation as well. Besides, King and I were ultimately tied to one another for life. No matter what, it was time for me to start playing the role of his baby momma and not just the random groupie I started off as.

"Rayna Ray, pop the trunk real quick," Cameron called out to me, snatching me out of my personal pity party. Waltzing out the store with a plastic bag in each hand, she'd been up to no good, you could tell. Her cousins were close behind with one bag in each hand, and Tiana brought up the rear with just a few packs of cigarillos. "If you thought your baby shower/welcome home party for

K.J. was off the chain, just wait until tonight. We're about to turn up until we pass out. Ol' boy behind the counter let me use my food stamp card to load up on a bunch of bottles of good shit. I don't know how the kids will eat this month, but Mommy will be drunk tonight."

"You're a mess, girl," I responded, popping the trunk as she requested. I couldn't help but smile and laugh at Cameron. She always found a ghetto hookup wherever we went.

"I don't care how much gas I have to burn out to come back to this store when my food stamps load. I swear I'll be back." Tiana slid into the back seat, amped up. "Shit, I could even start selling liquor on the sly for a few extra dollars. I might've found a hustle coming to handle Rayna's business," she snickered.

Tiana's wisecrack put me straight back into the hot seat and right back into my thoughts. It was no secret she'd never been a fan of my relationship with King, especially after he sent me into labor early, but my business wasn't hers to meddle in. It fa'sure wasn't her place to make it a mockery in front of everyone. As a friend, I thought, she was supposed to have my back when it came to being a comforting shoulder to cry on and an open ear for my vent sessions, not the judge and manipulator she was being. The shade she was throwing was irking me.

"What's your problem? Why are you acting all salty toward us like we didn't just ride out on a mission for you?" Tiana questioned, obviously picking up on my agitation with her.

"I appreciate y'all riding for me no doubt. But what I don't appreciate is how you keep throwing shade at me, trying to be funny and shit," I clapped back.

"Girl, what? Throw shade at you? Get the fuck out of here playing that victim role. I ain't King, baby boo. I've done nothing but be a best friend to you." Tiana sounded shocked and appalled by my statement. She'd gone straight into defensive mode.

"Whatever, sure you have," I grunted out of irritation from hearing her say King's name again. "If that's what you call putting me on blast in front of ya dude and possibly ruining my chances with my baby daddy, then fuck yeah, you've been one helluva pal." I was clearly being sarcastic.

"Naw, as a matter of fact, my definition of a friend would be a person who keeps me from losing my baby, stays up all night listening to me cry about a no-good nigga, and doesn't smack the shit out of me when I say dumb stuff," she growled at me. "I swear, Rayna, I'd put my hands on you worse than his wife did if I didn't love you. Did you forget who peeled you off the ground when King left you there slit open?" Turning from me, she leaned up into Cameron's ear. "It's gonna be a scrap session going down in your back seat if you don't hurry up and get us back to the PJ's."

Tiana kept putting me out there. I was embarrassed but more so caught up in my emotions. As wrong as I felt she was, I also felt where she was coming from. It was true she'd been there for me plenty of days and nights when King was home with Samira, in addition to getting me to the hospital twice because of him. Still, the way she was cutting into me and had strong-armed me earlier was straight out of pocket. If I didn't break the bullshit now, it would never be broken.

Everyone including Tiana was waiting on my reaction, so I gave them one. "You don't have to drive no faster, Cam. Just pull over and let me out. I need some space from this so-called best friend of mine," I sarcastically spat. "Plus, I'm a big girl who can handle my bullshit including finding my own way home."

"All right, y'all, that's enough. Tiana, quit picking on Rayna and, Rayna, I'm not pulling over to let you out. I don't know what lovers' spat y'all back there having but quit acting like my bratty-ass kids," Cameron chastised us.

"Whatever, Cam! You don't have to play the peace-maker right now. If she wants to get out, let her." Tiana was insistent on having the last word.

While Cameron was busy running her mouth, I was busy watching our surroundings. We'd just approached a red light. The car hadn't even completely stopped yet. I took that as my sign from God to make the next move. Talk is cheap, but actions are priceless. Opening the car door, I hopped out before Cameron could pull off.

"Are you serious right now, Rayna? Get ya ass back in this car right now. Whatever beef y'all got can get handled back around our way," Cameron begged. The light had changed, and she was now holding traffic up. Other drivers were blowing horns and beginning to yell obscenities out their windows.

"Fuck her if she wanna make a scene, Cameron. Pull off. If she wanna act like she knows how to wear big-girl panties all of a sudden, let her," Tiana spat. "She's only starving for some attention since King won't give her ass any."

"Yeah, cuz, ya girl is tripping. Either you can pull off on her or I'ma get out and walk the other way. You already know I've got warrants behind my name. Sitting in the middle of the street waiting on two bickering bitches will not be the highlight of my day or the reason I get harassed by the cops," one of her cousins chimed in.

Cameron looked at me apologetically then gave me one more chance. "I know you're caught up in your feelings, Ray, but if you don't suck that shit up and get in the car this very instant, you will get left. Not only do I have to look out for myself, but I've gotta look out for my family, too."

"Yup, that's right, Rayna. The sun don't rise on your round ass." Tiana threw her two cents in again.

"Fuck you, Tiana." I flipped her the middle finger, then turned my attention to the one person who was trying to remain neutral. "You've gotta do what you've gotta do, Cam. Just like I do. I'll catch up with y'all back in the PJ's." I waved them away.

"Damn, Rayna Ray, maybe you should be taken off the list of chicks I'd ride or die for. Tiana is right. You're acting ungrateful as hell," Cameron spat, then pulled off.

The brake lights on Cameron's car never popped on, which meant she didn't have any intention of reversing or coming back for me. I wasn't salty since I told her to go, but I knew she was no longer neutral between Tiana and me. Now that I was out here absolutely solo dolo, I realized just how alone I was. In just forty-eight hours, I'd lost my man, even though he wasn't mine to claim exclusively, my best friend, even though she was a flip-flopper, and my clique. All I saw was myself going out the world half-ass backward.

I spun in circles a few times, trying to figure out my next move. I wasn't sure about the bus routes on this side of town and didn't have enough money for a taxi. My dumb ass should've waited until I got back to the PJ's so I would've at least had my car. There was a supermarket a few blocks down. I headed toward it with hopes there'd be jitneys parked out front waiting on shoppers with groceries and no cars. I had enough to pay them for a ride to the hospital.

None of this would've happened if I hadn't left him in the first place. I was his mother, and he deserved to have me right by his side. It was a battle keeping my emotions bottled in.

"Where ya need to go?" the driver asked as I slid into his passenger seat.

"Hutzel Hospital, please."

Chapter Twenty-two

Samira

"Fuck, fuck, fuck," I whined, hitting myself upside the head, then burying my face in my palms. "How could you have been so stupid?"

I didn't care that I was drawing attention to myself. There would be more of a scene anyway whenever King arrived since he knew about me sleeping with Johnie. I'd gone from having control with him begging for my forgiveness to him probably hating my guts more than ever. I didn't know how things were going to play out between us now that his ego was bruised.

Although I had a reason to react irrationally, that was the lowest blow I could've ever served him. What I thought was a good idea at the time was nothing but an explosion waiting to blow up in my face. Just like the one I'd experienced with my house.

"Quit staring at me and mind ya damn business." I rolled my neck at a few of the neighbors looking back and forth between my ruined house and me having a meltdown on the curb.

They walked off with their noses in the air, but I didn't give a fuck. Hell, part of me wanted to get up swinging on them. At least that would've helped release some of this pent-up stress and aggression that was bubbling within me.

I knew my house burning down right in between their homes instantly brought their property values down, but right about now, their worries were the least of mine. My whole life was nothing but a mess. If anyone should've had an attitude, it should've been me. I was sure anything in their middle-class lives wasn't as dramatic or tumultuous as mine.

"Ma'am, our crew of firefighters was finally able to put the fire out. However, I'm certain the house is unlivable. Someone can escort you in to see what valuables or memorabilia you can recover. Do you have renter's or home-owner's insurance? If so, you might need to call an agent for a claim."

"Damn, I can't believe this is happening to me," I cried out. "Everything I owned was in that house. Now I don't have a pot to piss in or a window to throw it out of."

I'd been hysterically breaking down off and on each time I took a breath of smoky air, looked at my totaled car, or faced the harsh reality that I was now homeless. I couldn't believe I was going through all this behind the hands of King's trash-ass baby momma. Not even the president himself could've told me she wasn't behind this madness.

"Come on, ma'am, it's okay. I know this is a rough experience, but you'll get through this," the firefighter said, trying to be compassionate.

If only he knew this house and my car were only added stressors to my already-long list of bullshit to deal with. "You're right. I shouldn't be laying my burdens on you anyhow. Your job isn't to be a social worker."

"It's okay, ma'am. I'm used to dealing with situations like this. As horrible as everything may seem, I'm sure you'll bounce back on your feet in no time. When you're ready, we'll take that walk inside." He gave me a friendly motivational pat on the back.

"There's no sense in prolonging the inevitable. I might as well walk that green mile now," I groaned. I closed my eyes, took a deep breath, and tried gaining my composure to see exactly how much damage was done.

The house my parents handed down to me, but still kept their name on, was completely ruined. The living room I'd decorated like something from out of a ritzy magazine was burned to a crisp. That was expected since the cocktail came through the front window. All the pictures of me and King, all the memories we shared on holidays and late nights, and all the hands-on recollections of my childhood were nothing more than ash and rubble.

"There's more to salvage upstairs, but keep in mind the fire spread pretty quickly. I am very sorry for the personal items you have lost, but at least you made it out safely. You can always rebuild your life," the firefighter reminded me.

"You're absolutely right, and I appreciate you trying to shed some light on this dark situation. You just don't know how great that advice sounds." I honestly thanked him. My whole life had crumbled down, not just this house. I didn't know how it was about to be done, but I had no other choice but to start over.

The downstairs level was burned the worst. All the furniture, decorations, and personal items were all crispy items that couldn't be salvaged. The upstairs revealed more smoke damage than anything to our valuables, but the flames that managed to spread damaged the actual housing structure beyond repair.

Seeing everything my parents slaved for and handed down to me brought tears to my eyes and had vomit swirling around in my stomach. They'd never forgive me, and I couldn't blame them. Of all the disappointments I'd presented them with, burning down the home they bought as newlyweds would be gut-wrenching. Digesting my misfortune was all too much.

The firefighter stayed ten feet back while I went through my emotional downpour and collected what I could salvage. There wasn't much. I was mostly upset about my clothes being ruined. Although they hadn't caught fire, they reeked of heavy smoke. I was walking up out of here with just the clothes on my back.

Falling down to my knees, I picked up one of the charred frames that held a picture of me and King, and I cried. Everything that I loved was seared. I might've not wanted King, but I feared starting over alone. What I really wanted to do was drop everything and go back into hiding within a hotel room.

King

"What up, nigga? Holla at me 'cause it's a few words I need to spit at you. Don't delay." I got grim then hung up.

Tossing my phone into the passenger seat, I was disappointed that I only got Johnie's voicemail. I was amped to get at him man-to-man about his sexual relations with my wife plus end our musical ties. That motherfucka was sneakily coming up in the game behind my back, and it was time to put an end to his ass all around. My main goal was to get him blackballed.

Traffic was thick on Livernois Avenue because of construction, but I maneuvered the best I could until arriving on my block. None of this shit was believable. The more smoke I smelled, the more I realized I really wasn't getting punked.

"Yeah, that bitter bitch has gone too far." I slammed my fist on the steering wheel, pissed all the way off.

There was nothing Rayna could tell me to make me believe she didn't have a hand in this. Of all the groupies

I'd screwed, nothing like this had ever occurred. So there's no coincidence with the timing concerning this event. Rayna was bitter, angry, and looking for a way to get revenge on Samira, and hell, vengeance on me too. Truth be told, she was doing one helluva job.

Instead of me calling or texting my baby momma to serve her up with more promises and threats, I took in the depressing scene around me. The Detroit Fire Department was working hard, making sure the perimeter was blocked off and there weren't any injuries. I was looking hard but didn't see my messy wife anywhere.

Sitting across the street from the home I once shared with Samira, I was in total disbelief at the damage that was done besides Samira's car being totally wrecked. The windows had burst out, exposing the charcoal-colored living room, plus the gutters, siding, and even the roof were damaged. *Damn, I hope Samira made the insurance policy payment 'cause I'm sure I'm fucked out of all my music equipment.* Climbing out of the car, I coughed on the thick smoke that was heavily lingering in the vicinity.

"Sir, you can't come near here. Please step back," a firefighter quickly addressed me while trying to block my path.

"Back up, boss. This is my house," I responded with agitation. Quickly taking him in, I tightened up my stance, prepared to run him over if need be. "I'm looking for my wife. I just talked to her. She was here when the house caught on fire."

I'd been drinking like a drunk at the hotel with Jamila and even in my truck on my way over. I knew he could smell each word I spat.

"Oh, that's my bad. I'm just doing my job, sir," he apologized then moved to the side. "Your wife is in the house assessing the damage with a partner of mine. I'm sorry about what you two have lost." He pulled back the yellow caution tape and let me through.

Almost tripping down the basement stairs, I couldn't wait a moment longer to assess the damage in my man cave and studio. I knew everything was probably ruined by the smoke and fire, but if by luck there was a chance for me to salvage something, I wanted to. Building everything over from scratch wouldn't be a cakewalk. My eyes fell at what I saw.

"What in the fuck?"

Looking around the room where I'd made hits and spent countless hours relaxing, I was no longer infuriated only by the fire but by the wreck underneath it all. My video games, television, and worst of all of my music equipment were destroyed, and it didn't take a rocket scientist to figure out this wasn't a consequence of the fire alone.

Picking up my MPC, I saw all the buttons were popped out. Taking note of a few of my speakers, I saw holes were kicked in them. A few of the CDs I'd mixed with songs that were unreleased were split in half. Even the HDTV screen I'd just gotten Samira to get out of layaway was shattered. Naw, there was no way in hell a fire did all of this. This tragedy looked like the snapback of a scorned woman who'd been on the warpath.

Either Rayna and her posse tore it up before setting my house on fire, or Samira had gone completely crazy wanting me to feel some pain behind how I'd made her feel. Whatever the case, the person behind this wanted me to suffer and build from scratch. The fucked-up thing was that they succeeded, and everything I owned needed to be replaced. It was time to find my wife so I could start piecing together what in the hell really happened to our home.

Samira

"Samira, where are you at? Yo, Samira," King yelled through the house.

My heart fluttered. I was anxiously nervous to see him. I hadn't laid eyes on my husband since our wedding day when he walked out our front door to become a father to Rayna's son. What worried me the most about this moment was that this was the first time he'd look at me knowing I'd fucked the artist he was producing. Both of us were wrong, so which one of us could judge? That was at least my hope for how he'd view it. My time for thinking was up. He was standing right in front of me.

"You didn't hear me calling your name or something? Please don't tell me I have to change my name to Johnie in order to get a response up out of you," he crudely commented, disgustingly eying me from head to toe. With everything we shared around us ruined, his repugnance for only me was beyond evident.

Although I felt dirty for the deed I'd done, I wasn't getting ready to let him size me up when he was the one who stepped out first. Fuck that old saying "two wrongs don't make a right," especially when in mathematics two negatives make a positive. The firefighter was witnessing our dysfunctional conversation. I was flushed red with embarrassment. Since I knew there was no calming down King's reaction even though I wanted to, I gave him just what he wanted: a response.

"Only if I get to change my name to Rayna. Speaking of ya baby momma, what's her last name anyway? I'll need it for the report to list her as a person of interest of who threw the Molotov cocktail into our front window." Now that K.P. had me started, I was surely on a roll.

The firefighter cleared his throat, unsure of what to say or how to react. I'd said something pertinent to what he and I discussed in private earlier, and now he was reminding the both of us of his presence. King instantly picked up on what the firefighter did then responded to me.

"Don't dig yourself deeper into some bullshit by throwing her name around, Mira. That girl wouldn't dare do no dumb shit like this, for one. For two, bringing her up doesn't help your case. You fucked my boy, Samira. That shit was dirty, foul, low-down, disgusting, trifling—" He was bold, running down a list of degrading adjectives.

I cut him off when I couldn't take hearing any more. I didn't deserve the tongue-lashing, he did.

"Wow, I'm always everything but the only woman you're loyal to. I'm supposed to be your wife, your backbone, and your motherfucking soul mate. Even when I ride with you to the moon, my nigga, you find a way to make me feel like shit. Even when you say I'm winning, I'm the runner-up. So tell me, K.P., how does it feel to get played at your own game? It ain't so fun when the rabbit got the gun huh?"

"I'll fucking kill your ass, Samira."

He rushed toward me. His hands were around my throat before my eyes blinked and my mind could catch up with the moment. All the hate, animosity, and resentment he'd built up for me was felt through the grips of his fingertips. Not even the firefighter could stop him from attacking me.

"This shit is not a game. You're fucking the help, and you're supposed to be my queen. I swear I'll choke the life out of you for playing me like that," King spat through his clenched teeth. "Do you feel so brazen now? Why aren't you still spitting out cocky bullshit?"

"Get off of me. Let me go!" I tried pulling his hands from around my throat. "You're hurting me."

K.P. was cutting off my oxygen. I could barely speak or mutter a word, and I had to get him off me. It was obvious he'd been drinking because his breath reeked of the spicy smell of liquor. Because he was slightly drunk and out of his rabbit, I was fearful of what he'd do to me. I didn't mean to get this reaction from him.

"Hey, man, that's enough. You've gotta stop," the firefighter finally intervened. I got the weird feeling he didn't want to.

"Get your motherfucking hands off me, dude," King roared, finally releasing my neck. In the same motion, he threw the firefighter off of him and squared up to take him down. I'd never seen him act like a raging bull, but he was in full form. "You don't know shit about what's going on, so don't step in between a man and his wife."

The firefighter threw his hands up, not wanting to feel King's wrath. "My job here is done. If either of you would like to file reports or statements on who might've done this to your home, follow up with the police. I'm out of here. This seems way too messy for even a book. Plus, I have enough drama of my own." With that, he exited the room. King and I were alone.

My throat was stinging, my face was covered in tears, but my heart ached more than anything. We'd been each other's worlds. Hell, I'd made King into the man his groupie-ass baby momma couldn't let go. It was unbelievable that we were at the point of total ruin. I was attempting to beat him down with my words while he was trying to kill me with his hands. If this was what the preacher meant by for better or for worse, I needed an addendum to our vows.

"I can't believe you put your hands on me, King," I sobbed. "Not like that." I figured he'd be pissed and irate, but I never expected him to manhandle me or cause me physical pain.

"Yeah, well, you reap what you sow, and I can't believe you fucked who used to be my boy. Come on, Mira! Real talk, how'd you expect me to react off some news like that? Did you think I'd coddle and forgive you? That was some low-down shit you pulled, Samira."

Since there weren't any ears around to hear our emotional conversation, we both let our guards down. He didn't have to be a man in front of the firefighter, and I didn't need to play the victim simply because I was a woman. It was time to have the conversation we'd both been dreading.

"I'm sorry, King. I know I was foul for what I did with Johnie, but what you did with Rayna hurt me to the core too. Truth be told, I'm still torn off that shit." Only having the truth, I chose to put my heart on the line. "You had a baby by another woman, King. I wanted to be the only woman in the world to give you babies. Me. Me. Me. You're making me share that privilege."

"What in the fuck makes you think you'll still have the privilege to have my kids?"

His words were meant to hurt me, and they did.

King

"Yeah, you weren't expecting that cut-throat shit right there huh? You thought I'd get all mushy and soft 'cause you're stringing a violin and humming a harmonica? I swear on everything I love, Samira, I wanna choke your ass again." The liquor I'd guzzled at the hotel room with Jamila was still flowing through my system. I was thankful for the boost it was giving me to go hard without limits.

"Then you better choke the life all the way out of me. I don't care what you don't want to hear, King. You ruined us." She completely broke down. "I gave you all of me, worked my ass off to flesh out your dreams, and was even willing to help you raise the baby you had on me. I ain't humming no harmonica. I'm breaking the truth down to your ungrateful ass."

I didn't know seeing Samira was going to be so emotional and tough. There hadn't been enough time to process her dirty deed between me screwing Jamila and getting the call our home was burning down. Not to mention seeing the tragedy in my man cave, which I still hadn't brought up.

What I did know was that I couldn't keep playing the good guy when I'd still been creeping. 'Cause real talk, if Samira ever found out about me fucking her friend, I'd be every name but the child of God. But surely I'd be a hypocrite. Part of me had to accept I'd created this wild wave of bad events.

"Look, let's table this discussion until after we take care of whatever needs to be taken care of with this house. Nothing is about to be worked out right now, that's for sure."

"Fine," Samira huffed. "Let me see your phone so I can call my parents. The first thing that needs to be done is an insurance claim. We've lost everything in this fire. All I've got to wear is the clothes on my back but not even a pair of shoes. My purse, cell, and even the car keys to my ruined car were burned too."

Knowing my phone had all types of naked pictures, inappropriate text messages, and numbers of girls I hadn't had the chance to hit yet, I hesitated to hand it over. Me and Samira had enough drama to sort out. Her snooping through my phone would only make matters worse.

Samira snatched the phone from my hand before I could hand it all the way over. She wasn't a fool. She knew exactly what my hesitation was for.

"Oh, and ya better believe I'm giving them Rayna's name as a person of interest. In my opinion, she took being a home-wrecker way too far."

"You better not mention that girl's name, Samira. You don't have any evidence to back up what you're saying. Besides, even if you did, you can't press charges, because that will leave my son without his mother. We can handle whatever needs to be handled between us. Let me take care of it."

"What? After all this?" She waved her hand around our wrecked room. "You want me to fall back? You want me to care about her motherly duties to y'all son? Let me ask you this, King, if she cared so much about being a mom, why wasn't her ass at the hospital nursing him instead of firebombing where we live? Jesus Himself couldn't stop me from dropping her name to the cops. Fuck her, everybody from her ratchet clique who were probably involved, and those who want to protect them." She looked me square in the eye.

Samira was on ten. I was sure all of our nosy neighbors could hear our argument, and if they didn't know there was a person of interest before, they did now. Nine times out of ten, Mira was right, but I couldn't let an already-messy situation get messier. Instead of letting her continue to rant, I cupped her mouth closed and fought against her trying to get free.

"I'm not letting you go until you calm down. You know good and damn well you can't give that girl's name even if she did it. Let your husband finally put her in her place." I lowered my voice, kissed her forehead, and then rubbed my nose against hers.

I wasn't ready to forgive Samira, but I didn't have a choice. I was between a rock and a hard place with no other option but to manipulate the situation. Right about now, I'd give Samira the world to keep her from snitching Rayna out.

Releasing all of her weight as I held her in my arms, she was emotionally and physically drained from fighting me. I continued to hold and rock her tightly until her limp body completely collapsed and gave in.

"Please get me out of here, King. I can't take being here anymore."

Chapter Twenty-three

Jamila

"Thanks for towing my car and helping me out. I really appreciate it." I sincerely expressed my gratitude to the tow-truck driver who'd stopped to help me.

If it weren't for him having sympathy toward me, I still would've been trying to get the engine of my broken-down car to turn over. Johnie shaded me, King rode past without even looking back, and even my ex laughed and hung up the phone before I fully got my plea out. Karma was the baddest bitch I'd ever encountered for sure.

"Not a problem, beautiful. The side of the road is no place for a woman."

"I'm sure glad there's a man out here who still feels like that," I responded genuinely. "You're one in a million."

He chuckled, knowing I was right. "I'd like to take up for my brothers, but I already know it's a lot of 'em coming up slacking. Hopefully, you won't keep running into the wrong ones."

With my legs tightly squeezed together to help conceal the after-smell of sex, I sat back in the passenger seat while my car swayed on the back of his tow truck. It felt good to breathe, but I only felt a little relief. The many problems in my life that needed fixing were beyond my control. Wasn't shit I could do but wait and see how things would ultimately play out. My car was still not starting, which meant I'd have to come out of money I didn't have for a repair. That was only an added stressor to the fact that I'd been played by both King and Johnie.

It was beyond time for me to do some self-analyzing. Not because I was foul as hell for sleeping with the man who was married to my alleged best friend, but because I was getting too old to still be lonely making dumb decisions. Women my age could scream that "team single" bullshit all they wanted to. Good for them. I wanted a man on my team and a ring on my finger. Despite me not wanting to be miserable, I couldn't help myself. Snagging a man of my own seemed impossible. No matter what I did or how available I made myself, I was never good enough for a long-term title. Who wants to be the jump off, side chick, mistress, and other woman forever? Damn sure not me!

Once we dropped my car off at the auto repair shop for a diagnostic, the tow-truck driver was nice enough to bring me home, too. I rushed into the house, stripped down to my bare skin, and leapt in the shower to wash away the sex smell of King and of course all my sin. Almost using the whole bottle of body wash, lathering up, I couldn't wash away that I'd been used again.

Grabbing my Summer's Eve douche, I rammed it up my coochie, not pulling it out until the bottle was empty. As the suds and semen ran out of me into the drain, I wished the last week of my life would've gone with it. I finally dragged myself out after the water turned ice cold, and I headed straight to the kitchen for a stiff drink. I'd put myself in a fucked-up position. I'd gone from being a cool girl of the crew to a pitiful outcast.

Johnie

A nigga was feeling good about himself. Not only had I bagged two bad bitches, one of whom was my producer's chick, but my name was ringing in the ears of those who loved music. My time of living in the shadows was coming to an end. I hadn't planned for things to play out the way they were, but I was making moves based on how the opportunities came.

Yawning while rubbing the crust boogers from my eyes, I'd been sleeping good, but it was time for me to rise and grind. I was sure my timelines, friend requests, and downloads were on slap since I'd done the interview. That meant I couldn't waste another moment not capitalizing on the opportunity.

Once I turned my phone on, I went in search of my computer so I could retrieve the stolen tracks I'd ripped off from King before banging Samira. Since he and I weren't supposed to meet up at the studio until eight, I still had time to remix a few songs to make them mine. I wasn't claiming that I wasn't talented or creative enough to come up with my own original music, but I could double my worth with having extra songs on deck. Plus, I didn't have enough funds to pay for the studio time or a bad bitch like Samira to sponsor me.

As my emails loaded, I checked my voicemails. That's when I heard King sounding like he had a problem. He said, "What up, nigga? Holla at me 'cause it's a few words I need to spit at you. Don't delay."

"Naw, homeboy. You're gonna have to wait it out for a few until I handle some business," I spoke out loud to myself, powering my phone back off.

Instead of responding to notifications and blowing my name up more, I had to get the songs remixed before King and I parted ways. Judging by the tone in his voice, we were gonna have problems with one another before we had peace. There was no question in my mind if he was pissed about me doing an interview behind his back. I'd gone against the code 'cause we were supposed to be making money together.

Opening the first track from a Detroit artist, I was feeling the beat and the verses so much so that it was easy for me to put my own spin to it. Bobbing my head and writing down flows in my notepad, my heart was pounding with the anticipation of blowing up big. At this point, I couldn't see failure in my future. I was too busy feeling myself.

Chapter Twenty-four

Rayna

"I'm so glad you're here, Mom. It's truly important for you to bond with your son as much as possible, especially since he doesn't get to go home with you and Dad yet," the nurse said, welcoming me into the nursery.

"I'm trying, although I don't know the first thing about being a mom." I couldn't help but be honest. "All I know is I want to bond with him and make sure he knows I love him more than I love myself."

"Oh, honey, there's no manual to being a mom. We all will bump our head over and over again raising our babies into kids then our kids into adults. If you're lucky enough, you'll help raise your grandkids, too. It'll never stop, but neither will your joy at the end of the day. You've got the first part down so far, and that's simply showing up to bond. You'll be fine." Her words were comforting and enlightening.

The nurse was very compassionate and loving. You could tell she loved her job being around people and was a nurturer by nature. Being in her presence put me at ease but also made me sad. Her being a representation of a motherly figure made me wish upon a star there was a mother, grandmother, aunt, or even a fairy godmother to be a role model in my life. It never crossed my mind before, but I didn't have a strong woman in my life to help me with motherhood or train me how to properly raise my son. If King left, I would truly be a single mom.

As we walked through the nursery, I felt crappy notic-
ing the incubators and cribs decorated specially for the
babies. It made me feel sad and worthless that I hadn't
taken the time to do something so simple but had made
time to fight his stepmother and destroy his dad's home.
The more I thought about my decisions in life, the more
disgusted I was with myself. K.J. wasn't a week old and
was already lacking as a result of my bitterness. There
wasn't a choice for me to do better. I had to do better. I
just didn't necessarily know how.

"Have a seat, Mom. I'll get him out for you to hold." The
nurse slid over the rocking chair.

I got overly emotional after she placed him in my arms.
Although he was still extremely small, he was getting a
tad bit darker from the light, bright complexion he was
when they pulled him from my belly. It looked like he
was getting better. I rubbed his fingers and kissed his
nose. He smelled so good, felt so soft, and smiled at the
angels in his dreams.

"You're perfect, absolutely perfect, baby," I whispered
to him sweetly.

"He sure is, Mom. You should be proud of your little
slugger. He's drinking more milk and responding very
well to the medicine the doctor has him on. He'll be ready
to go home very soon."

What she thought was good news actually threw me
into a panic. Don't get me wrong, I wanted K.J. healthy
and home with me, but I was scared of failing his needs.
Tiana and I were at each other's throats, so I knew the
tension would be thick between us at home. Not to
mention the countless issues with King, who wasn't
even welcomed on the projects premises anymore, at
least without there being friction from a few folks. There
wasn't one good thing I could think of that I had to offer
my little one besides me, and even my mentality needed
some work.

"Okay, Mom, tell me what you're thinking and what's wrong. I've been raising kids so long that my senses are picking up on your discomfort. I'm a great-grandmother. When you get to be my age, you'll be able to read minds too."

Part of me wanted to keep my feelings bottled up to spare me any embarrassment. I wanted to tell her I had everything for him prepared to come home and was ready to take on being a mother full-time. Yet the wiser side of me fought through to tell her the truth. I needed help, and a quiet mouth ain't never got fed. That motto is what got me fucking King in the first place.

"Come on, girl, and talk. I'm too old to hurt you, and I can only help if you let me."

For the first time in a long time, it felt like someone genuinely cared about me. She was a complete stranger but seemed completely invested in finding out my inner thoughts. The feeling felt too good to pass up the opportunity to get the "Big Ma" I needed and wanted.

"I'm scared. I love this baby more than life itself. I just hope and wish I can give him everything he needs." My lips trembled with each word.

"Okay, sweetheart, you're gonna have to do more than hope and wish to give him his necessities. Giving him a lot of love is vital, showing up for him is important, but providing for him is going to require a firm foundation along with hard work to maintain it."

A complete stranger was reading me like a book. Biting my lip, I looked down at K.J. and let fall the tears I'd been holding in. The more truth she spoke, the more tears of admittance I answered with. Finally, I broke down, telling her the truth from start to finish. I even told her about the fight between my baby daddy and his wife. If I thought there was empathy or sympathy felt from the nurse who seemed so compassionate toward her job and even more concerned toward me, I was completely thrown for a loop by her next statement.

"You're in no position to provide that baby with all that he needs. I think you should speak with the hospital's social worker for some assistance."

Tiana

"What's up with ya girl? Is she going through postpartum depression or something?"

"To be honest with you, Cam, I don't know what her problem is. As much as I've been there for her, you'd think she be more thankful. I'm done, though. She's on her own for all the games King is certain to play."

Getting drunk with Cameron and her cousins, I wasn't thinking about Rayna throwing a tantrum or trying to jump dumb on me. If she wanted to act like I was shady when all I'd done was have her back, to hell with putting my neck out there for her again.

"All I know is that both of y'all friend better not pin no bullshit on us for having her back. I don't know her like that, so I have no problem popping a bitch." Cameron's cousin put her two cents in.

"I doubt if she'll throw shade at us like that, but when it comes to King's ass, you'll never know." I shook my head, swishing the liquor around in my mouth. "If either of them does, though, Jesus better be a fence."

We all shared a few more laughs, a few more drinks, and a few more Kush blunts. The more of a buzz I got, the more in my feelings I got about my and Rayna's argument. I'd had her back when King turned his on hers, so I was actually more salty than upset about her playing me to the left. Before she found him on the internet doing songs then stalked him to become his groupie, it had been me and her having fun. I swear I can't stand a change-up chick. *I'm about to text her and see what tip she's on now.*

Me: What's up? You still acting funny?

Three minutes passed, and there still wasn't a reply. I took a sip from my cup then texted her again.

Me: Helllloooo, you don't see me texting you?

Me: All this over that nigga King?

The more I sipped and waited on my phone to ring with her response, the more agitated I got. After about ten text messages of me being absolutely messy, I called Rayna's phone but got sent straight to voicemail. That's when I really lost my cool.

Me: You brought all this shade on ya'self. See ya when you get back to the PJ's.

"Hey, y'all, I'll be right back," I announced to Cameron and her cousins.

Rayna knew firsthand how vindictive and malicious I could be, so I didn't know why she wanted my wrath turned on her. I walked out onto Cameron's stoop and started going through my phone for the phone number I needed.

Rayna moved into my subsidized town unit with me a few years back when she couldn't afford nor get a place on her own because of her fucked-up credit. She didn't have a job, wasn't dating a "get money" type of nigga, and didn't even know how to scam the system for food stamps. Me being her girl, I didn't judge her, though. To be honest, I felt her struggle. Until the projects schooled me on how to get over, I was in her same predicament.

I taught my roommate all the tricks of the trade that came along with being a PJ chick. Our rent was barely $200 a month, both of us were pulling in close to $200 in food stamps, plus a few different hustlers who kept the projects pumping with weed and dope connected with her on the strength of me. By the time I was done schooling Rayna, she knew how to survive by the skin of her teeth. She owed me more gratitude than what she was expressing, and fuck if it seems like I wanted her to kiss my ass. I did. I'd helped her come up, but she wasn't giving a bitch credit for shit. The same way I'd made her life better, I could make her life hell.

"Yes, I'd like to either speak with or leave a message for the hospital's social worker, please." I put on the best imitation of a proper voice I could. Being a true product of my environment, my first language wasn't English but Ebonics.

"One moment," the operator responded then put me hold.

I quickly went over what I was going to say in my head so I wouldn't stutter. What I was about to say needed to sound believable and urgent.

"Hello, this is Mrs. Janice Thompson," the social worker answered my call.

Taking a deep breath so I could sound as educated as possible, I began acting out my malicious plan of payback. "Hi, I'd like to give a report anonymously. There's a baby who's been born who doesn't have a safe place to go home to. I know it's your job to make sure homes are adequate, mothers are stable, and babies are safe. If you let King Wallace Jr. leave the hospital with Rayna Robinson, I can assure you he won't be safe. Don't have another case similar to that chick whose kids ended up in the freezer."

If she didn't get goose bumps from my final sentence, she was immortal as fuck because I did. Disconnecting the call, I hoped the social worker got both names and heard my complaint loud and clear. Wrong or not, it was fuck friendship, because my loyalty to Rayna had played out.

Rayna

"Oh, hell naw!" I jumped toward the nurse, shouting. K.J. was still nestled in my arms, and I didn't care about the babies I'd interrupted and made cry. The nurse needed to be checked because she must've been out of her rabbit-ass mind. "You must be plum-nigga nuts if you think I'm about to tell a social worker any of what I just told you. Naw, matter of fact, I must've been crazy for trusting your ass." I was ready to physically explode on the nurse, and my hand was itching to slap her. I would've done it if K.J. weren't in my arms fa'sho. I was tired of people backing me into a corner.

"Whoa, sweetheart, stop creating a scene, because I promise I'm not trying to upset you." She frantically looked around. "Everything is fine, everyone. Please just get the babies back resting. There was just a small misunderstanding, but it's all under control." Waving away the nurses who were coming toward us, she then turned toward me with the same warmth and glow that made me trust her in the first place. "Listen, sweetheart, I heard every single word you told me, so I understand you're questioning everyone's loyalty to you. Especially when a li'l ol' lady drops the words every young black girl hates to hear. However, the social worker is a friend of mine, another dear old lady." She sounded convincing.

When she placed her hand on my shoulder, my tension melted. I looked down at K.J., who was looking wide-eyed at me, and knew I didn't have a choice but to trust someone. My responsibility was to give him the world, but all I owned were the belongings in my shabby bedroom. King was in the wind, Tiana kept putting me in my feelings by constantly throwing shade, and at the end of the day, I didn't have parents to fall back on.

"Listen, all I have is the little guy. I'd kill myself if we were separated from one another. If you fuck me, old lady, I'll fuck you right back. Respectfully speaking, you better take those words to heart."

Although my attitude was fierce and I was directly breaking the code of respecting my elders, I needed the nurse to be trustworthy and a woman who stood up to her promises.

"There'll be no need for that," she chuckled. "Finish your visit up with your handsome son, then come get me from the nurse's station. From there, we'll go down to meet my friend, Mrs. Janice."

The nurse was gone, so I was busy bonding with my son. He was absolutely precious. I fed him, burped him, rocked him, and of course took a million pictures of my li'l creation. I wanted to post a few on my social sites and even send King some, but there still hadn't been any communication from either of us since that text. I knew all signs of him and Samira's house going up in flames pointed toward me, so my plan was to play it low-key until the truth hit the fan. What else could I do?

My phone was blowing up, and it was Tiana. In spite of me wanting to see how she was feeling and how our friendship was lying after the blowup in Cam's car, this wasn't the right time. I had to finish up visiting with K.J. so I could see what the Mrs. Janice chick was all about. I'd call her back once I left the hospital, but for now, I sent her straight to my voicemail.

Tiana

"Remind me to never get on your bad side," Cameron half-ass joked with a judgmental look on her face. "I knew you were a raw bitch but not that raw."

"Whatever!" I threw my hand up. "Ain't nobody tell you to be eavesdropping on my conversation. When you heard me on the phone, you should've stepped back from the door and given me my privacy."

"And you should've taken your ass on across the parking lot to your own spot. You know I'm not the type of chick to keep my opinion to myself. That was foul. Rayna Ray didn't deserve for you to throw shade on her like that. Trust me, it ain't no joke to have child protective services running through your business. I've been there plenty of times." Cameron puffed on a blunt and looked at me, shaking her head like I'd turned her in.

"I ain't trying to hear no speech on shit, Cameron. What's done is done, and sometimes you've gotta teach lessons the hard way. I'll get at y'all later. I'm not in the mood to get chastised by no project chick."

"Well, get the fuck on then. You ain't stopping no party, and I ain't in the mood to be around no fake chicks today. See ya later," Cameron popped off.

I stood up with an attitude. The rage in me wanted to fly across the room and beat Cameron's ass, but I knew I couldn't beat both her cousins, too. It was cool, though. I'd get at Cam once she didn't have them here. I was smart enough not to get jumped.

After stomping across the parking lot to my unit, I hit the stoop and called my dude to come keep me company. I was tired of being around pussy and needed some dick to balance my hormonal ass out.

Chapter Twenty-five

King

The hotel room was quiet besides Samira's snores. Sitting in the chair across from the bed, I had my legs crossed and my eyes locked in on the woman I'd made my wife. It was hard accepting what she'd done to spite me. She'd been in my corner for so long that it didn't feel right knowing she'd played me just as grimy as I'd played her and still was. I guessed I should've never taken what I had for granted and underestimated what levels of revenge she'd go to once shit became too much for her to endure.

Samira was knocked out in the same bed I'd slept with Jamila in a few hours ago. Sure it was a doggie-dog move and a trifling thing to do, but she'd fucked my boy in our house. She deserved some type of payback. Truth be told, Samira was lucky I didn't choke her soul out of her body. The harder I tried not thinking about Johnie stroking her pussy cat, the more I thought about it.

I might've been trying to let shit slide, because I knew I'd started the domino effect of pieces falling and I ultimately didn't need Rayna turned in, but the foulness behind Samira's actions was still beating me in the gut. It wasn't a shocker, but each time I tried thinking of reasons to stay with Samira, I found myself listing reasons why I should make my family work with Rayna.

It was just hard to up and bounce on Samira given our history, though. No matter what she was guilty of doing, I knew what skeletons were in my closet. I was just as grimy. Me fucking Jamila evened the score. The least I could do was give her the chance she'd given me several times. Today just wasn't about to be that day.

Not being able to lie up under Samira, I'd gotten up and showered and gotten dressed. I was ready to hit the streets. Johnie hadn't hit me back yet, but that was all the more reason why I needed to start making some moves on my end. He wasn't about to keep standing up in the music industry on my shoulders. All the beats I'd produced, hits I'd made, and connections I'd linked him to were about to be severed. It was time I started pulling strings like the fuckin' boss I was.

"Babe, I'll be right back." I shook Samira lightly to wake her. "I've gotta go to the studio to handle the mess you've helped create. I shouldn't be long, but I'll at least be a few hours."

"Nope, King, that won't be happening," she hissed, popping up like she hadn't been asleep at all. "Now that we seem to be back on the right track, I'm not letting you out of my sight. I'm going to the studio if you are. Hell, you're lucky I'm letting you pee without standing over you like a warden."

I snickered at Samira although I knew she was serious. "This is all work, Mira. There's no reason for you to feel insecure or like you've gotta watch over me."

"Like hell I don't. If I would've been on your shoulder like a parrot back when you met ol' girl, we wouldn't be down to scraps living in a hotel room now. I might've made a major mistake with Johnie, but leaving you free to mingle with these bitches won't happen again."

Before I could contest her claims, Samira was out of bed, putting on the only clothes she owned. I knew an argument would follow if I disputed her wants any further, so I sat down quietly and gave in for the first time to my wife. I definitely needed a joint and a double shot. It was about to be a long day.

"Why don't you take a hot shower while I ease my nerves for a bit, Samira? You've had a long day, and I need to get my mind right before going out to handle business." Pulling out the bottle of Patrón Jamila brought with her earlier, I was popping the cork before she responded.

"You better not pull a slick move and be gone by the time I come out." She looked at me suspiciously.

"We already have more than enough problems to sort out. If you've never believed a word from my mouth, trust that I'm not planning on leaving this hotel without you. Don't take this the wrong way, but I'm not the only one in this room who requires a close watch."

"I guess I deserved that," she huffed, rolling her eyes. "And I also guess it's gonna be a long and gruesome time before your disgust for me dies down. I've been with you long enough to tell when you're pissed and trying to swallow your pride." She read me without hesitation.

"I can't lie and say it won't be, Samira." Taking a swig straight from the bottle, I needed liquid courage for the conversation staring me dead on. "I know I fucked up by bringing a bunch of bitches to your platter to deal with. I also know it was a helluva gut-wrenching blow for one of those chicks to end up pregnant. Hell, I'll even be honest and say I knew it tore you to shreds to have me run out to be by Rayna's side the day she gave birth. But none of that is comparable to what you did with Johnie. Of all the niggas you could've fucked and thrown in my face, why him? Not only did that taint my ego but it tainted my business."

The tears that were once gathered in her eyes were now falling freely down her face. She came closer to me. I thought she was gonna try to hug or kiss me to make the situation less tense, but she grabbed the bottle and took a swig.

"What do you want me to say other than sorry? After all these years of me being loyal and holding you down, that's all you've managed to say to me. Why do you think you deserve something more than that? I'll say it again, though. I'm sorry," she brazenly spoke. "You just ran down a list of things you knew you were wrong to take me through, yet you still continued to do them. You've always admitted to crushing my heart, and I've always taken you back without putting up a fight. Now you want me to fall to my knees and beg for your forgiveness because I fucked someone close to you?" She raised her voice with the last question. I could tell she wasn't gonna let me play the victim or hold her head in the mud for sleeping with Johnie for as long as I planned.

"Naw, that's not what I want you to do, Samira. What I want is for you to skip ya ass into the bathroom, take a shower, and leave me alone to get some peace for at least twenty minutes. You want me to say fuck what you did and move on? Fine. Fuck what you did. I'm over it."

I was lying, but it was worth it just to kill the noise. Arguing wasn't on my agenda for today. She swallowed my bullshit knowing exactly what it was and gave up arguing without saying another word. Maybe today wasn't gonna be as bad as I thought.

Once Samira locked herself in the bathroom, I got deep into my smoke session. I couldn't let time keep ticking by with me sitting still. Still trying to get in touch with Johnie, I sent him another text letting him know we needed to link up quick, fast, and in a hurry on the music tip. I even followed it up by saying there were hella moves we needed to make that could take both of us to the next level. I figured he'd be quicker to touch base with me if there was a promise of advancement in it for him.

Leaning back in the chair, letting the thick smoke cloud my lungs, I was mentally trying to debate if I'd touch base with Jamila as well. Since she and Samira were best friends, I knew the whole situation had the potential to get messy. I wanted to know where her head was at and if I could manipulate it. Knowing it wasn't smart to leave a trail of text messages, I had to think of a way to get rid of Samira so I could see what was up.

I was worried about Rayna the most. She was honestly the only woman I was truly connected to because we shared a child. The damage she'd created in my life proved her resentment toward me. I didn't know how things between us were gonna end up playing out.

Samira

Although I didn't have any clothes or even a pair of clean panties to put on my ass afterward, the hot water cascading down my body was just what I needed. I'd been begging for relief. I let the tears I was shedding behind my pain over me and King rinse down the drain along with the suds. Once I got out of here, I would have to keep my game face on. I'd barked at him, called his bluff about not forgiving me, and I knew that I'd have to deal with a heap of bullshit within the days to come. Done were the days of me being weak.

I climbed out of the shower and wrapped a towel around my body tightly. Wiping the steam from the shower off the mirror, I stared at my tired-looking expression, wishing I could glam myself up. In addition to the bruises that hadn't healed from my fight in the projects, there were circles around my eyes, bags underneath them, and redness inside of them. I looked drained and beaten up from life all together. Grabbing a washcloth,

I let it run under the cold water before placing it on my face. If it weren't for ol' hot-finger Rayna, I would've had makeup to conceal my scars and look of defeat.

Instead of going back into the main room of the hotel King and I were sharing since we didn't have a home, I sat on the side of the tub. I knew he needed space. Hell, I did too. Unfortunately, that didn't matter 'cause I was still about to tag along. I'd do anything to keep avoiding the conversation I needed to have with my parents.

Since their name was on the house and insurance policy, they would be privy to knowing how the fire started, so I couldn't expose Rayna. I'd be exposing the problems between me and King, making them dislike him more. When my parents found out what side of town he came from, that he didn't have a degree or a dollar, and that he stayed in the house all day while I worked, they made sure I understood how disappointed they were in me.

Somehow, they knew he'd cause me a tremendous amount of pain. Had I only listened . . .

Sliding on my dirty clothes, I was about to make King take me shopping for new ones no matter what he had planned. That was the very least he could do. From head to toe, I looked unkempt. Without a comb or brush, all I could do was use my fingers to comb through my hair in an attempt to look presentable. All I'd done was waste my time.

"He might as well get prepared to spring for a trip to the hairdresser as well," I spat to myself, then walked out of the bathroom with the same amount of attitude I'd walked into it with.

King didn't want me out on the streets and most certainly on his arm looking like a peasant, so he didn't put up a fight about taking me shopping. Unlike many

of the times we'd torn the mall up with our hands inter-
locked, today we walked side by side like two strangers.
The other thing out of the ordinary was that he was the
one treating. Although I couldn't because my purse had
burned up, I was happy not to be running up my charge
cards. Thankfully, Rayna couldn't destroy my cash that
was in the bank or the credit I'd been granted with good
ol' Visa.

Hitting up Macy's, I got a few outfits, shoes to match,
and a couple of bags. It was gonna take a while to replen-
ish my entire wardrobe, but this was a good start until I
got a closet of my own. Once I'd spent about $1,000 of
his cash, I hit the MAC makeup counter up and stocked
up with concealer, eyeshadows, lip glaze, and mascara.
His mouth dropped at how much money I kept holding
my hand out for. As far as I concerned, this wasn't nothing but payback for all the racks I'd spent on multiple
shopping sprees for his ass. K.P. owed me much more.

"I think you've put a big enough dent in my pockets
today, Mira. Besides, I've still gotta make those moves,"
he spoke with irritation in his voice.

"Damn, don't be like that, King. We wouldn't be here if
it weren't for your baby momma." I threw the same irritation back at him. "If you wanna be pissed at anybody,
be pissed at her. Now, if you don't mind, let's go replace
my cell phone then swing back by the hotel so I can get
dressed and do something a little more decent to my hair.
I can't be looking like a scallywag running errands with
you."

He huffed and puffed like the Big Bad Wolf but didn't
deny my request. King knew better than to act like this
situation was any of my fault.

Chapter Twenty-six

Rayna

The nurse walked me up to her coworker's office, which was in a completely separate area of the hospital. I could barely hold a casual conversation with the nurse from feeling like two tons of bricks were sitting on my chest. Anxiety had completely taken over. I could hardly breathe. Part of me felt like this was the right thing to do because I needed some assistance to actually become independent from both King and Tiana. The other part of me felt like I should've never opened my mouth in the first place. Every step I continued to take was for my li'l man.

She knocked on the door to the office then entered with me on her heels. The two women greeted each other with warm smiles and brief but meaningful hugs. It was obvious to me they really shared a rapport.

"Miss Janice, this is my young friend I called up to you about. Rayna, this is my good friend and coworker, Miss Janice," she pleasantly introduced us.

"Come on in and have a seat, Rayna," Miss Janice greeted me, sharing the smile she was giving the nurse.

"Thank you." I was hesitant, but still, I sat across from her.

The two of them shared small talk about things that didn't concern me while I took in my surroundings. Her office seemed welcoming enough. Along with a few plants, there were pictures everywhere of who I assumed was her family. She was in a lot of them. In addition to that, there were several awards lining the wall along with both her master's and bachelor's degrees in the study of social work from Spring Arbor University. Janice P. Thompson was her government name.

Once their mini-conversation was done, the nurse tapped me on the shoulder then left the office. An awkward silence was left behind. After about sixty seconds of Miss Janice typing into the computer whatever was written down in her notebook, she turned and faced me dead on.

"How are you today, Rayna?"

"I guess I'm okay," I answered, fidgeting in my chair.

"I know it's a natural reaction for you to feel uncomfortable given the position you're in." She relaxed her stance, picking up on my body language immediately. "But I'm not a threat to you at this point. What I mean by that is unless you tell me you have intentions of harming the baby or yourself, I won't be breathing a word of our conversation to anyone. Besides me signing a confidentiality agreement, I am very close friends with Miss Samantha, and she seems to have a genuine concern for you. Just do me a favor by being honest and straightforward. I can't help you if you don't allow me to."

"Okay," I murmured. Gripping the sides of my chair, I took a deep breath, trying to calm down. I'd come too far to go back now.

"Good. Now, of course you know Miss Samantha told me a little bit about what you mentioned to her, but I need you to give me the detailed version." She got straight down to the nitty-gritty.

Miss Janice was cool, but I didn't bond with her like I'd done the nurse. So I didn't emotionally break down or show the same signs of distress as I'd done earlier in the nursery. She claimed our conversation was casual, but it felt professional as I talked about me and King, me and Tiana, and the worries I had regarding being a mother to K.J., while she jotted down notes. I wasn't sure what she was writing, but I kept on talking until I felt like everything was explained thoroughly. I basically asked Miss Janice for help getting a fresh start.

"You seem like a really nice girl, Rayna. I'm really happy for that, but there's something important I must share with you before proceeding. We have a bump in the beginning of the road we must get over before I can provide you with any help."

I knew her helping me was too good to be true. "Okay, enough stalling, lady. What is it? Why'd you let me pour out my business to you for nothing? That's the exact bullshit I was talking about." Disappointment had set in before she even opened her mouth. I couldn't hold back my mini-meltdown.

"It's my job to feel you out, Rayna. I had you talk to me upfront and without the bit of information I'm about to tell you because I didn't want you sugarcoating anything." She paused then read from the notebook she'd just been using. "I got an anonymous call from someone naming you to be unstable and unfit to be a mother. They made accusations that your son wouldn't be safe in your care and a formal investigation should be done before King Wallace Jr. is released from the hospital. If you had known that ahead of time, your whole demeanor would've been even more braced than it already was."

"Someone what?" My eyes were bucked wide in disbelief. I was shaking mad. That bitch-ass wife of King's moved hella fast in getting revenge. The only person I thought could've done something so wicked was Samira. I didn't know if this was payback for me setting her house on fire, but I knew she had more than a few reasons to despise me and even my child. "That was probably my baby daddy's girlfriend being vengeful. She hates me for obvious reasons, of course. I swear on everything I love I'm not a bad person and I won't be a bad mom to my son. Me being up in your office asking for help oughta help prove my good intentions for both him and myself. You've gotta believe me, Miss Janice. That bitter bitch is lying!"

In spite of me being pissed that she'd withheld telling me about the call, I understood why. This might've been a favor to her friend, but this was still her job, and she couldn't take a chance on bending the rules without feeling me out. The whole harsh reality of everything made me sick. There was no way the State could have my son. I was desperate for Miss Janice to see things my way.

"I know it may be hard to do, Rayna, but just relax. Like I told you earlier, part of my job is to observe the people I work with in order to draw my own conclusions. From my many years of experience, you don't strike me as the type of woman who shouldn't be a mother. Trust me, there's a lot of cases out here that should make the news."

No matter what she was telling me about other people and their cases, I only cared about mine. I was amped and infuriated. I was sure the emotions were written all over my face. "So are ya just gonna forget the phone call?"

"Well, I can't go that far, even though I'd like to," she sighed. "Unfortunately, my hands are tied, and I have to establish a case and investigate the claims made against you before releasing your son into your care. My career will be over if whoever made the complaint follows up and I haven't followed protocol."

I got ready to respond, but Miss Janice threw her hands up to cut me off. "I know that's not what you want to hear, Rayna, but there's a bright side to this. I'm not working against you. We've established the initial point of contact, and your story sounds legitimate. This very well could be an act of revenge against you like you've said. As the one assigned to your case, I'll be able to close it quicker plus request emergency benefits for the necessities you need. I'll do my part. You just need to make sure everything checks out on your end."

I knew it was a bad idea trusting these motherfuckas. I can't tell this fuckin' lady no even though I want to. I swear I can't win for losing. And if ol' girl told the cops I was responsible for setting her house on fire, I am really gonna be fucked.

"Yeah, well, hopefully I'll get some assistance at the end of all this. 'Cause my need for that is the only reason for me not rising up and beating both your and Miss Samantha's asses. It don't matter what you say. I feel like I've been bamboozled," I said, blurting out my raw emotions.

A little over an hour passed of my life that I'd never get back before I was able to leave the hospital. I'd rushed out so fast that I hadn't stopped to say goodbye to my li'l man. Hell, I didn't even know if that would've been allowed, now that I thought about it. Clutching a manila envelope of paperwork I needed to complete for the case, I looked around for the nearest bus stop so I could get the hell out of dodge.

Everything within my mind was jumbled up after hearing Miss Janice run down the long list of hoops I'd have to jump through to take K.J. home. That meeting was our first point of contact, but we still had more sessions to go through before this case could be swept underneath the rug. She had to come to my home and investigate it for safety, cleanliness, and other state standards, which now involved Tiana. Although this woman claimed she wouldn't be hard on me and was ultimately gonna help, I still had to make a good impression.

All this did was add another thing to Tiana's list as leverage to bitch at me about. I was dreading telling her she couldn't smoke within the house or have Deon's drug-dealing, two-strikes-having ass lying up for the next few weeks. She was gonna be piping mad that my unfortunate drama was pouring over into her life yet again, especially because Samira was the initiator behind all of this.

A big part of me wanted to call King to tell him all that was unfolding with K.J. and the child welfare case, but we hadn't exchanged words since he'd rightly accused me of being an arsonist. I didn't have it in my heart to blame him for not reaching out with all the tension we had brewing between one another. Yet and still, I was frustrated by him not doing so. I loved King. It was hard for me whenever we didn't talk.

Right about now, I didn't know who was in my corner 100 percent. I felt sad, incomplete, and confused. Plopping down on the bus stop bench, I was mentally drained from dealing with life. I needed to get my mind right. I couldn't wait to get back to the projects for my stash of Kush.

Chapter Twenty-seven

King

Samira tiptoed around the hotel room like she was a princess walking on fairy dust. She'd taken an hour doing her makeup and hair and was now trying on every outfit she'd gotten me to purchase from the mall. I leaned back against the headboard with one leg propped up on the bed, slightly annoyed.

"Come on, Samira. You're doing too much. We ain't doing nothing but running a few errands and going past the studio. You ain't gotta look like a celebrity. Do me a favor and hurry up."

"Don't rush me, King," she argued back. "Your little music career won't be over before I'm done fixing myself up."

If looks could kill, Samira would've died a thousand deaths at that moment. I couldn't understand why she wanted to keep playing hardball with her words when she knew I'd get gully with her ass right back. I'd been playing it cool thus far. That nice-nice shit was a wrap!

"Ay, you might need to stay your ass here and get ya mind right off some of this green. Your crazy ass is bugging if you think you're about to ride out with me after making comments about my music career being little. That's some hater shit to say. Ol' girl and her friends must've really gone upside ya head."

Swooping my keys off the bed, I leaped up, ready to make good on my word. Samira's ass was as good as left. She knew I was swallowing a lot already by allowing her in my space in light of her fucking Johnie. So to diss my entire career was definitely off-limits. I didn't care if my response was a low blow or if my reaction was petty. As far as I was concerned, Samira needed to be checked before things went too far left.

"Don't play, King. You're not leaving this hotel without me." She called my bluff, then leaped up, grabbing her purse.

"I'm not playing with you, Samira. Don't follow me out this fuckin' door. Being around you and your smart-ass mouth ain't for me right now. I'll be at the studio."

Recognizing how serious I was, all she did was mumble something under her breath. She knew better than to keep testing me.

"Good job," I said then slammed the door.

Samira

"I know this nigga didn't just walk out the door and leave me standing here looking dumb," I growled in disbelief.

I waited about five minutes then made my way to the parking lot to see if he'd really left or was playing with me. Egg was on my face when I realized another car parked where his truck once was. King was constantly playing me. He knew good and damn well I wasn't trying to shade him maliciously. So that whole argument was a play for him to get from under me. I knew better. Things between us were notably different.

Continuously calling him a few times, only getting his voicemail, I gave up, knowing he was invested in a game of hardball. He and I couldn't get on the same page for shit.

Ring, ring, ring!

I jumped to answer my phone, thinking it was King proving me wrong, but it wasn't. To my surprise it was Jamila. The way I was feeling, my tongue was gonna get to spitting some real shit, so I was hesitant about answering. *What does this broad want anyway? I swear I'm not in the mood to play games or front with her fake ass.*

I was on my way to the spa the last time I'd spoken to her. She was all giddy and acting weird trying to get us to hook up. I don't care how you spin it. Her knowing that both of us were fucking Johnie and not saying anything was questionable, to say the least. I didn't care if her car ended up being ruined. There weren't enough vengeful plots I could think of to make me feel justified.

Ring. Ring. Ring!

Before the call went to voicemail, I answered it dryly. "Hey, Jamila. What's up?"

"I was just calling to check on you. We haven't talked for real in the last few days, and I missed my best friend."

Her fakeness made my skin crawl.

"I've kinda had a lot going on. It's been hard adjusting to King, Rayna, their new baby, and that I fucked Johnie."

I knew I already told her the night it happened, but I wanted to drive it home. Apparently, it worked. I heard Jamila suck in her breath. That's exactly how I wanted her to feel: shocked, caught off guard, and uncomfortable that I'd brought it up again.

"Yeah, that's a big pill to swallow. I can't believe you got freaky with your husband's artist, but what's done is done now. Ain't no sense in crying over spilled milk. Everything will work out with you and K.P., Samira. It always does. That nigga might play in the streets with these bitches, but he's not getting ready to leave home.

Trust and believe that man is very much in love with you."
There was a hint of bitterness in her voice.

I would've poured out my heart and all my business to
Jamila, looking for her advice, had this been any other
day. Matter of fact, I would've gotten her to pick me up
to get out of this compact-ass room. Too bad the bond we
shared was broken as far as I was concerned. It was only
a matter of time before I called her out. Instead of leading
the conversation with stories about me, I got her talking.

"So, now that you've got me, let's kick it." I decided
to see how far her charade was gonna go. "What's been
going on in your world?"

"Slow motion as usual. I would say we should link up,
but my car is in the shop. Ol' Bessie died on me earlier
and had me stranded on the side of the road," she whined.
"My ho-ass ex even hung up when I called asking for help.
I was stuck tripping for almost an hour when a tow-truck
driver generously stopped to assist."

"Aww, that's fucked up." I acted like I felt sorry for
her. The truth was that her misfortune made me smile.
"Wasn't that nigga just at your house giving you long
strokes and bubble gum? Damn, he played you scurvy
for real." I put her on blast with the lie she'd told me the
other day about her ex randomly showing up.

"I'm always gettin' played. I swear I attract some of the
lamest niggas. That's why I want you and K.P. to work it
out so bad. Ain't shit out here, Samira. You better keep
your nigga. All men fuck up, but not all men go home."

Jamila was giving me the pep talk I wanted to hear
but hadn't asked for. It was weird she was acting like
King's campaign manager when it came to preserving our
relationship.

Beep!

My other line clicked in, and it was my parents calling.
One of the neighbors probably called them trying to be

nosy about the house and ratted me out. Despite me not wanting to, it was time for me to face the music.

"Hey, Jamila, let me call you right back." I clicked over without giving her a chance to respond.

Jamila

Samira was acting funny. It made me wonder if she knew about me and King fucking. I'd only called to see where her head was at and to low-key see if K.P. was around her booed up after our little escapade at the hotel, but I got shaded. She'd hung up before I found out anything.

Now that I'd relaxed with a few glasses of wine in me, I was ready to face the world, at least a little bit. I was sitting on the porch, letting the warm breeze blow away the smoke from my blunt, while watching the young girls across the street being fast-tail for a group of boys. I reminisced about doing the same things back in the day and getting beaten by an extension cord when my momma caught me "being grown." From that day on, I'd been a freak on the sneak tip.

I opened a notebook I often scrabbled stuff in that I needed to remember, and then I called the mechanic shop to find out about my car. I was praying it didn't cost an arm and a leg to get fixed because I simply didn't have it. I wasn't working, and the little money I did come up on was tied into the business Samira and I were starting. My dumb ass didn't think about that when I ran to bang her husband. That whole venture would end up being a bust if the truth ever came out.

"Gettin' 'Em Back on the Road Automotive," a woman with a hard, raspy voice answered.

"Hi, yes, my name is Jamila. I'm calling about a 2005 Sebring that was towed in earlier. Was the diagnostic done yet?"

"The mechanic just finished up. It looks like there was some type of fluid mixed in with your gas. The engine will need work but possibly a replacement. Your estimate is with me at the front desk, and I'll be here all day. The mechanic can discuss anything further once you get here." She ran down the speech, sucking the air from my lungs.

"Oh, wow! How much am I looking at spending?"

"It won't be any less than about a thousand dollars, and we'll take the sixty-dollar diagnostic fee off of that. But like I said, the mechanic will talk with you about all the details once you get here. He makes the final prices and will be able to give you a better idea."

"Okay, thanks."

I hung up deflated. I didn't have a grand sitting around to pay for an auto repair. Nor did I have anyone to call for a loan. Samira would've usually been my backup plan, but obviously, that was out of the question now. Something had to give 'cause I needed my car up and running. I poured another glass of wine and tried plotting on a scheme to come up.

Chapter Twenty-eight

King

Part of me started to go back to the hotel so me and Samira wouldn't be on bad terms, but I wasn't trying to be up under her. There was animosity between us for good reason, and I didn't want things to get worse.

Johnie still hadn't answered the phone or called back, but I was done leaving messages. That nigga knew he was foul because he would've hit my line up by now any other time. But fuck that snake nigga. We'd have to meet sooner or later, so I'd save my energy regarding him until then. I still had a producing career to tend to along with a blackballing scheme to mastermind.

There were a few voicemails lingering over the last few days from both males and females following up with me from passing them my business card at Flood's. I called each of them back, scheduled meetups, and then drove toward the studio to start flushing out beats. Since I was about to kick Johnie off my moneymaking roster, I needed an artist who was cold with their lyrics to fill his shoes. I had to come out on top somehow or another from this fucked-up situation.

K.J. crossed my mind. I'd been so spent over Samira and Johnie that I hadn't even focused on my son. I looked at one of the pictures Tiana sent me from the day he was born and thought twice about calling Rayna to check on him. He was supposed to be coming home in a couple of days, so I wanted to make sure he had everything he needed. I wished I weren't caught between a rock and a hard place, 'cause I was serious as hell about putting her up in a nice crib within a decent neighborhood. It was a bad deal that shit was up in the air for all of us.

Things between us would probably never be the same. I knew her bitter ass was the one who set my house on fire because there was no one else in the world who would bring that drama to either me or Samira. The only thing I knew for certain was that my li'l man couldn't get caught up in the never-ending bullshit between me and his momma.

I went straight into grind mode once my feet stepped into the studio. All the madness I'd been going through with the peeps closest to me must've been fueling my creative process 'cause beats were flowing off the top of my head with ease. Within two hours of me cutting the whole world off, I had five solid sounds and even a dope-ass hook. My adrenaline was pumping. I was in the groove and ready to work all night.

The first artist I'd scheduled a meetup with came fifteen minutes early, prepped with his own USB drive full of songs. He was looking for someone to manage him and take to the top the career he'd been establishing for a few years on the solo tip. It was cool and all that he knew some of the ropes and how to hustle, but I didn't need another cat like Johnie on my team. The joke had already been played on me for backing disloyal clowns. Ol' boy might've not been an opportunist, but I wasn't fucking with him either way. He got sent on his way with a handshake and the generic one-hitter-quitter line: "I'll be in touch."

The two interviews after him were also a bust. One of the girls reminded me of Teyana Taylor, but her voice sounded like a hyena. And the third guy was barely subpar and probably wouldn't make a lot of money. Even with two more meetups left, I'd given up on the search and started scrolling through my email on my phone, checking for a few more potential callbacks.

That party created a lot of buzz, even by Johnie's own admission, so I knew there'd be more inquiries than normal. I'd managed to jot down ten more people to call for meetings before the last two artists showed up. It was the third girl I interviewed, who went by the stage name of Lyric, who stole my attention.

Lyric was cold both musically and physically. She came in admitting she didn't have any experience but got major likes from her followers on Instagram when singing. I let her sing the hook over one of the beats I'd made today, and she floored it almost instantly. Li'l momma had singing skills, was looking to get molded, and had a sexy Dej Loaf swag with a little extra pizazz. The music media would eat it up. I was pissed at myself for not having a contract for her to sign right there on the spot, because she was just that hot.

"Let's say we meet up tomorrow and go over what I can offer you, what you can do for me, and how we can benefit one another in a partnership," I smoothly kicked it to her.

Leaning back into the chair, the playa in me was coming out. I felt like an imitation Stevie J. Although I was trying to keep it strictly business, I couldn't help but stare at her curves. She was fine as hell with a flawless body that would entice any man. *Chill out, King. You've got more than enough messy shit going on in your life. Don't get caught up trying to dig out another pussy.* Common sense was trying to win the battle, but I was thinking with my dick.

"That sounds good, K.P. I've been dying to work with you. Your name has been getting dropped at almost every party me and my girls have been at. All you've gotta do is let me know the time, and I'm there. Just promise not to geek me up to let me down." There were undertones of flirting in her voice.

"Naw, baby girl. Trust when I tell you I'll see you tomorrow. Working with you is my first priority. I'm already thinking of some major moves we can make if you're down for real."

If I didn't get myself under control fast, Lyric and I were gonna have some trouble straight out of the gate. Shifting back into business mode, I straightened my relaxed stance, making this move more about money and less about pussy.

"I think you'll be pleasantly surprised to see just how down I am." She smiled. "I'll see you tomorrow."

My dick thumped at the sight of her delicious-looking ass walking out of the room. I massaged it down and hit play on the verses she laid down a few minutes ago so my mind could refresh back to the hustle. Ol' girl was destined to be a star. I was about to get paid.

The last artist came in a little late but surprisingly had major flavor too. There wasn't a doubt in my mind I wanted to sign him after listening to his first prerecorded track. This dude's name was Fresh, and he was cold with his skills. He was born and raised in Detroit but had a Southern flare with controversial verses like Pac. Today was turning out to be a good look for me productively. Between this cat Fresh and li'l momma Lyric, my brand was gonna get more exposure than since I introduced it to the D. Fuck Johnie. He hadn't stopped shit but his own career.

"I'm digging your music, my dude. I can see us doing business and making major bills together." I was up front with Fresh.

"Dat's what I'm talkin' 'bout. Makin' moves and gettin' my bread up. I got kids, ya feel me? Let a nigga know where ta sign the line." Fresh was straight hood, but it would sell.

"Let's meet up here tomorrow for all the paperwork. We can shake on it now then test this song out if you feel like it."

"No doubt. I'm here, playa." He pulled out a blunt and lighter then looked at me for approval. When I nodded it was cool, he lit up quickly then passed it to me. "Let's put in dis work, boss."

Fresh was a lyrical beast. I let him listen to the same track Johnie and I worked on the last time we were in the studio, and he came hard with a rhyme to accompany it without hesitation. The flow was so good I ended up recording it then told him to just chill back and freestyle. Fresh would have a mixtape in no time at the rate we were going.

Fresh was spitting some real shit. The music was so loud and I was so caught up in his flows that I didn't hear the door open. It was Fresh's eyes looking up in question that made me turn around.

"So, what up, nigga? Is this what you wanted me to see? You giving my beats away to a wannabe rapper?" Johnie's voice sickened my stomach.

"Don't come up in my studio trying to front on me, ma'fucka. All you know is how I am when it comes to music. You have no idea what grim shit I'll send ya way." I bossed up, offended that he'd walked up in here like he owned the place.

I might've cleaned up my swag and carried myself more like a professional rather than a hood nigga since I'd become a producer, but I was born into the struggle. I was a street nigga by nature. Samira found me looking scruffy on the corner, so ya better believe I knew how to put in work. It was in my roots.

"Slow ya roll, King the Producer," Johnie antagonized me. "I'm not really worried about none of this lame shit going down in ya little studio. I was just shooting a move through here 'cause you left so many messages. I take it you heard the interview and didn't like me branching off doing my own thang? What's the word? Holla at me." Standing across from me, smirking, Johnie was smug and cocky.

His demeanor made me more pissed. I was itching to rock his jaw for being brazen enough to bang my broad then step to my face man-to-man. Johnie must've taken me for a weak-ass pushover when he should've pegged me for a monster. While he was busy looking at me arrogantly, I was busy sizing him up so I could one-up him when we scrapped.

"Yeah, I heard ya little whack-ass interview, bro. It was cool and all for you to branch out. What wasn't cool was you fuckin' Samira." I put the shit on the table.

"Yo' messy ass left the opportunity open for her to be fucked."

Sliding my chair back, I stood up calmly then rushed across the room like a bull. Right before he could properly brace himself, my forearm struck his neck and knocked the wind from his lungs. Fresh rushed in right as Johnie hit the floor from me clotheslining him. I'd been so caught up in trying to take Johnie out that I'd forgotten all about my session with Fresh.

"Yeah, ma'fucka! What's all that shit you were just talking? I'll put my size-twelve shoe up ya ass on the real."

"Fuck you, K.P., and that's my word," he spat, trying to get up to battle me.

I wanted him to fight back, so I loosened my grip from around his neck. He came out swinging. He landed a quick two-piece to my jaw. Either the blows were soft like baby taps or my adrenaline was pumping too fast to feel them. Either way, we scrapped it out and tussled on the floor like madmen. He was able to get a few solid blows in, but I took over the fight and started molly-whopping him with no remorse. The thought of him sliding into Samira was gonna make me kill his ass.

"You better stay the hell away from my wife and anything I linked you to in this music game, J. I swear to God we're always gonna have motherfuckin' problems."

"On my life, nigga, you're gonna be the one with the problem." He tried catching his breath. "You ain't shit, and ya wife is community pussy."

My fist landed dead in the center of his face and came back speckled with blood. I'd cracked the skin between his eyes open to the white meat. My knuckles were throbbing from connecting with his bone.

"Aw hell naw, dis shit crazy than a motherfucka on da real," Fresh laughed out in the background. "Ay, dog, ya better keep cool, 'cause fella right here lookin' like he'll leave ya in a body bag or some shit like dat."

Fresh shook his head at Johnie with a hood smirk on his face. Lighting a blunt up, he took a seat in my chair and played back the track he'd just been spitting. Yeah, Fresh was a cool dude. There was no question about that.

Through the blood trickling down Johnie's face, I could see the rage he still had inside for me. I was sure it was no match for the aggression I was ready to work out on his ass, though. This nigga had gone against the grain in the worst way. I could tell he was debating leaping toward me but thought not only twice but a third time, too. That punch to the face must've knocked some sense into his high-yellow ass. Looking back and forth between me and Fresh, he swallowed his pride then walked out of the studio without mumbling a word. I'd won the war this time, but me and that cat were gonna scrap again. I knew it.

"Yo, Fresh, that right there wasn't even cool, but ol' boy drew blood a few days ago that required me to step out of character," I began explaining to him. I didn't want us to start out on the wrong foot.

"Oh, we tight, brody. Hunnad grand on that. It's good ta know ya know how ta jump gutter on a nigga. I'm 'bout making bread, not jumping in niggas' beefs. Dat shit ain't got nuthin' ta do wit' me."

"I respect that. Good looking. And on that note, let's get back to laying that track."

He jumped back in the booth, and I stepped right back into my producer shoes like nothing happened. This cat made my job easy by doing all the work. I was angry at myself for letting my personal drama interfere with this new business venture, because quiet as it's kept, both Samira and Johnie should've been old news the moment Jamila let the cat out of the bag.

I kept blinking out between lines and verses, thinking about Johnie and what he'd said about Samira being community pussy. The more his words played over in my head, the angrier I got. Samira wasn't supposed to spread her legs and give away my goods no matter how much dirt I did with bitches in the streets.

I was tensing back up at the thought of putting hands on Johnie again. It was a good thing Fresh came to grind and was passionate, because he was the only reason we finished the song so quickly.

Johnie

With a busted face and hurt pride, I rushed out of the studio with vengeance in my footsteps. If K.P. thought this was the last he was gonna see of me, he was more brain-dead than his ditzy-ass wife. She'd made him, and

I'd destroy him, just not by the power of my fist. I wasn't a fighter. I was a singer and a ladies' man.

Whipping out of the parking lot, headed home, I was about to put together a revenge song so cold it would demolish him in the music world. I hurried and accepted all of my pending followers so I'd have more of a platform to clown in front of. Since K.P. wanted to play hardball, I'd give him the fight of his life.

I'd shown up at the studio to flush out a few of the songs I'd remixed from earlier, and I ended up running into him surprisingly. The tension in his voice was immediately heard loud and clear on my voicemail, but I hadn't expected him to ambush me on some punk shit. He and whoever ol' boy was who was rapping over my beat were both gonna get it on my comeback, believe that.

I went extra hard on a diss track, putting all of King's business out there without saying his name. Once it got a buzz on the internet, I knew people would start questioning what ho-ass nigga I was talking about then go crazy finding out it was him. The song was like Usher's song "You Got it Bad" from back in the day. Hopefully, cats would want follow-ups from my shot at stardom, too. This was a win-win situation for me because the shine would be on me by the time I dropped my album. King might've wanted to scrap with me like an animal, but I was mentally focused on ruining his entire brand.

Chapter Twenty-nine

Samira

"I'm not going to sit on this phone listening to you blame that boy you are foolishly attracted to for all your misfortune, Samira. I raised you better than to be some man's doormat, chile. For some reason, you like what doesn't make sense. I'm so angry I can't even talk to you." My mother sounded gravely disappointed.

She'd been berating me for the last thirty minutes straight about King, their house, my choices, and how this was the final straw. It was so bad that I withheld the fact that I was married. I took the tongue-thrashing with a lump in my chest. They weren't wrong for refusing to help me any further, since I'd let burn the first house they purchased as a newlywed couple.

"Well, Samira, you've ruined your mother's day and probably her whole week with this devastating news. I'm not that thrilled with you myself. That house had a lot of sentimental value for us both." My father sounded more disappointed than my mom did. "But you knew that and didn't care."

"I did know, and I did care. I'm so sorry, Daddy," I sympathetically apologized. "Please know that my intentions were never to hurt you or Mom. I know I've frustrated you over and over again by not following your advice, but this is the worst. I know it'll be hard to come back from this."

"Quit with the speech, Samira. We've heard it time and time again since you've met this boy. We can't control who you love, but we can control our actions. Giving you a safety net is like us helping you support him. That scruffy failure of a man met you with nothing but lint in his pockets, and you cleaned him up. You busted your ass working at the hospital and have even screwed up your credit with all those student loans just to help him become a record producer. Ha! I don't know where we went wrong raising you, but we'll be right from this point on. Whatever monies are paid out by the insurance company for personal property within the house will be yours. From there you can start a new life. The payout for the structure will be ours."

I'd always been a daddy's girl and spoiled rotten by him. I knew he was hurt behind my behavior with King. He always taught me that a man was supposed to provide for, protect, and cherish his special woman, and here I was accepting everything otherwise. They were teaching me an ultimate lesson by cutting the cord. I'd never not had the help of my parents, so who knew how this shit was about to go.

My mom didn't get back on the phone, and my dad chewed me out for only a few additional minutes before ending the call. I knew they'd be infuriated. That's why I tried avoiding the call altogether. Now that it was said and done, all I could hope was that the insurance company would replace all of my and King's personal property. The premiums had always been paid on time and not a cent short, so maybe they'd issue a check as quickly as they'd cashed 'em.

Besides the checks I'd get from working, I wouldn't have anything else to start over with. I only had about ten grand set aside. Saving money hadn't been possible since K.P. was always needing shit. The music business he was taking so seriously better start popping enough to carry more weight. 'Cause without my parents, things were about to change.

Ripping my clothes off, I jumped in the bed, quickly snatching the covers over my head. I felt an anxiety attack coming on. My whole life was in shambles because of my addiction to King. This shit was déjà vu. I was just crying in a hotel room, trying to sort my life out, and now I was crying because I didn't have a life to sort out. I didn't have a house, a car, or the backing of my parents to hold me down. I let my tears soak the pillow and my cries fill the hotel suite.

King had been staying here to supposedly clear his mind, but he was the one responsible for all this bullshit. Both hurt and anger consumed me. I hated being stuck while he was free to run the streets. He still had a vehicle, wasn't out of much with regard to the house 'cause he hadn't invested much, and was gonna run to fuck Rayna as soon as she healed. It was time for me to come up out my private pity party, because he wasn't living in one.

Instead of calling King to be ignored again, I grabbed the complimentary notepad along with the pen off the nightstand and began writing down a task list to complete in the morning. So far, I'd plotted to call a claim in on my car and the renter's insurance I'd been paying, call my job to pick up a few more hours once I returned, and call the financial institutions to reissue my credit and debit cards. I also was gonna inquire about the process for getting a small loan just in case I ended up needing one. The final thing I did was think about where I wanted to live. There was no way I was staying within the confines of this room longer than I needed to. Something was about to give big time.

Chapter Thirty

Tiana

Me and my dude had just gotten done smashing smoked sausages, French fries, and damn near a whole pitcher of grape Kool-Aid. Our bellies were on swoll as we lounged across the couch watching back-to-back episodes of *Power* on Hulu. Me and Deon had been off and on for almost a year, but he'd only been acting right for the last three months.

When he was lucky enough to stay out of jail, Deon had commitment issues when it came to moving out of his momma's project unit and at least into his own. So, whenever I got tired of him lying up in my shit without lifting a finger or offering rent, I started tripping. That's when he got to cheating. I couldn't tell you how many hoes' heads I'd had to knock off behind him dipping his dick behind my back.

This was the longest we'd gone without repeating the cycle, and he was talking a good game about getting his own spot. The only reason I didn't invite him here was because Rayna was my roommate. But if things kept going downhill with that bitch, she'd get put out, and I'd be on his back about him staying booed up with me twenty-four seven.

"Come here, girl, and show daddy some special attention." Deon pulled his shorts and drawers down.

I eagerly slid off my clothes, ready to oblige. His dick was still limp, so I knew what had to be done first. Dropping to my knees, I put my head into his lap and put my mouth to work. I slurped, sucked, and tugged at his balls until he was hard enough to fuck me right. That's when I climbed on him like a cum-chaser and rode him like a horse.

Deon loved for me to get freaky, and I loved him giving it to me rough. He yanked my hair, gripped my neck firmly, bounced me up and down on his manhood, and then spread my booty cheeks as far apart as they could go so he could drive his dick in farther. Deon was hitting spots within my coochie that I didn't even know existed. I loved when he was a thug with my pussy.

Rayna walked in, but I didn't let that stop my hips from rotating or my pussy lips from clamping down on Deon's dick. She could keep it moving if she had a problem and address it with me later. Getting my nut was the one and only thing I cared about. I heard her smack her lips then stomp up the stairs, but I never heard her speak a word.

Five minutes later, my thighs were sore from all the riding I'd done while my coochie was rubbed raw. He'd rammed me relentlessly to the point my period was probably gonna come down early. We were both sweaty and sticky from cum. I peeled myself off him and trailed my happy, naked ass upstairs to get our shower going. Deon was right behind me but was sliding on his shorts. Rayna was used to seeing me nude, but seeing my nigga wasn't an option.

Rayna poked her head out her bedroom door. "Um, Tiana, we need to talk."

"Can it wait? I'm kinda still in the middle of something." I gave her a dumb look because she should've picked up on what was going on.

She slammed her door then turned her music up even louder than it already was instead of giving me a verbal response. I didn't care about that petty shit. The louder Future rapped meant the louder I could moan while me and Deon got down with some seconds. So hey, she was doing us both a favor.

I got the shower temperature just right, climbed in, and waited on him to join me.

Deon didn't end up leaving for a few hours. We finished the whole first season of *Power* and even grubbed on some fried chicken I ordered from the "you buy, we fry" store. Rayna never came out of her room or turned the music down. I did smell some strong-ass loud lingering from upstairs, though. I couldn't help but wonder if she'd gotten word about the anonymous complaint I'd called into the social worker.

Once he was out the door to deliver a few dope packages, I eased up the stairs to my bedroom and got prepped for the talk Rayna wanted to have. There was no way of me knowing if she and I were gonna beef since we almost scrapped in Cameron's backseat. So I wasn't about to take any chances. I pulled my weave into a ponytail, replaced my tiny booty shorts with a pair of leggings, and put a sports bra on underneath my spaghetti-string shirt. If Rayna wanted to pop off, I'd fa'sho clap back.

Music was still blaring from her room when I knocked on the door. "Yeah," she called out, turning the sound down.

"Deon just left. Are you ready to talk or nah?"

Swinging the door open, she let out an exasperated breath. One look at her face and I knew she wasn't the tough girl she'd played the role of earlier. Rayna's pitiful, puppy-dog expression reminded me of how our dynamic started in the first place. Her eyes were red, puffy, and full of tears. There were even dark circles around them and black bags drooping beneath. Part of me felt bad for pulling that snake move on her earlier, but the other part of me was satisfied she was broke down. All I wanted in the first place was for Rayna to be grateful for all I've done to hold her down.

"What's wrong with you? Are you in there having an emotional breakdown over King or some shit?"

"Nope. I haven't even talked to him since the phone call in Cameron's car. He hasn't texted or nothing, not even about K.J." She sniffed.

"That's 'cause he's busy consoling that bitch and licking his own wounds from us clapping back so hard. That nigga probably lost a lot of shit behind that fire," I chuckled. "He'll get over it though, so don't trip. I'm sure that uppity-ass wife of his has insurance."

"You're probably right, T, but he could've at least called to check on his son. Shit is crazy. You don't know the half of it." She shook her head then began breaking down some more. "A lot of stuff popped off at the hospital earlier, and long story short, the social worker got an anonymous call that I was an unfit mother. She won't release K.J. into my care until she investigates the complaint."

"What? Are you serious? Get the fuck out of here." I acted shocked when really I was only playing it off.

"Yup, I'm serious. It's fucked up, right? I've been down in the dumps ever since I met with the lady. I swear I'm tired of going through bullshit. If it ain't one thing, it's another."

"I'm sure everything with that social worker will die down. Try to stay cool. K.J. will be home in no time, crying and screaming and keeping us both up all night." I tried to lighten the mood some.

Rayna wasn't acting like she knew I was the caller, and I wanted to keep it that way. The only way to do that was to manipulate her and the situation. Since she and King weren't gonna reconcile anyway, I threw heat his way by suggesting him as the culprit.

"Maybe that's why your funky-ass baby daddy ain't called. Do you think he could've been the one who flagged you since you threatened him with child support?"

"Wow! That never even crossed my mind. I know you're gonna call me dumb, but I don't think he'd be that coldhearted toward me. King knows his role in all of this drama. I just can't see him doing something as foul as trying to take my son from me. At least I don't think so." She was trying to reason with me while convincing herself. It was evident in the tone of her voice that my suggestion made her question herself. "But his arrogant-ass wife, she has every reason in the world to."

"I swear, if that broad started this bullshit with K.J., it's gonna be me and her but mostly me. You won't be able to even calm me down, Rayna! My nephew don't deserve to be in the middle of y'all drama or raised in a foster home behind ol' girl being jealous. If that bitch couldn't have his baby as long as they've been kicking it, that's her dumb-ass fault." I was going in.

Rayna was eating my reaction up and should've been. I was acting my ass off, to the point where I was actually starting to believe myself.

"You always have my back, T. And I'm gonna need you to keep holding me down until this investigation is closed. I owe you an apology about earlier. I was pissed, but I do appreciate you." She seemed sincere.

"Don't worry about it, sis. Whatever you need, I've got you no doubt. I know you've got a lot on your plate. So that's my bad for flexing on you in Cam's car," I apologized back. If only we could've had this conversation earlier.

No doubt I was foul for lying in her face about being the one who was making her life more miserable, but I had to do it. I'd gone too far to go back. At this point, I sorta felt like scum 'cause I'd let a silly argument between us put K.J. in harm's way. It might've been too late for me to right the wrong. The only thing I could do was play along with everything she needed me to do with the social worker.

Chapter Thirty-one

Rayna

Tiana and I sat up talking like we used to back in the day. I cried on her shoulder about my whole relationship with King, the drama with Samira, and how afraid I was of the social worker finding me unfit. I knew she said she'd help me, but I couldn't help but be fearful. Fuck all the drama I'd endured since delivering him. The only thing that mattered was that my li'l man came home.

When Deon came back from selling his stash of pure white weight, Tiana excused herself but not before giving me a Valium. I eagerly popped the pill, praying it would stop my constant crying spells and anxiety attacks. At one point, it felt like my chest was caving in.

The steamy hot shower water I'd been standing in for the last forty-five minutes was now quivering cold. The temperature was uncomfortable to my body, but my mind was somewhere else. Pill or no pill, I couldn't stop feeling like I had the worst luck ever. The Valium didn't stop me from thinking. It prevented me from reacting. Sliding down the wall, I sat in the tub with my legs pulled up to my chest, letting the cold water run down on me. In some weird way, it was soothing.

Forced to snap out of the trance I was in once my Cesarean incision began throbbing from the position my body was in, I got up and turned the water off. Having a staple pop out would've been horrible since there were so many things on the table for me to handle. There was nothing I could do about this situation but play the hand I was dealt, so it was a must for me to quit wasting energy having meltdowns.

Bring your love, baby, I could bring my shame
Bring the drugs, baby, I could bring my pain
I got my heart right here

Hearing The Weeknd playing from my phone, I did my best to rush out of the bathroom to answer it. It was K.P. calling.

King

Even though my day was productive at the studio, it was still hectic, to say the least. Fresh and Lyric were the two new artists I'd planned on signing tomorrow, and already we were making moves. They might've been using me to get a start, but I was using them to get my name even further out here as a talented producer. All I had to do was stay focused and keep my mind sewn into the game. That was gonna be hard since shit with my personal life was so dysfunctional.

I hadn't expected Johnie to show up at the studio, but I was glad we'd met and gone head-on. Now that nigga knew where I was coming from. But I'ma g'on and be honest by saying he had me in my feelings even more than I'd been initially about him and Samira. He'd dirtied her up with more mud. I was still wigging off him calling her community pussy. The same woman who was a wife to me was a ho for him. It was hard to admit it since Mira had been my backbone for so many years, but our relationship was probably close to over.

Turning up the pint of Hennessy I'd stopped at the store and gotten, I was starting to feel horny off the buzz I'd gotten. The perfect way for me to end the night was to be off in some skins. But I didn't want the used meat between Samira's legs. Matter of fact, I didn't even wanna see her face. The one person I knew would answer was who I dialed.

"I didn't expect you to be calling me anytime soon." Rayna didn't sound defensive but surprised that I'd called.

"Yeah, I didn't think I would either, but I need to see you," I openly admitted. "Are you up for making that happen?" No matter what was unspoken between us, I still cared for Rayna a great deal. And my dick cared even more than that. I was trying to get at her on some "hit it and quit it" type shit.

"Don't pull up with ol' girl or on no disrespectful shit, King. I've had a long day." She smacked her lips.

"Naw, it ain't even like that. We can discuss what transpired another time, ya feel me? I'm on another tip tonight."

She waited a few seconds then responded. "Okay, call when you get outside, and I'll open the door."

"Naw, how about you be on the porch when I pull up in approximately ten minutes. I ain't trying to chill up in your house or in the projects after all that beefing." Between Tiana, her wannabe man, and whoever the other rat was who'd run up on Samira and me, I wasn't getting ready to get caught slipping.

She smacked her lips but agreed to be on the porch waiting. I knew Rayna wasn't about to turn down the chance to see me. She never said no.

I pulled over at the nearest gas station, rolled a blunt of weed up, and took a few more generous swigs of Hennessy. It's like there was a miniature figure on each of my arms trying to dictate my decision on having a nightcap with Rayna. One kept telling me to fall back 'cause Rayna was most definitely responsible for that Molotov cocktail flying through my living room window. But the other one kept telling me she was my baby momma, and we'd be banging eventually, so I might as well appease my stiffness now and whenever it was convenient. With pussy and a slob job on my brain, the later voice sounded more on point. Before my mind played tricks on me again, I whipped out of the lot, headed toward Rayna's.

Rayna

I'd wanted to call King since I walked out of the hospital earlier, but I didn't know how he'd react. Now this nigga was calling me for a nightcap. I wasn't dumb. As much drama as I kept going in his life, he still couldn't stay away from me. My pussy must have had heroin in it.

Still very sluggish from the Valium and drained from the long shower, I pulled myself together so I could be on the porch when K.P. pulled up. It was easy for me to admit it to everyone in the world: I loved his dirty drawers and the sweat underneath his balls. Whenever he beckoned, I'd be running.

Throwing on a pair of lightweight jogging pants and a T-shirt, I couldn't jump sexy because nothing was supposed to rest on my incision. And since my hair was a mess from the shower, there was nothing I could do but throw a hat on. It wasn't often I allowed King to see me looking rough and ratchet, but I'd just had his son so he'd have to understand.

Deon and Tiana had dozed off on the couch. There was a funky smell within the living room that didn't just smell like weed, but I wasn't sure enough to question it.

Either way, I was glad they were passed out so I could leave without Tiana's badgering. I knew the first thing she'd bring up was how I planned to deal with the K.J. situation. Sadly the answer was that I still didn't know.

I leaped in the passenger seat of King's truck before he barely shifted the gear into park. Not only did I understand him not wanting to linger around after all the commotion yesterday, but I also wasn't trying to get questioned by onlookers like Cameron who'd for sure run back with gossip to Tiana. K.P. might've been wrong for leaving me on the pavement to run after Samira, but he was still my baby daddy. They had their issues with niggas, and obviously, I had mine. None of us were in a great position to judge. I'm just saying.

"So, what's up? Where are we headed? The studio?"

"Naw, not tonight. Look up the Red Roof Inn in Warren for their number then call to see if they have any $49.99 rooms available. If they do, tell 'em we're on the way."

"Dang, you're pulling out the bells and whistles tonight," I laughed, whipping out my phone.

"Don't start with ya mouth, girl, unless it's speaking into my mic." He tapped on the crotch of his pants.

Twisting my lips and rolling my eyes, I giggled again. His weak ass couldn't deny a good head job if his music career depended on it. "I'll give you a sample of what's to come after I make this call." I didn't know why he was with me instead of Samira, but I wasn't about to question a damn thing. My main objective was to seize the moment.

K.P. was dressed fresh to death as usual and smelling even better. Stealing a few glances, I thought about how much our son would probably favor him. I was lucky to have a baby by a man so fine. Every time we were around each other I was reminded why I fell so hard for him in the first place.

Initially, he was only supposed to be a trick I'd keep in my back pocket for VIP entry to clubs, concerts, and whatever other perks he was privy to by being a producer. That plan changed after he blew my ego up by making me his main groupie. My dumb ass slipped up thinking that meant I was his wifey.

Thankfully the Red Roof Inn had rooms. My coochie was starting to tingle at the thought of getting stroked good, but I knew King wasn't about to fuck through blood. Desperate times called for desperate measures, so when I finished getting him off, I'd use my pocket-sized dildo to relieve myself of an orgasm in the shower later.

"A'ight, the room is taken care of. Let me see what that mouth be like." King reminded me of what I promised I'd do.

I didn't know how long it took us to get to the motel 'cause I was too busy focusing on not getting a neck cramp or tearing my stiches open by leaning over the middle console of his car. It was like bobbing for apples. K.P. swerved a few times, but that might've been from all the weed and Henny he was taking in.

By the time we walked into the two-star room, I already had cum breath and a sore throat. But K.P. wasn't close to satisfied. He immediately forced me down onto the bed, whipped his hardness back out, and asked me to take another shot of his semen for the team. The way we were going at each other, you would've thought we were long-lost lovers. He was moaning, I was gagging, and both of us were out of breath from kissing and panting so hard. I swallowed two nuts and damn near a third before he snatched my pants down.

I was sure there was blood down there, but it was mixed with the juices he'd been making my vagina produce. Since it was pitch-black within the room, I wasn't embarrassed or nervous about him calling me out. I went with the flow and damn near passed out when K.P. stuck his stiffness inside of me. He must've really been horny or had a rough day. After about the seventh pump, he pulled out and jacked his last nut for the night all over my back. By the time I slid out of bed to clean up and get him a soapy washcloth, he was already snoring, with crust forming in his eyes.

Chapter Thirty-two

King

Rayna was curled up on my chest with her nails dug into my skin. My head was slightly pounding from all the Henny I'd drunk, plus the showdown with Johnie at the studio. I might've taken the win like a champ yesterday, but I was paying for rolling around on the floor scrapping today. It might've been a new day, but there was still old nonsense to be hashed out and addressed.

Ring. Ring. Ring!

My phone was blowing up, back off the hook. It had rung all night while I was getting freaky with Rayna, but I hadn't checked it once. I knew it was Samira going nuts about my whereabouts, and this was probably her again. Just like I didn't want my buzz and mood blown then, I didn't want my day starting off wrong. I was comfortable with Rayna's body in my arms. For now anyway.

Ring. Ring. Ring!

Rayna jumped up, annoyed at the sound of my phone ringing again. "Damn, King, if you're not gonna answer whatever bitch keeps calling you, at least turn your volume down. I'm not trying to be woken up and bothered just like you're obviously not." Rayna reached over my chest to the nightstand and handed me my phone.

I snatched it from her hand before she got the bright idea to answer it herself. Looking at the caller ID in curiosity and surprise, I couldn't believe it was Jamila calling and not Samira. My face curled up in a frown. *What in the fuck does this crazy broad want?* Not knowing where the conversation would lead, I answered the call anyway.

"What up doe?"

Jamila paused, laughed, and then replied, "'What up doe'? Straight up, King? That's all I get for real?" She had the nerve to sound surprised.

"It's too early for word games, Mila. You called me for something, so what is it?"

"My car ended up going into the shop yesterday after you put me out of your room. They said my engine is probably ruined. I know you saw me stranded on the side of the road," she spoke with aggravation, attitude, and sarcasm. "It was foul of you to leave me there, by the way."

"Yeah, and so? I had somewhere to be. Why are you calling me at the crack of dawn telling me about your car? Just like you being on the side of the road ain't have shit to do with me, how you get your car fixed ain't my problem either."

"It might not be your problem, but you can do me a favor by looking out. I'ma need a few dollars to get it fixed. That's why I'm calling you." She revealed her want.

"Bitch, please. You better get off my phone talking crazy," I shouted. "I can't believe you rang my phone this early on some more thirsty shit. What's wrong with you, girl? I've given you all you've got coming, believe that!"

I should've known better than to have sex with Jamila, knowing she'd been digging me for a while. But I was too busy trying to even the score because Samira slept with ol' boy. Rayna, who was at first rolled over facing the wall, jumped up, staring me in the face with shock painted on hers.

"Oh, I see you woke up feeling ya'self," Jamila snapped back. "Let's not forget I can blow your whole spot up by telling Samira what went down between us," she threatened.

"I ain't forgot, baby girl. The truth is that I ain't worried. She fucked ol' boy, and I fucked you. It seems like all I did was even the score. So after you call and let her know you ain't shit but a grimy bitch who's been faking as her homegirl, hit me back up so I can laugh. But I still ain't giving you no dollars."

I ended the conversation after those words. Setting my phone back on the nightstand, I was about to catch a few more winks of sleep, but Rayna wasn't having that.

"Hold up, King! I know you were shooting cum all over me last night, but I didn't think any clogged my ears up. Did I hear you right? Did you have sex with Jamila? The same Jamila who dragged me up out of Flood's, acting like the perfect prototype of a friend to Samira? Helllll naw!"

She seemed more shocked that I'd slept with my wife's friend than about her sharing the dick with yet another female.

"You heard the conversation, Rayna. Now either put ya mouth back to good use or cuddle up with a nigga so I can get a little shut-eye. I've got major moves to make today," I replied, not willing to go into details about that part of my life.

"Boy, bye, you're not getting ready to get out of this that easily. You're damn right I heard the conversation. Who did Samira sleep with? It looks like your sacred wife ain't so sacred after all, huh?"

Sitting back up, I knew the chance of me getting any sleep was blown. I'd just have to grab a Red Bull to put some pep in my step, 'cause I was about to put Rayna in her place.

"You wanna talk? Are you sure about that? You ain't got room to judge Samira while yo' ass running around setting fires and shit. I might've slid up in your medium-rare-ass pussy for a few seconds, but don't think I've lost my mind and forgotten. Instead of asking questions, you better get to answering some ya damn self."

"I knew it was a mistake to come out with your ass last night, King. I swear your Gemini personality be having you flip-flopping with your mood swings too much," she huffed, ignoring everything I'd just laid on the table. "You haven't even asked me about Junior."

"Don't try that diversion shit on me, Rayna. I might've not asked about K.J., but you sure as hell haven't brought him up." I threw the ball back at her.

I picked up on her being tense almost immediately. Instead of looking me in the face, she looked down. Instead of running her mouth smartly at me, her lip was quivering. And instead of her looking at me with venom in her eyes because I hadn't asked about K.J., she tried hiding them because they were red and tearing up.

I might've been pissed that she'd set my and Mira's house on fire, but I was still soft on Rayna. I didn't want her hurting if I could prevent it, especially because she was my baby momma. Most dudes didn't understand the concept of making sure the mother of their child was straight. If the woman suffered, the kid suffered. And there's no way to get around that. I didn't want that type of dynamic for my family, even though she and I weren't together.

"Whoa! I know you ain't call me out for my mood swings then jumped straight into one. What's up with yo' ass?"

She shook her head like she was scared to talk. I'd never seen Rayna's tongue stuck from movement.

"Some serious shit popped off when I went to see K.J. yesterday," she whispered. "I saw a social worker about getting some assistance with subsidized housing and other stuff and ended up finding out someone called in saying I'd be an unfit mother."

"What in the fuck? Are you serious with me right now? That ain't no shit to play with." I jumped up, ready to explode.

"Don't you think I know that?" She jumped up just as quickly as I had. "I wouldn't play about nothing like this. I've got a case open against me, King. Until I can prove I have everything K.J. needs, have a safe place for him to come home to, and am mentally stable, they won't be releasing him into my care. The social worker is claiming she'll look out for me as a favor to her friend, but I hate having my back against the wall."

Rayna kept saying this wasn't a joke or a way for her to manipulate us being together. I flew into a rage. This was the last thing I ever thought would happen. True enough she was living in the projects and scheming the system to get by, but she wasn't a bad person. Rayna loved hard, and there wasn't a doubt in my mind she'd love our son unconditionally. Overcome with frustration, I paced the room then punched the wall 'cause I was tired of getting hit in the head with bad news.

"Who in the hell called? Who you got beef with?"

"Nobody but Samira." She threw her hands on her hips with defiance. "And you ain't gotta think about it long for it to make sense. She has every reason to. That bitch probably thinks if K.J. is out of the picture then I'll be too." Rayna was coming at me from left and right rationalizing my wife's guilt. Sadly all of it made sense.

"Give me a minute." I threw up my hand for her to be quiet. I needed a quiet second to think. Rayna was right. Samira did have the ammunition to report Rayna as a bad mother, especially since she worked at the hospital and knew the ropes. I didn't want to put the blame on her, but it was too convenient to agree that she was bitter enough to do so.

"All right, your minute is up. Tell me what you think, K.P.," she huffed.

I wasn't getting ready to tell her she was probably right. That would've caused even more drama between them, and that wasn't necessary. If Samira couldn't make it through the planned interrogation I had in store for her later, then I'd be on her head. For now, me and Rayna had to team up so I could get her off of craps. Ultimately, the priority was for our son to come home from the hospital.

"I think you should just stay focused on getting that random-ass case closed. Let me handle the rest. Ain't no son of mine about to get raised by the State, so don't even worry on that tip," I tried to reassure her. "Just trust me."

"I'll trust you, King. I know you want the best for our son." Rayna's mouth was saying one thing, but I could tell her mind was processing another.

"Come here, girl. My word is bond when it comes to this. I can tell you're still tripping, but I've got you and K.J. 'til the day I fall off."

I pulled her close to me, and she collapsed against my chest like I'd relieved the weight of the world from her shoulders. I couldn't help but squeeze her tighter. Rayna cried a lot to get her way, but I knew this potential problem about K.J. was a lot for her to bear.

"I'm not any less of a man or gonna be a piece-of-shit-ass father just because I can't keep my dick in my pants, Rayna. I told you at the hospital he'd always be straight. Believe it."

I coddled her for as long as she needed me to. Like I said before, her being A1 meant Junior would be gravy as well.

After the contracts were signed with Fresh and Lyric, in addition to Samira getting paid out from the insurance company, I'd divvy up a portion for Rayna and my li'l man. Intentionally holding my plans in to get her a one-bedroom apartment, lace it up with toys for K.J., and pay up her rent for a few months so she'd have time to get a job, there were a few things that I needed to fall in place first. I was gonna financially help Rayna get off craps.

"A'ight, come on, girl. Get ya'self together so we can go grab some breakfast at that Coney by your spot before I drop you off."

Rayna backed up from my grip and got dressed even though I could tell she didn't want to. She always acted sad when it was time to part ways.

"Are you gonna try going by the hospital today? I have a case, but you don't. You should be able to see K.J. without a problem."

"Yeah, I'ma swing by to see my li'l fella plus check out the vibe of folks down there. Did they suspend your visitations until the case is over?"

"The social worker didn't tell me I couldn't visit him. I would say we should go together, but maybe it'll be best for us to go separately so you can see what's up on your own."

"We'll see. It might be best for them to see us being parents to K.J. together. I'll let you know what move to make after I'm done taking care of some business. Are you cool with that?"

She seemed a little more relieved. Probably because I'd given her hope that we'd stand hand in hand with our son.

"Yeah, that's not a problem. I'm cool with that. Now let's go grab that Coney. My stomach is grumbling like a kidnapped hostage."

"Damn, slow ya roll! You ain't pregnant no more with ya greedy ass," I joked with her. "Give me about twenty minutes. I gotta make sure my dick and balls are squeaky clean, especially after that nasty shit I did last night."

Chapter Thirty-three

Samira

When I first woke up at 1:00 a.m. with the lights on and my to-do list still in front of me, I realized I'd fallen asleep from pure exhaustion. Everything in the room was the way I left it, which meant K.P. hadn't been back and probably wasn't coming in at all. Just to say I did, I called his phone twice. Then I powered my cell off altogether. I had to play the game smarter than before, so I stopped myself from overreacting.

Hours later, now 8:00 a.m. and broad daylight, I was up and dressed, waiting for the cab I'd called. I barely got a wink of sleep with my mind wandering about King's whereabouts. Apparently, he had somewhere to stay, but I didn't. The game was over with regard to our living situation. I wasn't about to spend another night without options, alone or not. If today went well, I'd be signing a lease.

After making sure my makeup concealed the bruises Rayna and her crew left on me, I grabbed the biggest purse I'd gotten yesterday for all the things needed for my day of errands. My first planned stop was my job to get copies of my ID, social security card, and birth certificate. Then I'd order originals of all three. Those were the essential things I needed to get things back on track.

Walking into the hospital where I'd been a registered nurse for the last couple of years, I welcomed the early morning rush. Wallowing in my own pity was starting to drive me crazy. Had I not needed time to bounce back, I would've come off vacation early for a taste of normalcy. Just to be out amid the hustle and bustle of people was therapeutic. I swiped myself into the emergency department then made my way toward my manager's office.

"Hey, Mira! I thought you were off for the next week." My coworker Gabi greeted me with a wide smile. Gabi and I worked many shifts together. She was a cool girl, but I didn't consider her a friend. I kept all my relationships on the job friendly yet professional. Things had the potential to get messy when you mixed the two.

"I am. I just had to come up here for a few things. Trust and believe, I'll be right back out of that revolving door in no time. That waiting room is on bump today," I lied, still feeling the urge to punch in.

"Tell me about it. I've already had a wannabe sick-ass chick clown on me 'cause she felt she waited too long in the waiting room. I told her ass she wasn't gonna get no better if she didn't be quiet. I'm probably gonna get written up for snapping on her," she giggled. "But I don't care. I'm tired of these messy, Medicaid-having-ass motherfuckas."

"I know you didn't! Girl, you are a fool. Let me get what I came for and bounce before something else pops off," I joked with her then moved on about my way.

"Yeah, I don't blame you. It must be a full moon because no one is safe today. I'm dreading even calling another peon back here to piss me off."

I giggled. Whenever we were on shift together, Gabi always made me laugh and kept the moods of the entire staff lightened. The comradery was good within my department, at least between the nurses.

"Don't laugh. You know I'm serious. I'ma need a whole bottle of liquor after this shift. Speaking of that, my brother is in town from Vegas because he just purchased a bar here. We're gonna hit it up either tonight or tomorrow. Are you down to club?"

I wanted to jump at the offer. With all the stress I'd been under, I needed a night on the town along with a few drinks. But I knew the way I was living was bold, and I needed to focus on getting right. Depending on how everything played out today, I wanted a reason to get out of the hotel room and up from under King's thumb. He didn't need to know where I was at or what I was up to at all times. I'd tried giving him a dose of his own medicine, yet it was clear he needed another.

"I'd like to say yeah, but I won't know for sure until I finish running a few time-sensitive errands. I might be on vacation, but I ain't been catching a break."

"I feel you on that not catching a break tip. You know how that old adage goes, 'If it ain't one thing, it's another.'"

"You ain't never lied." I sucked my teeth and shook my head. "I'm gonna need a vacation just to recuperate from this vacation."

"Girl, don't let stress bog you down like that. I wasn't gonna say anything because it's not really my place, but you look like you're carrying the weight of the world on your shoulders. Let whatever it is go for tonight so me and my brother can show you a great time. To sweeten the deal for you, don't even worry about having to buy drinks. Since my brother owns the club, we'll be getting the celebrity treatment, and all drinks will be free."

"Wow, now that sounds live," I admitted. "You're right, that did sweeten the deal. Make sure you hit me up with the details."

Going to the club with Gabi and her brother was looking more promising knowing that I wouldn't have to be responsible for a cover charge or a drinking allowance. As long as everything went smoothly with the tasks on my to-do list, I wouldn't stand her up.

"I'll be calling you for sure. Just make sure you answer."

Gabi and I had never hung out one-on-one at a club before. The only time we've seen each other outside these hospital walls, besides walking to our cars, was hitting the mall on lunch for the quick sixty minutes we were allotted. Gabi was a firecracker while on the clock, so I could only imagine how she'd be in a free environment. I was sure it was gonna be an interesting night.

I couldn't help but laugh thinking about Gabi's crazy behind as I made my way to my manager's office. She was always going head up with patients, never practicing a good bedside manner. The hospital gave her several verbal warnings, write-ups, and even sensitivity training. Nothing worked. Gabi remained Gabi.

The one thing nobody could take from her was that she did her job damn near perfectly and could float throughout the whole hospital assisting short-staffed departments with ease. She could be a surgeon behind all the surgeries she's assisted with and sat in on. Gabi never stopped going to school, researching, and working. Despite her attitude, she was an asset to the hospital, and they knew it. Gabi used that to her advantage to give even less than a fuck about being pleasant.

My manager had copies of everything I needed and didn't have a problem with approving additional hours, so it was a quick in-and-out visit. With my personal documents in hand, I headed downstairs to the credit union that was reserved for hospital staff and their families only. Hopefully, they'd let me withdraw some cash and handle my business with just a copy of my ID. They knew me, so I wasn't planning for a problem, and I was right. I got all the information I needed about the loan and a few stacks from my account, and I took King's name off everything I'd given him access to. It was easy taking back my independence. *I should've done this a long time ago.*

My funds were limited, so I didn't waste money catching another cab who'd gyp me by stopping at every yellow light and yield sign. I caught the bus to Acorn Motors to put a down payment on a car. Money talked and bullshit walked at this franchise. Things like a job, a license, and a credit score meant nothing when it came to leasing a like-new vehicle from them. Since I had stubs, proof of a license, and two grand in hundred-dollar bills, I knew they'd let me sign and drive without a hassle.

The lot was full of trucks, cars, and vans ranging from 2005-2014 models. I wasn't trying to do it big by getting the most expensive vehicle on the lot. I just needed a dependable means of transportation that was worth paying a car note on. I test drove three different cars, finally picking a 2013 silver Malibu. It was close to the car I'd just had, just not as new. When the insurance money for my car kicked in, I'd take the difference for my savings account.

I might've arrived on the bus with a transfer ticket in hand just in case, but I drove back up W 8 Mile Road toward the insurance company in my certified-used whip after just ninety minutes. It felt good to be back on the road. If Rayna tried tearing this car up, I'd be renting one to ride and roll all over her ass.

Thinking of Rayna, of course, made me think of K.P.'s trifling ass. He still hadn't called, texted, or sent so much as the Bat-Signal to check in with me. He didn't care if I was okay, and he damn sure didn't care how I perceived his behavior. Fighting the urge to call, I tossed my phone on the floor of the passenger seat then turned the radio of my new car up on blast.

The agent at the insurance company was extra friendly because I'd just helped him make a few dollars of commission with the car insurance sale. He made sure the paperwork was submitted for expedited processing and even gave me a few tips about filing my personal claim so I'd get the maximum payout back. I was thankful for him looking out because I sure as hell needed the hookup. As sour as things had been, finally they were looking up.

Rayna

"I see you're back to sleeping with the enemy." Tiana smacked her lips at me as soon as I walked through the door.

"Don't start, T. Me and King have problems just like you and Deon. We can't help who we love," I said, trying to brush her off.

Arguing with Tiana about my late-night rendezvous wasn't high on my must-do list. Making a beeline for the kitchen, I was ready to smash my Coney Island breakfast special 'til every drop was gone.

On my heels like my shadow, she was resilient about being in my business. "Well did you even talk to him about what happened at the hospital and how his stank-ass wife probably got the bullshit started?"

I wanted to tell Tiana to give me fifty feet, that she wasn't my keeper, and to quit coming at me with a million questions. But it was my fault she felt so comfortable doing so. I'd put her in the position to know too much. Therefore, she felt like her opinion mattered more than it did.

She was my personal "Captain Save a Ho," making me feel better whenever K.P. and I got in a tough spot, and she was my personal cheerleader whenever I needed an ego boost to demand more from his ass. However, when things got better with me and K.P., I wanted her to back away and keep her opinion to herself. Clearly, I couldn't have it both ways.

Successfully ignoring her while I added condiments to my breakfast, I sat down at the table then broke down my and King's conversation about K.J. and the social worker. Tiana kept rolling her eyes, slouching, and twisting her lips up like she couldn't believe King was being supportive. I did my best not to be irked by her disposition, but once again she was making my skin crawl. For some reason, Tiana was only a friend to me when I was down in the dumps.

The rest of my breakfast was uneventful. Tiana got tired of me taking up for King and excused herself outside. Then I locked myself back inside my bedroom to go through all the baby stuff Samira purchased. It was taking everything in me not to be resentful and toss it all in the trash, but I needed the majority of it so Miss Janice could see I was prepared. King would be proud of me for taking the high road given the situation. Getting a family out of all this had always been my motivation.

I cleared out two drawers of my dresser just for K.J.'s stuff. One was for his onesie undershirts and pajamas, and the other one was for all his bibs, burping cloths, receiving blankets, and socks. Since I didn't have any baby hangers, I used mine to drape the few outfits he had across them, and I hung them in the closet. I was on a mission to transform my space the best way I could.

There wasn't a lot of room for his bassinet, yet I managed to cram it in a corner after rearranging my room twice. I even put some sports stickers up by where'd he sleep to make the tiny area more baby friendly and personal for him.

For extra show, I stacked the few gift boxes and body-care sets on the dresser, replacing my Victoria's Secret smell-good collection. If Miss Janice wanted to see I was ready for K.J's arrival, she would. Anything I didn't have, I'd ask King to get later. Let him tell it, he had us. I was about to put his ass to the test super quick. Satisfaction of how things were coming along helped ease my nerves. I didn't have a lot, but you could tell King Jr. was cared for.

My next two hours were spent cleaning the entire townhouse from top to bottom. I scrubbed the bathroom until it sparkled, washed the walls down of all the built-up smoke, and scrubbed the refrigerator out after tossing all the old, spoiled food we'd been too trifling to throw away. There was much more to be done, but I'd gotten off to a good start.

"Hey, bring ya ass over here, girl," Cameron shouted from across the parking lot. She was sitting on the porch with two of her kids while they colored. I'd just come outside to get a breath of fresh air from all the cleaning solution I'd been using. I walked over to join them. Just as I expected, she wanted to give me her two cents about how I acted yesterday.

"Sup? I guess you wanna read me about how I acted yesterday, huh?" Taking a seat across from the kids, I picked up a crayon of my own and started helping her youngest daughter color a picture of Minnie Mouse.

"Yeah, that's first on my list," she replied sarcastically. "I don't care what you and your roommate have going on, I risked a lot plus put my family in your drama. If nothing else, you could've been a little more grateful for us riding hard for you. I mean damn, Rayna Ray, do you know what would've happened if we'd gotten caught? Low-key, there's still a possibility of that as quiet as it's kept. The next time I have your back, you better have mine all the way to the end. That means the only way we split up is 'cause we have to. Got it?"

Cameron wasn't holding back how she felt, but I wasn't salty about anything she was saying. Unlike Tiana being emotional over how I acted with King, Cameron was more concerned with getting me to realize how I'd played her and her cousins shady by jumping out.

"No doubt, Cam. You ain't making nothing but sense, and I respect you for keeping it real with me. My bad about yesterday. That shit will never happen again."

I wasn't above admitting when I was wrong. We dapped it out as a truce.

Cameron was initially Tiana's friend, but she'd grown to be one of my best friends too. No, I didn't tell her all my personal business, cry on her shoulder, or gossip about how I got down as a groupie with King. However, we did chitchat often about fake bitches, drama in the projects, and ironically our dreams that stretched further than the hood.

Not many people thought red-cup-carrying Cameron wanted to be anything but barefoot and pregnant, but she was secretly writing books trying to weigh in as an author. Even I thought it was a joke until I read the first story she submitted to some e-book publisher. Everyone has hidden talents, and writing was hers. The story was bomb as hell!

Me, on the other hand, I was trying to enroll at a community college to get some credits underneath my belt on how to run a business. I didn't think I had the attention span to finish a whole two years to be awarded an associate's degree, yet I did think I could stomach a few semesters so I'd know a few key things successful owners practice. I hadn't shared my plans with K.P., but I wanted to own a little boutique that sold sexy women's clothes and shoes. Women in the D liked to dress to impress, and that's exactly what I wanted to call it.

"Okay, Mikey Jr. and Marlissa, go in the house and check on your siblings. We'll go over to the playground after I finish with this grown folks' conversation." Cameron waved her two oldest into the house. They got up and scurried off quicker than I could blink. Cameron kept her kids in check by the power of a belt and the authority of her fist. She didn't play about kids being disrespectful and not minding her, being a single mom. Her rationale was that they weren't gonna end up running over her by the time they were teenagers. It seemed logical enough.

"So, how are you and Tiana? Y'all squash that petty beef yet?"

"Yeah, you know we fight like sisters sometimes, but we're good now," I replied, confused as to why her face was frowned up.

"Oh, okay. I guess that's what's up," she sarcastically countered.

"Whoa, slow ya roll, Cam. What do you mean by you guess that's what's up? Don't start holding back on me now."

"It's not that I'm trying to hold back on you. I'm just careful about whose business I put myself in the middle of. I don't want you and Tiana beefing or no shit like that, but I won't be fucking with her like I used to."

"Quit talking in riddles, chick. Just spit out what happened and what you not fucking with her has to do with me and her beefing." I'd just gotten done scrubbing the house, moving furniture around, plus slobbing K.P. down all night off a Valium. I wasn't trying to get mentally drained figuring out where Cameron's conversation was going.

"What up doe, Cam? Hey, roommate. Y'all two tricks ain't trying to get the party started without me, are you?" Tiana had come from nowhere.

First, she and Cameron were eyeballing each other, then both sets of eyes landed on me. Cameron was the first to speak, though.

"Well, Rayna Ray, I'll holla at you later. I've got some things to do with my kids. We didn't get to talk about K.J., but I hope everything is okay with him."

With that, she ashed the cigarette then marched into the house. When her door slammed and the lock clicked, Tiana and I didn't have a choice but to march away looking dumb.

"What happened between you and Cameron? It's obvious y'all got into it," I questioned Tiana.

"Kind of. She was pissed about how I flipped on you in her car. She should just get over it, especially since we have. But you know how Cameron is, always exaggerating and blowing shit out of proportion."

I shrugged her explanation off. Somebody wasn't saying something, but there were always bitches bickering around here. My focus was getting back to the house. I'd left my phone in my room all this time and could've missed King's call.

Chapter Thirty-four

King

After dropping Rayna off at the entry of her housing project, I pushed it to the max toward midtown so I could find a computer and print shop within the university area. Lyric and Fresh needed contracts so we could officially be partnered up. I'd have two new avenues of income within a few hours. The thought of that alone made me feel like a boss even though nothing else in my life did.

Speaking of that, I was shocked Samira hadn't called but a few times early in the morning, yet not a single time so far throughout today. Maybe Rayna was right about her being the one who called the social worker. If she was, things between her and me would absolutely be over.

My mind was still spinning over the bomb Rayna dropped about her having a case open with the State. That piece of drama was more complicated than anything because it was the one part I ultimately couldn't control. All I could do was play my part as a man and fight hard against any unfavorable determination. My responsibilities had tripled in just one short week. From this point on, I couldn't see life slowing down.

I'd professionally gotten to the pub thirty minutes earlier than scheduled so I could order appetizers, the first round of drinks, and spread the paperwork out for Lyric to sign. All the sections that required her signature were highlighted in yellow and already had my initials beside them, including my manager/producer fee of 12 percent. I expected this meeting to go swell with no glitches.

Lyric walked in on time, looking like a sex kitten. This girl was gonna be trouble. Dressed in a spandex crop top and matching pants with a pair of simple flat sandals, every curve on her body looked juicy. There was little left to the imagination to process but how to rub all over her. Lyric's body was absolutely perfect.

I stood up to welcome her into the booth as she got a few feet from me. She gave me a friendly hug that could've been an innuendo for so much more, and then she took a seat. The dog in me had to keep my tongue in my mouth.

"I hope your day is going as good as you look," I complimented her.

"I'm glad you noticed with your corny ass," she giggled. "I see you're just as eager to get me signed as I am to get signed." She picked up the contract packet.

"I've got a lot of plans for you. The longer we wait, the more of a disservice we're doing ourselves. With both of our talents linked up, we can make some noise within the industry." I was laying it on thick.

"All right now, K.P.! You better not be selling me no dream. I'm gonna hold you to everything you've been promising me, plus more." Wearing a devious grin, she began validating our musical contract with one another by inking it.

Instead of feeding off her flirty girl ways, I kept our interaction professional so there weren't any distractions. With me having heavy responsibilities with Rayna to take care of, I didn't have time to be slanging dick around Detroit. Lyric and Fresh had to feed a lot of mouths associated with me. When the last designated line was initialed, it was time to celebrate.

"Waiter, let me get two glasses of your best champagne and that package I left with you earlier, please." I had a small surprise for Lyric. "We're about to skyrocket straight to the top. Make no mistake about it."

The waiter returned with the bouquet of lilies and pink roses I'd picked up. Both Samira and Rayna loved flowers, so I knew this gesture was nothing but icing on the cake for Lyric.

"Oh, my God, King, these are absolutely beautiful." She beamed. "I'm enjoying the perks of this contract already."

The rest of the lunch meeting went on without a snag. Lyric was actually good company who could hold an intriguing conversation. Not only did we vibe about sports, but she was well versed about things that interested me like music from different genres, artists, and generations.

I found myself getting caught up in spite of me not wanting to. It felt kinda good having someone give a fuck about things I gave a fuck about. Both Samira and Rayna were lacking when it came to doing anything other than complaining about how I'd done them wrong. Between us eating and toasting, I hadn't even thought about the chaos that was waiting on me in the real world.

By the time I was done wining and dining her, the bill totaled out close to $150. It was cool, though. You have to spend money to make money. Dropping two crisp Ben Franklins on the table, I knew it was a floss move to tip the waiter an extra $50 spot, but that was my intentions. The more Lyric was impressed with me, the more she'd trust in every move I told her to make. I had one more thing up my sleeve.

Lyric sat snuggled in my passenger seat as we rode out toward Somerset Mall. Part of the contract was an obligation from me to provide her with a branding photo shoot accompanied with clothes. She was happy, and I was glad to have the ball rolling.

Keeping my eyes focused on the road, I used the time to start breaking down our next week's calendar. I wanted to get her in the studio ASAP. The sooner we started flooding the web with her sweet sound, the better it would be for the interviews I'd get planned. That was part of the reason why I needed a fresh photo shoot: exposure and promotional material. I'd mapped out a thorough game plan for Lyric that was about to have her name buzzing all over the D.

She went crazy in the first store we walked in. I sat around for at least an hour while she tried on outfits, different accessories, and shoes to put together for a hot look. She tried modeling for me so I'd notice her sexiness, but I was too busy handling business via my phone.

Fresh still planned on meeting me at the studio to work later, but he was signing his contract now through DocuSign so there wouldn't be any distractions. My guarantee to him was an album within three months and a mixtape within one if we kept grinding like how we'd started. The quicker I got Lyric and Fresh squared away, the quicker I could get down to the hospital about my son.

"You ain't that attentive for a manager/producer, K.P.," Lyric hissed, snapping her fingers in front of my face. "Don't make me regret signing a contract with you on the first day."

Another woman I've gotta find a way to please. "Naw, Lyric, come on now. Don't be like that. I'm just trying to lock in a few deals for us next week plus the studio time I told you about earlier. I don't have a big entourage, so I've gotta multitask whenever I can. But trust, I'm working for you." Women required soft touches and much more attention than men. Lyric was gonna make

me a lot of money, but she was gonna require double the
time of Fresh.

"You better be." Her voice softened. "I narrowed it
down to a couple of outfits that will be fly and envied. I
know you're ready, so we can go now."

"That'll be $492.19," the cashier properly announced.

Instead of bagging the items, she stood with her hand
out, waiting on me to pay. I wasn't shocked by her behavior. That was how most of these uppity white people
acted out here in this city and at this mall.

I knew I didn't have enough cash to pay for the bill, so
I passed her my debit card to cover the cost. *Yeah, let me
get this girl into the studio quick, fast, and in a hurry.
She ain't about to break my bank.*

"I'm sorry, sir, but your card has been declined. Do
you have another form of payment or would you like me
to run this card again?" The cashier was trying not to
look awkward, but you could tell she hadn't said this to
customers often.

I was thrown off. "Naw, try running that card again.
There's money on there so it must've been a glitch with
your system."

Lyric stood off to the side trying to act like she wasn't
with me, while I was damn near leaned all the way over
the counter. I watched her run the card three more times,
but it kept coming back declined. Two additional customers were now behind me, seeming impatient about
being held up. This shit was mad embarrassing.

"Sir, it's not going through. If you don't have another
form of payment on you right now, I can hold the items
until close." She was trying to be nice. Reading the look
in her eye and her agitated posture, I knew she wanted to
tell me to get my broke ass out of her line.

"Naw, you don't have to hold nothing. I've got another
card right here." I whipped out a credit card Samira

and I kept for emergencies. It had a $5,000 line of credit so I knew there'd be $492 available. The people behind me smacked their lips, and one even went to seek out another line. Lyric seemed even more embarrassed than I did and had even slightly covered her face with her hand. I was about to save face, though.

"Sorry, sir, this card has been declined too."

"What in the fuck?" I couldn't hide my sudden frustration and surprise.

"Please step to the side, sir, and let me handle the customer behind you. I'll try running your transaction over after that. Maybe you can call the institutions to see if their systems are down," she suggested.

"Give me my damn cards." I got rude and belligerent.

With humiliation written all over my face, I snatched them out of her hand and moved to the side. I knew it wasn't her fault, but I hated looking like a fool. And here I was appearing like one in front of Lyric and some white people I knew were judging me as a bottom-class black man.

"Let's go, girl," I called to Lyric as I angrily headed toward the door.

She was on her toes then on my heels at the sound of my voice. Following ten paces behind, she was still acting mortified to be with me. I couldn't blame her, though. I'd arrived at the store like a boss but was leaving like a peasant. I knew I was looking like a slime-ball-ass manager in Lyric's eyes.

"Wow! That was embarrassing. Are you gonna have the funds to pay for the photo shoot and the studio time you promised me or nah?"

Lyric was being an asshole, but rightfully so. I would've been too if I'd just signed to a manager who appeared to be broke.

"Yeah, you'll be good. Let me get you back to your car so I can go get my ducks back in a row. I know shit seems shady right now, but I'ma handle all this confusion before the day's done."

I was short with Lyric because I was on another tip. Samira was the only one who had access to the cards other than me. She was the one I really wanted to talk to.

We rode in silence all the way back to the restaurant. I was busy consumed with my thoughts and Lyric was busy typing away on her phone. I suspected that she was telling someone about me and what had just gone down, which infuriated me even more.

This shit was all bad, and the gut-wrenching feeling in my stomach wasn't a good sign that things were about to get any better. Once I turned into the parking lot, shit hit the fan. Lyric jumped out of my truck before my foot fully hit the brake.

"I know times are rough, K.P., so you ain't gotta idle and possibly run out of gas. I don't want that shit on my head. I'm good. Holla at me when you've got shit straightened out," she sarcastically spat.

This chick had me fucked up for real.

"Yo, Lyric, you can kill those smart comments. Like I said earlier, I know thangs look rocky, but I'm about to tighten those ropes back up. In the meantime, do me a favor and keep those lips locked unless they're making songs to fulfill our contract."

I wasn't trying to be at odds with Lyric since we still had to work together, but she'd crossed the line first. I was gonna end up with another wannabe-controlling crazy broad on my hands if I didn't put my foot down now.

"Oh, you've got me twisted, King. On the real, don't talk to me like that. I know people," she threatened, or at least called herself doing so.

I chuckled. "If you did, you wouldn't have trotted ya hot ass into the studio yesterday looking for me to make you a star. But that's neither here nor there in the grand scheme of things. We both have obligations to meet so let's not burn bridges with one another." Reaching in the back, I grabbed the bouquet of flowers and handed them to her. *Yeah, gotcha ass.*

She snatched the flowers then dropped them to the ground with a snarl that could've killed. All that cool shit we were vibing on earlier was gone out the window. Lyric was just as self-absorbed and psychotic as my baby momma and wife. Slamming my truck door, her little ass actually made the vehicle shake. The east-side nigga in me almost had me jump out on her ass. Thankfully for her, I had other things to handle. I was calling Samira by the time Lyric made it to her car.

"Hello," Samira answered, sounding nonchalant and carefree.

"What's wrong with the accounts? Why aren't my cards working?" Not wasting any time with greetings or small talk, I wanted to know what she'd done right off rip. "I mean, did you cancel them 'cause your cards were burned up or what? That shouldn't affect my shit, though."

"Damn, straight like that? You're not even gonna acknowledge that you left me alone all evening and night? You stormed up out of the room with your ass on your shoulders over me making an irrelevant-ass comment, then you come calling almost twenty-four hours later, acting like I owe you some answers. I know you're not serious."

She might've not been calling, but Samira was definitely feeling some type of way about me disappearing.

"Ain't nobody about to nurse your wounds right now. I was in the middle of taking care of business with a new artist when my cards got declined. I've got obligations and responsibilities as a manager, Mira. That shit can't be happening because it discredits me and gives me a bad name no one will respect. How in the hell am I supposed to put on like a boss when I can't pay a five-hundred-dollar tab?"

She snickered. "You ain't the real MVP, King. Don't you think it's about time you quit fronting for everybody? I took your name off all the accounts because I needed all of my money to start over. There's a lot of things you missed when you left and didn't check in with me."

I damn near crashed my car trying to get to the hotel. I couldn't believe Samira pulled a move like that. With barely $200 in my pocket, she was leaving me out here dry. That shit wasn't about to fly.

"I'm about fifteen minutes away. Be ready and in the parking lot by the time I pull up so we can get to the bank before they close. You ain't did nothing but waste your time 'cause you're about to put my name right back on those fuckin' accounts!"

"Oh, that won't be happening. Like I just said, things changed while you were lost in the streets. Whoever you were with last night, I suggest you see if they can add you to their accounts."

"Don't make me hate you, Samira. That wasn't even all your mon—" I stopped in midsentence when she began screaming over every word I tried spitting out.

"Wow, so now you hate me 'cause I ain't letting you milk me bone dry anymore? Hmm, that's some helluva shit to say. I bet you don't hate me more than I hate your raggedy ass. You ain't gotta keep showing me your true colors, King. I finally believe you ain't shit."

I went to retort but heard the background change. There was dead silence. She'd hung up. I pushed the gas pedal to the floor in a rage to get back to the hotel room I'd left her in yesterday. Samira has never pulled a stunt of this magnitude before, but it fa'sho had me thinking she could've also been vindictive enough to call the social worker on Rayna. It was time for me to dead this situation once and for all.

Ring, ring, ring!

Of course, it wasn't Samira calling back. She was too busy feeling herself and trying to prove a point. It was the DJ from the radio station I'd connected with, Beats. I threw my game voice on and was ready to talk business.

"Yo, Beats! I hope the tracks been spinning and shooting up the charts."

"Oh, fa'sho. That's part of the reason why I'm hitting you up right now. Is this a good time to chop it up?"

"Never better. What's the word, my manz?"

"Ya boy Johnie came down here the other day and spat an interview out. The lines were off the hook, he was cool with the callers, and even dropped a few dope verses live over the air that hyped up the mixtapes you dropped off for spins. I thought shit was cool until I got a track this morning in my email from him. Dude, I ain't trying to be on no messy-chick shit, but are y'all still making money moves together or nah? That cat seems to be spazzing."

Infuriation was an understatement to describe how I felt. This rat bastard was gonna keep coming for me until I gunned for him. If he wanted the thuggish nigga to come creeping back outta me, then so be it. I might've cleaned up well for the sake of my career, but I was still bred to go hard like a beast. Samira came along with money and softened a nigga up. Caught up in the moment, I replied to the DJ with too much emotion.

"To keep it one hundred with you, me and that bitch-made nigga got into a scrap session last night at the studio. I'm done putting his ass on. Matter of fact, do me a solid and pull those songs off rotation. I'll be through there by the end of the week. I've got some new things in motion."

"Whoa, K.P., I know you're heated about whatever beef you and ol' boy got going on. However, you can't expect me to step in the middle of that shit when it's money on the line. If I get the request, I've gotta make the play. Ya boy has already struck his first move so he can easily take that song to another station. Then I'm fucked on ratings. C'mon, man, you already know the rules." Beats was being honest. "The most I can do is send you the link so you can be prepared with a comeback."

Ol' boy was right. He had me feeling like a punk on multiple levels, and truth be told, I deserved it. As a man, I couldn't ask him to do something I wouldn't do. For all I knew, he could've had mouths to feed too. Yet even if he didn't, it wasn't my place to count the dollars in his pocket. He'd already done enough by putting me up on Johnie's snake move. Not wanting my reputation smeared any further, I fell back.

"My bad. Let me play my position, 'cause you're right. This shit ain't got nothing to do with you, but good lookin' on sending that track. I've gotta dead this shit quick, fast, and in a hurry before it causes a problem with my career."

"As long as you know it ain't personal, we're cool."

"I'm out my feelings, bro. Me and you are good fa'sho. Please believe I'll be getting at you before the week is over."

"A'ight, you know how to find me."

The call ended, but my tension didn't let up. It was really fucking me up that this nigga Johnie was trying to clown me like Meek. He wasn't about to body me with his wannabe-Drake-singing ass.

The hotel room was dark, quiet, and still. No wonder Samira felt so comfortable talking reckless after pulling that stunt with our accounts. Her suddenly sneaky ass wasn't even here. Flicking on the light, I threw my keys across the room in anger. She'd gone mad wild, tearing up shit in here.

"Oh, bitch, you're done," I yelled out in madness.

Pacing throughout the room, I continuously called Samira's phone back-to-back, but it kept going to voicemail. It might've not been her in the flesh, but the sound of her voice during the greeting made the hair on the back of my neck stand tall. I never thought I could hate Samira as much as I did right now. Fucking my boy was a cold, harsh move. Yet fucking with my money was unforgivable. As far as I was concerned, she'd taken revenge to the next level and was trying to take me under.

All the stuff I'd gotten her from the mall yesterday was gone, my clothes and shoes were cut up and tossed around the room, and everything of fabric material within the hotel was shredded as well. Samira had done more than proved her point. She had a nigga listening and at attention fa'sho. My thoughts weren't in her favor, though.

The one trigger that kept popping off in my mind was her banging my boy. She was probably getting down with that nigga and laughing in my face with his ass at this very moment for pulling the wool over my eyes. It was just too damn convenient that my fist pounded into his face yesterday and now Samira was going against the grain once again. If she thought she was gonna start putting Johnie on, especially with my money, I was gonna put my hands on her too. All rules were off.

This time when her voicemail kicked on, I left a vulgar message so she'd know where I was coming from. "Where in the fuck are you at that you can't have your phone on? I'm back at the room and found your little surprise, Mira. You're foul as fuck. I should've expected that since you let Johnie bust it wide open with your trifling ass. Get at me when you spit that nigga's nut sac out ya mouth. Please believe I got something for you, on behalf of my li'l one. Yeah, whatever. I ain't worried about you or that bastard. I'll be waiting on your comeback. Peace."

The End